# By the Grace

## Sine Peril

Copyright ©2020 by Sine Peril

Printed in the United States of America

ISBN 9798694680561

For Mrs. Walker and Mrs. Merriman, two of the best teachers I ever had, who knew how to work with my quirks before I did.

Also for Kae, without whom Julia would be a very different person.

# Forward

When I first started writing this book in 2017, I'd never heard of a corona virus. Covid-19 wouldn't exist for another two years. SARS was something people got in other countries, not a global pandemic.

After a year of querying *By the Grace* and running up against brick walls, I had just made the decision to publish on my own when the reports of Covid came out of Wuhan, China. I had no idea that within weeks, the entire country—and most of the planet—would be on lockdown.

I spent four months sitting on this manuscript before I decided to move forward with it. My intention in writing it is not to objectify pandemic victims or to profit from such a horrible situation, but to shed light on untold stories. In the years I have been writing horror and historical fiction, I have learned two things: The adage about those who don't learn from history being haunted by it is true, and sometimes diving head first into the darkness makes it easier to find the light on the other side.

I sincerely hope that if you are reading this, you have not felt the personal impact of this disease, but I know that is statistically unlikely. Please know you have my heartfelt sympathy and best wishes that you and yours remain unscathed.

For two years now, KnotMagick Studios (which encompasses all of my work, both literary and design-based) has been supporting The Navajo Water project, which brings electricity and clean water to some of the most marginalized people in the United States. The Navajo nation has been hit particularly hard by Covid-19, with the most cases per-capita out of all ethnic groups in the US, and more deaths than any US state. Additionally, most do not have access to clean running water, electricity, or ambulance services, and have to drive for two or more hours just to get groceries or see a doctor. I am donating an additional percentage of the proceeds from the sale of this book to the NWP to assist in improving sanitary conditions, as well as helping the Navajo nation recover from the devastation the pandemic has left behind. If you would like to contribute personally, you can do so at NavajoWaterProject.org.

*By the Grace* was a labor of love to write, but it was also fucking hard, and that was before the world turned into a dystopian novel.

The book you are about to read is narrated by an autistic young woman who has fallen into a set of circumstances even neuro-typical people would find challenging. In 1918 the word *autism* did not exist as the diagnosis we know today, and the general understanding of how to work with or accommodate people with neurological differences, learning disabilities, and other issues was essentially nonexistent. I have done my best to depict the attitudes Julia would have encountered during this time period, both the good and the bad, but please be aware that this book contains physical and verbal abuse of autistics and children, though I have refrained from making these scenes too graphic.

For more on the history of autism and the depiction of it in this story please see the historical note at the end of the book. If you would like to know more about the influenza pandemic and how it shaped America and the rest of the world, I recommend the books *Very, Very, Very Dreadful* and *The Great Influenza.*

# Chapter One

The Chillicco

Friday, October 18, 1918

## Chillicothe Under Quaranti

As the influenza outbreak rages in nearby Camp Sherman, officials have placed the city of Chillicothe under quarantine.

Soldiers are banned from entering the city proper and attending public entertainments in theaters and dance halls.

All residents must wear a mask when in public. These can be procured from any Red Cross location throughout the city.

Citizens are encouraged not to enter public spaces unless necessary, not to loiter when away from home, and to return home before dark.

Rer
foll
imp

The
that
rela
the
beh
of a
exp
in l
its
heh

## Saturday, October 19, 1918

We found the body at dawn.

Well, Enid found it. *Her*. She went to ring the morning bell to wake us, and found Ada face down in the fountain. Instead of the bell ringing at seven o'clock, I woke to screaming.

The teachers pulled Ada out of the water, but it was very clear she was dead.

The infirmary was just above the back door. I sprang out of bed like a shot at the sound of the screams. Once I realized we weren't being invaded—Why would the Kaiser bother to invade a girls' school in Ohio?—and the building wasn't on fire, I looked out the window. Saw Ada's fiery red hair spread out in the water, half frozen.

I was one of the first ones down, wrapped in my quilt, barefoot and in my night dress. Frost covered the flagstone patio, so cold it burned under my feet.

Ada wore her civies, instead of her uniform. There were red marks on her face and neck where someone hit her, and blood on her nose and lips.

But my eye was drawn down to the handprint on her thigh, where her skirt rode up before the headmistress pulled it down again.

Headmistress Davenport and Nurse Spencer pulled her out of

the fountain. By then, other teachers gathered, trying to send us back inside, but I remained glued to the spot. My feet were numb. My whole body was numb. Even my mind went numb. I couldn't tear my eyes away. Ada's face burned into my retinas, and the handprint on her thigh.

***

Somehow, I got back to my room. I don't remember how. I had a vague recollection of a teacher leading me upstairs, and then I was on my bed, shivering, with the curtains drawn against the scene outside.

I looked down at my feet. They were blueish-purple with cold. Horrified, I stuffed them under the blanket, chafing them with my equally cold hands until the color returned.

Blinking, I stared around our room. Nothing had changed since I went to the infirmary the night before, but everything felt foreign.

There was still a table in the middle of the room, under the window, which Ada and I shared and used as a nightstand. My glasses and flu mask rested on top of my copy of *The Yellow Wallpaper*. Ada had marked her place in *Cosmopolitan* with a hair pin; there was a pile of them next to the lamp. We'd been reading passages to each other before bed. Me, lines about a woman driven slowly insane as she peeled back the wallpaper in her attic room, and Ada from the Edgar Wallace thriller advertised on the cover of the magazine.

The table was framed by our beds, both rumpled. The shiny black boots Ada always wore with her uniform were underneath, one laying haphazardly on its side, next to her slippers. Her dressing gown hung over the foot of the bed.

Our beds faced the door. On either side was a desk for us to do our homework, and on the remaining walls we each had a wardrobe and a small bookshelf. Each half of the room was a mirror image of the other, but they were vastly different. Ada hung pictures of actors from moving pictures on her side, along with portraits of her family. There was a glamour shot of her mother that could have come out of *Life* magazine, she was so beautiful.

My side of the room was nearly bare. I had my books, of course, all arranged alphabetically by author. But the only thing on my wall was a piece of framed embroidery I'd done last term, of a cardinal and a sparrow perched on a flowering branch. Ada used to tease me that it was a portrait of us: bosom friends, her with her red hair, and me with my plain brown.

I stared at it, as if I'd never seen it before. The red of the cardinal was the brightest thing on my side of the room. I stared at it, lost in the overlap of the stitches, tracing each one with my eyes.

There was an area where the thread was too tight, and the warp of the linen out of square. I frowned, trying to decide if it bothered me enough to take the whole thing apart. I hate it when things that should be perfectly square don't line up at ninety degrees.

Crawling to the head of my bed, I pulled aside the curtain and peered out. Someone had brought the headmistress her coat and gauze mask, or she'd gone in to get them. She was talking to two policemen. Nurse Spencer knelt by Ada's head. Someone had covered her with a blanket, but in my head I still saw her damaged face. Saw the bruising on her temple, her split lip. I saw the frost on her eyelashes and hair and the blue-white hue of her skin.

*You could have prevented this. It's all your fault*, I thought, letting the curtain drop back.

My feet weren't blue anymore, but the rest of me still felt numb as I climbed out of bed and retrieved a clean uniform from my wardrobe: ankle length navy blue skirt, navy blouse. I thought the sailor collar looked childish, but no one asked me my opinion about anything. They also hadn't asked my opinion about making the entire uniform out of wool. I had a red mark around the base of my neck where I couldn't stop scratching. Under the uniform, I wore a silk slip to make it less itchy.

I braided my hair in two tails. I tried pinning them up the way Ada used to do for me, but the ends always stuck out, and I could tell the right side was crooked and would fall down the first time I took the stairs too quickly. I took out the pins and left it, allowing the braids to fall down my back.

Even in thick wool socks and my sturdy brown boots, my toes still felt cold. I pulled my fingers into the sleeves of my blouse, curling them into fists. Why was I so cold? I must have been inside for over an hour, but our usually sweltering room—it was above the kitchen—felt like an ice box.

Before I left my room, I put on my glasses and my mask. There hadn't been any cases of influenza at The Mt. Sinai School for Young Ladies—yet—but if the police where here, that meant outsiders. Every girl knew someone who had died from the pandemic. I'd lost two cousins and an aunt already. When my uncle found out he didn't have a family to come home to, he climbed out of the trench and walked into the German line. The army sent back a casket, but I overheard Grandfather say there wasn't enough left to call it a real funeral. He had to be identified by his watch.

The clock in the dormitory parlor said it was half past eight. Everyone should have been leaving breakfast and on their way to their first class, but girls huddled around the couches, talking in small groups. Some were still in their night dresses.

"Julia!"

A dozen heads all turned to look at me as I entered the parlor. I stopped in my tracks. The girls flocked to me, all clamoring for answers.

"Oh, Julia! I'm so sorry!"

"You were her friend, weren't you?"

"You shared a room."

"Where did she go?"

"What happened?"

"You poor thing, you must be devastated!"

Someone put a hand on my shoulder. I took an automatic step back, pulling out of their circle.

The babble cut off abruptly. Why were they so interested in me? I'd started at Mt. Sinai the year before and had never been the subject of so much interest, not even on my first day.

"Give her some air," snapped Bernice. She was still in her night dress, the pink ribbons around her collar incongruous with her stocky, athletic figure and alto voice. The other girls listened, backing away. Bernice was pleasant enough, for all that she usually sounded like she was angry at everyone. She wasn't afraid to pick a girl up by her collar though, and teach her a lesson if it came to it. She did it once when Elvira Compton made fun of Sara Brown's new glasses. After that, everyone left Sara alone, and no one crossed Bernice.

"Are you all right?" asked Mary Ann. The prefect for our year, she always tried to mother us. She reached out to put a hand on my shoulder, and I took another step back.

I stared at them, still standing too close. I didn't know what to say, so I started with the obvious. "The police are here."

"Well, of course. Did you think the headmistress wouldn't call them?" Elvira might have learned not to pick on anyone directly, but it didn't stop her from treating the rest of us like we were below her.

"Have they talked to anyone yet?" I asked.

"No, not yet. Miss Comstock sent everyone back to the dorms to wait." Miss Comstock was the teacher in charge of our year.

"Miss Grace."

We all turned to see Miss Comstock standing in the hall. She gestured to me. "Come here, Julia. The police would like a word."

I followed her down to the first floor. Enid, one of the kitchen maids, was hunched over the bench in the entry hall, sobbing. Nurse Spencer tried to soothe her, rubbing her back. She was wrapped in an afghan I recognized from the formal parlor where we met visitors.

"Now, there's nothing to be afraid of. But as you're Ada's roommate, they want to talk to you."

I nodded dumbly. Everything was out of order. I hadn't seen so

14

many faces without masks in weeks. At first, it looked like Ohio would be spared the brunt of the Spanish influenza outbreak, but in the past few days it had reached epidemic proportions, even in our small community. Dozens of girls had already gone home, but many of us had nowhere to go. With the city of Chillicothe quarantined, I couldn't go back home, and sending half the girls away would mean sending them into homes with active flu cases.

So far, Mt. Sinai—the church and the boys' and girls' schools attached to it—had been spared, but we all wondered how long that would last. The area schools had been closed for a week, but we could stay open so long as no one left. Most of us had nowhere else to go, as leaving would mean going back to homes where someone was already sick. There was a sign posted in the dining room with all of the rules: no visitors, no leaving campus. All deliveries had to be made to the back door, and windows had to be open at least half an inch. Masks had to be worn to class, and our In Town days—the one day a month we could go to Chillicothe to shop or visit friends or family—were cancelled until further notice. Mt. Sinai Church started having services for students an hour early so we wouldn't interact with the public.

The policeman sat at the Headmistress's desk, scribbling in a notebook. A mask covered half his face. It was hard to read his expression over the gauze.

He looked up when we came in. "You're Julia Grace?"

"Yes, sir."

"You were Ada Brooks's roommate?"

"Yes, sir."

"Do you know what she was doing last night?"

"No, sir. I was in the infirmary last night. I get headaches sometimes," I explained.

"Headaches?"

I swallowed hard, fidgeting with my locket. I'd worn the back smooth over the years by rubbing it with my thumb. "Yes, sir. I had a headache most of yesterday, but it started to get worse just before bed. I couldn't sleep, so I went to the infirmary to ask Nurse Spencer for some aspirin. She told me I should stay in the infirmary for the night, since it's usually quieter and a little darker."

"When was the last time you saw Miss Brooks?"

"Around lights out, at ten o'clock." I pulled on the pendant until the chain cut into the back of my neck. I let it fall slack again, then repeated the process.

He scratched something into his notebook. "Did she say anything about going out? About meeting someone?"

I bit my lip and squeezed the locket harder. "Not particularly, no."

16

"What do you mean?"

"Ada…Ada had a boyfriend. From the Academy." Mt. Sinai Academy was the all boys' school on the other side of the woods. In between was the church. We saw the boys every Sunday, but otherwise we weren't to interact with them, except on special occasions, like the Christmas dance.

"Do you know his name?"

I shook my head. "She didn't say. They'd only been seeing each other for a week or two. She said she wanted to see where it would go before she introduced us."

His eyebrow went up. "You didn't ask for more information? I thought girls were gossips who told each other everything."

I glared at him. "Of course I asked, but she didn't want to tell me. And it was none of my affair."

"You didn't ask after her? Didn't try to find her letters or read her diary?"

"Why would I? It wasn't my business. I thought she would tell me in her own time, if she wanted to."

"But surely she would tell you something about him?"

I eyed him, unsure if he was just doing his job, or if he really thought I was hiding something. When I didn't answer right away, he tried again. "You were, I imagine, fairly close?"

"Ada was my closest friend." *My only friend.* The chain cut into the back of my neck again. I twisted it tight around my index finger.

"And friends tell each other secrets, don't they? Isn't that what young girls do?"

I dropped the necklace and let my hands fall into my lap. This was just too much. "Do you have any daughters, officer?"

He blinked at me, caught off guard. "No."

"Then let me assure you that while friends do confide in each other, every girl also has her secrets, something she doesn't want to share even with her closest friend."

The policeman sighed. "Very well. If there's nothing else you can add, you may leave."

For a moment, I thought about telling him. But the man was so off-putting. So I held my tongue and left.

One by one, all the girls in the eleventh grade were called down to talk to the police, but most of their interviews didn't last more than a few minutes.

Rather than be cornered by the other girls in the common room, I went straight back to my room and shut the door.

I peeled off my mask and threw it on the bed, glad to be rid of it. It made the bottoms of my glasses fog up when I breathed too hard, and the hot air trapped inside the gauze made it hard to breathe.

My eye landed on the night stand, and I thought back to the night before, when we'd been reading to each other. We both loved a good scary story. The house I'd grown up in, my grandmother's house, was haunted. Ada loved to hear stories about that house. I'd promised she could come visit over Christmas vacation, if her parents said it was all right. She was thrilled by the idea of staying in the old guest room, which once belonged to my great-uncle, who had consumption and went mad after two years of being bedridden. There was also a family legend that a maid hung herself in the attic after great-great grandfather forced himself on her. Grandmother said it was nonsense, but I'd seen her once, through the attic window one evening when we came home late. She said it was just a reflection, but I knew what I'd seen.

I went to the window, looking down at the fountain below. The infirmary was also on the third floor, in the little protruding wing on the back of the building. I could see it from our window.

My breath formed a cloud on the glass. What had possessed Ada to go out last night? It was so cold. A boy seemed a very poor reason to go traipsing around the woods in the dark and cold, but as Ada regularly reminded me, I was hardly an expert on such matters. Michael Weaver once slipped me a note in chapel asking me to meet him after the service. We walked the gardens around the chapel, but when he tried to hold my hand I pulled away. I suppose he was handsome enough, but I simply had no interest. The other girls spoke in dreamy tones of kissing boys and canoodling under the stars or by candle light. My only experience was last New Year, at my grandmother's party. A boy from down the street, Steven, kissed me at midnight. He wanted more. I found it wet, sloppy, and terribly awkward. Ada insisted it got better with practice. I didn't have anyone I wanted to practice with.

I looked down at her hair pins, the haphazard pile under the lamp. A few strands of red hair still clung to one or two of them.

On the other side of the room, Ada's wardrobe stood, the door cracked open slightly. I went around the bed to it, inhaling a whiff of perfume. When I opened the door, I saw the little case where she kept her cosmetics—strictly contraband, of course. Mt. Sinai girls were demure and reserved. We weren't supposed to paint our faces or wear perfume. Usually, the case crouched in the back of the wardrobe, hidden behind the hems of skirts and dresses.

On the top tray was the little teardrop shaped glass vial of perfume.

*"Isn't it divine? Mother will never notice it's gone. She has dozens just like it. She used to get them from France, before the war,"* Ada said, *holding the delicate bottle under my nose.*

If nothing else the perfume confirmed she was meeting a boy. She'd have been sent straight to the headmistress's office if she'd

20

worn perfume to class. We weren't even supposed to use scented soap, though some girls did anyway.

I put the bottle back in the case and pushed it to the back of her wardrobe, where the smell of cedar would eventually overpower the fragrance of roses.

Stepping back from the wardrobe to close the doors, my heel caught on a loose floorboard, and I stumbled. I landed with a thump on my backside, my head bouncing off of Ada's mattress.

With stars dancing in front of my eyes, I didn't hear the knock until Miss Comstock pushed open the door with her hip and it banged off my desk.

"Julia, what on earth are you doing down there?" she asked, dropping an empty crate on Ada's bed.

"Nothing. I tripped, that's all," I said, scrambling to my feet and brushing down my skirt.

"Are you all right?"

"I'm fine, Miss Comstock."

"Good. I brought this…The headmistress contacted Ada's parents. They are unable to come to collect her things. Concerns over the epidemic, you know. The headmistress has asked…that is, if you're feeling up to it, if you would pack up Ada's things. I can help you, if need it."

I thought of the perfume, the makeup. "No. No, that's all right.

I can do it."

The teacher raised an eyebrow. Had I answered too quickly?

I shifted my weight, my heel rocking back and forth on the loose floorboard until it slid back into place with a *snap*.

Miss Comstock cocked her head. "Are you sure you're well, Julia? Do you need to see Nurse for a headache powder?"

I took a deep breath, counting as I exhaled, trying to regulate my breathing, my tone, my words and cadence.

"I'm fine. Really." Pacing each syllable to match the ticking of the clock on the nightstand, I waited, hands clasped behind my back.

"Well, if you're certain."

I nodded, holding my breath until she left.

As soon as the door closed, I knelt down, prying the floorboard back up. I'd thought, for that brief moment I was sprawled on the floor, there'd been something underneath...

There! The board came loose in my hand and under it I found a stack of letters tied with a blue velvet ribbon. I recognized it—Ada wore it two or three weeks ago to church, and said it was from an admirer.

I suddenly wished I'd paid more attention to her wistful anecdotes of stolen kisses in the churchyard, where the overgrown trees and bushes and the plethora of stone monuments provided ample hiding places, away from the eyes of teachers and Pastor Brown.

Pulling off the ribbon, I unfolded the first letter.

# Chapter Two

*May 5, 1918*

*Ada,*

*I lay awake last night thinking about our last conversation. I don't know how you can be so cold.*

*My birthday is in July. Write to me over the summer. I don't know when I'll be called up. I might even volunteer. I want there to be a girl back home to fight for.*

*I don't know if I'll be back at school in September. But please, think about it?*

*You know where to find me.*

*Yours,*

*J*

"Do girls really find this engaging?" I wondered, making a face at the writer's description of Ada's *flowing, flaming locks* and *eyes of purest midnight blue*. Then I read a bit further, blushed, and quickly folded it back up again. Really! What kind of boy would write such a thing? Clearly, he was no gentleman. Ada should have reported him for writing those things—he'd have been sent home straight away.

It was a horrible, crude thing to say, but…could the writer be the one who had killed Ada?

I bit my lip, unfolding the letter again and skipping the lurid details until I found an initial scrawled at the bottom. L. Who was L?

I ran through the short list of names I knew from the Academy. There were at least two boys name Lucas, and there was a Linden, or something like that. One of them had the last name Cash, but I wasn't sure which one it was. Then there was Lance…Lance Moore, I thought.

I should have been ashamed, I thought, sitting there reading her letters—her hidden letters, that she hadn't even shown to *me*. We'd been sleeping within arm's reach of each other for months. We shared the same classes. Ate every meal at the same table. She did my hair in the morning, and I sewed buttons back onto her uniform.

Now I wondered how she managed to lose so many of them.

But as I sat there on the floor with the pages spread out around me, reading these profound declarations of love, I only felt—what?

It was the same sort of feeling I got when studying for an exam. The sense that every word was vital and had to be committed to memory before it escaped into the aether.

I traced my fingers over L's handwriting, as though by touching the words some sixth sense could tell me who the mystery boy who wrote it was. Unfortunately, while ghosts occasionally made an appearance, I could not seem to conjure up the face of the living boy who had lured Ada to her death.

I set aside the letter and reached for the next in the stack. Much to my surprise, the handwriting on this one was much finer; the spelling better and the grammar correct.

*February 26, 1918*

*My dearest A,*

*You looked so beautiful last week in church, with the ribbon I gave you. I can't wait until we are able to meet again, and I can run my fingers through your hair.*

*I will meet you at the end of the rainbow at Marie's, Sunday night. Wear the ribbon to church again if you can get away. I'll meet you at ten o'clock.*

*Love,*

*J*

"Ada, what have you been doing?" I muttered to the page,

sitting up a bit straighter.

Who was Marie? I'd heard some of the girls mention her before, but she wasn't a student. They talked about visiting her sometimes, but when I asked they just giggled.

I sifted through the notes, quickly picking out three different sets of handwriting—AB, J, and L. AB's notes were all at the bottom of the pile, interspersed with a few from L. The top of the stack alternated between J and L. Few of the letters were dated, but as I read I gathered that her correspondence with L was the oldest, pre-dating my arrival at the school the year before. Then hopeful but timid AB began writing to her, seemingly unaware she already had a pen pal of sorts. Several of the letters mention Marie or the end of the rainbow. I scratched under my collar, puzzled.

Then the letters from J. A few at first, confident and plain. Then growing more and more impassioned. AB still wrote from time to time, begging favors. From his letters it would appear Ada was uninterested. He gave the impression of a small dog, nipping at one's heels and always following, underfoot.

*Ah. Andrew-with-the-spectacles*, I realized at last. He was always very attentive to Ada at church and when we had In Town days. Small, pudgy and freckled, he'd always seemed nice enough, but rather too earnest. He'd brought her flowers sometimes on Sundays, a daisy picked on the way to the church. She was polite,

27

but always turned him down. No matter how many times Ada asked him to go, he always turned up.

"Like a bad penny," Ada called him.

*So why keep his letters?* I wondered.

Andrew was clearly devoted; he seemed to write at least once a week. But his letters were eclipsed by the ones from J. Though he'd written only on occasion at first, there were stretches where there seemed to be two or three of his letters to every one from Andrew. But J apparently hadn't written for at least two weeks.

Outside, the bell for lunch rang. I thought about skipping it, but I'd already missed breakfast and my stomach growled. The smell of leek and potato soup wafted up from the kitchen.

Folding up the letters, I tied them with the ribbon again and put them back under the floorboard. If Miss Comstock wanted me to pack Ada's things, I would have to go through them in detail before they were sent off to her family.

\*\*\*

The energy at the lunch table hummed like a badly wired electrical socket. Girls with red eyes slumped over their empty bowls. No one was wearing a mask, since they made it impossible to eat. For a moment, I felt naked without it, as though everyone was staring straight through me. As if they knew I'd been going through Ada's things. As if they knew I'd lied to the police.

As if they knew I could have stopped her.

I went to my usual place, four seats from the end of the second table. There were three long tables for students lined up, and one for the teachers arranged perpendicular. The maids waited with their tureens of soup in the corner until everyone was seated.

The murmur of voices skipped a beat when I entered.

It was worse than that morning in the common room; now it was the entire school staring at me.

I reached for one of my braids, twisting the tail between my fingers and walked quickly to my seat without looking up.

"Is it really true?" asked Camille, leaning across the table to whisper to me.

"Is what true?"

Gloria, who was sitting next to her, bent her head toward the conversation. "What they're saying about Ada, of course."

"That she's dead? Of course it's true."

"That's not what she meant," Camille asked, pulling back quickly, a look of horror on her face. "How can you just say it like that? I thought you were her friend."

I looked down at my empty bowl, twisting my braid around my finger until the tip turned red, then purple. "She *was* my friend." It came out so quietly, I wasn't sure they could hear me.

"I heard that policeman talking, and he said she was *loose*."

"What do you mean, loose?" That was one of the ninth grade girls, twisted around in her chair at the next table.

Camille and Gloria giggled. "You know, *loose*. She went with boys."

"Went with them where?"

"Well, that's the question, isn't it?" Gloria whispered as Headmistress Davenport rose from her chair to address the assembled girls.

A hush came over the room. "As many of you will have heard, we lost one of our own this morning. Ada Brooks passed away. We don't know yet what the circumstances were surrounding her death, but the police are looking into it and will likely be speaking with most, if not all of you at some point. I entreat you to please give them your utmost cooperation in this matter, so that it can be resolved quickly. At present, there is no reason to think any of you are in any danger."

Her voice faded into the background. Vaguely, I was aware of a pain on the left side of my head; I'd wrapped my braid tightly around my right hand and was pulling so hard my head tilted to the side.

A hand on my shoulder made me jump. I released the braid, my hands falling into my lap.

"Are you all right?" Bernice whispered, concern on her face.

"I'm fine," I said quickly.

"You were rocking."

"I'm sorry."

"Don't apologize."

"I'm not supposed to do it." Grandmother always chastised me for it at home, and so did my teachers. Especially Miss Newton, the English teacher.

"It's okay. My brother does that a lot. My mother always yells at him for it, but it only makes it worse."

I glanced up at her through the fringe coming loose from my braids. She smiled. "My little brother, Benjamin. He doesn't talk. He does that when he gets upset. Yelling at him only makes it worse."

I bit my lip. "My mother does it." I hadn't even told Ada why I lived with my grandmother, though there were plenty of rumors. I had hoped she assumed my parents were dead. Between the Great War and the influenza, there were certainly enough girls living with grandparents or aunts and uncles or older siblings, or even just staying in children's homes or wherever they could find shelter.

Berniece nodded. "That's what I thought." When I looked at

31

her, one side of her mouth twisted in a wry smile. "There's no secrets at Mt. Sinai, you know. Girls talk. I heard…I heard there was a rumor about your mother. That she was…"

"Feeble minded." It was the kindest in a long list of terms the doctors, my grandmother, and our neighbors used.

"Yes."

The maids started coming around with the soup, ladling it into our bowls. The smell of onions was stronger than it used to be when I first came to the school. Onion was supposed to ward off the flu. We had some at nearly every meal. It felt like I'd used twice my usual amount of tooth powder since April, trying to get rid of the taste.

I glanced across the table where Camille and Gloria whispered to each other, sharing gossip about Ada, no doubt. Camille felt my gaze and looked up, then bowed her head closer to Gloria and whispered something I couldn't hear. They both looked my way and giggled. I stared down into my soup and tried to convince my stomach to accept the onion-laden broth, despite its protests.

Bernice's hand brushed my arm.

"You're not feeble minded. Eccentric, maybe, but not feeble minded." One side of her mouth curved up in a smile.

I looked down at my bowl. "Thank you," I whispered.

*** 

After lunch, I retreated to our room—my room, now. I would have to get used to that—to re-read the letters and begin packing Ada's things.

The first time I read them, it had been in what I thought was reverse-chronological order, starting with the most recent. The second time, I went back to the beginning, or as close to it as I could manage. I don't know what I was looking for, but I didn't find it.

At last, I set them aside. I knew I was delaying the inevitable. Presumably, Miss Comstock would return to pick up Ada's things tomorrow or perhaps the day after. Better to have it all ready to go.

As I pulled her uniforms from the hangers and folded her stockings, the numbness that had overtaken me that morning began to peel away, shedding the thin, hard layers that had protected me in the form of hot, angry tears. I sat on her bed, sobbing into her night dress.

*Ada.* The only friend I'd ever had. The only one who didn't hold my *eccentricities*, as Bernice put it, against me.

I missed dinner. I wasn't hungry, and just the smell of the liver and onions from downstairs made my stomach turn. The last thing I wanted to do was sit in a room surrounded by it, and gossips like Gloria and Camille, trying to keep my food down and pretending it

33

didn't bother me.

Bernice and Miss Comstock both came to check on me, but I sent them away. I told Miss Comstock I had a headache, which was true enough after several hours of crying.

I was sick of people asking me how I was. Sick of their pitying looks, before they whispered behind their hands about how horrible Ada was. A "loose" girl, implying we were all better off without her. She'd been vibrant, cheerful, but also talkative and occasionally standoffish when her dander was up. She didn't hold back on her opinions, and that meant a lot of girls disliked her. In her way, she'd been almost as much an outcast as me.

The bell for lights out rang at ten o'clock. I lay in bed, but sleep wouldn't come. I kept rolling over to stare at Ada's empty bed. I should have been able to hear her breathing, hear her tossing and turning until eleven or midnight, or else reading under the covers with her flashlight.

Instead, all I could hear was the ticking of the clock on the nightstand. It seemed unbearably loud in the silence. I'd always found the ticking of clocks and watches to be comforting, but tonight it drove me crazy. I climbed out of bed, shoving it under Ada's pillow. It muffled the noise until it was barely audible, but then the room was too quiet.

I rolled over on my back and stared at the ceiling, clutching the blankets in my fists as I fought back another wave of tears.

Something creaked on the other side of the room. Cautiously, I turned my head. The door of Ada's wardrobe swung open, as though directed by an invisible hand. I caught another whiff of her perfume and shivered.

The pain that had been building behind my eyes all afternoon suddenly exploded. I squeezed my eyes shut, covering my face with the blankets.

Footsteps. Footsteps, inside my room. I lay frozen, afraid to look. The door had been shut. I hadn't heard it open. Who had come in? Miss Comstock? Nurse Spencer, maybe, come to check on me?

A shadow passed overhead. Under the covers, it grew even darker, as someone blocked the meager moonlight from my window. I could *feel* someone standing over me, looking down. I couldn't move. It was like I'd been pinned to my bed like the butterfly specimens in the science room. My heart raced until I could barely breathe.

Maybe they would think I was asleep.

The squeak of floorboards trailed away as the person left. When I was sure they were gone, I pulled down the blanket, peering over the edge at the rest of the room.

It was just as it had been before, with the soft ticking from under the pillow in the next bed, Ada's wardrobe ajar. The bedroom door was still closed.

And attar of roses hung in the air around me.

I shivered, throwing back the blanket. Instead of getting up on the left side, the side by the night stand and the door, as I usually did, I nearly leaped out on the right, closer to the wall. I kept my back to my bookshelf and wardrobe, inching around the room until I got to the door.

I jerked it open, half expecting someone to be waiting on the other side.

The hallway was empty. Three doors down, Mary Anne snored away, just as she did every night. Sometimes, I think the reason she got to be prefect is because prefects don't share rooms. With so many girls gone, however, and concerns over the epidemic, Headmistress Davenport had divvied us up into as many private rooms as possible.

The wood floor was freezing under my bare feet, but I didn't want to go back for my slippers and dressing gown. I went to the common room, just across the hall, looking out through the large windows at the front lawn of the school. The pale gravel of the circular drive seemed to glow in the moonlight. The lawn sloped downhill, fading into tree tops and general darkness. I could just make out tiny lights moving around the town below as ambulances went on their nightly rounds to pick up the sick, the dead, and the dying.

My head throbbed. I went down to the infirmary. Most of the medicines were locked up in a cabinet, but Nurse Spencer always kept a packet of headache powders and some sticking plasters in the cupboard over the sink, and a small lamp on the table by the door in case someone woke up in the middle of the night, or just needed something small.

The rolling dividers were up around the last bed on the end; one of the girls not feeling well, then. Maybe someone else was as upset as I was, after all.

*Or maybe it's the flu,* an evil little voice whispered. I silenced it. If the flu had come to Mt. Sinai, there'd have been an uproar. The only reason the school was even still open was that we were effectively our own quarantine zone—only we seemed to be keeping the flu out, not in. It was so contagious, so deadly, Nurse Spencer and Headmistress Davenport wouldn't have been able to keep it contained, not even for a few hours. There were stories of people who were perfectly fine at breakfast going to school or work in the morning, and by dinner they were at death's door.

I rubbed my hands together, trying to chase the chill away. The last symptom was for the fingers and toes to turn blue, as oxygen was cut off to the extremities and the lungs filled with fluid.

I'd read all the pamphlets. It was one of the things that made me strange, according to the other girls, but I wanted to be a nurse when I left school. I'd asked Nurse Spencer to borrow some of her books, and she reluctantly agreed. I'd read most of them twice since coming to Mt. Sinai.

As quietly as I could, I opened a packet of headache powder and poured it into one of the glasses upside down by the sink. I tried to be equally quiet with the tap, but there was air in the pipes and it gave a little squeal before the water splurted out. I shut it off in a hurry, but there was silence from behind the divider.

I put the cup down, the evil voice whispering once again. That was loud enough, there should have been a rustle, a grunt, something from the end bed. But no matter how I strained my ears, I couldn't hear anything—not even breathing, labored or otherwise. No coughing.

Swallowing a knot of fear, I crept closer, until I was just on the other side of the divider. The lamp threw long shadows over everything. I watched mine play over the pleated fabric of the screen. Even this close, I couldn't hear a sound from the bed on the other side.

I screwed up my courage and peered around the metal frame.

# Chapter Three

*A,*

*I saw you trying to catch my eye in church. I know you think I didn't notice, but I did.*

*You were beautiful, with your hair up, and the light coming through the stained glass. Like an angel.*

*I think you and I both know you aren't one, though. So why don't we meet sometime, and you and I can show each other how wicked we can be?*

*L*

What I saw drew something halfway between a scream and a gasp, an awkward squawk as I stumbled back into the bed opposite. Clutching the frame for support, I stared at Ada's still form. Her wide, blank eyes stared at the ceiling. Her clothes were mostly dry now, but still smelled of damp wool. Her arms lay straight at her side; even without her eyes open, I'd never mistake this for sleep. She was too stiff, to uncomfortable. No one ever slept like that, least of all Ada. She sprawled in her sleep during the warmer months, limbs dangling from the edge of the mattress as they sought a cool breeze or bundled up in a ball when it was cold.

Once the initial shock wore off and my heart rate returned to normal, I inched forward, resting my hands on the curved metal bed frame. A hard lump balled itself up in my throat until I could hardly swallow. It didn't matter—my mouth was completely dry.

I stared down at her, unable to pull my eyes away. She was wearing her good shoes, the ones she set aside for church on Sunday and In Town days. Black and white brogue heels, with a little strap over the foot. One of them had a broken heel. They were horribly scuffed. She'd be so ashamed, especially since her stockings had come free of their garters and were pooled around her shins and ankles.

My eye landed on her hand, curled loosely at her side. There was something stuck to her fingertips. I inched around the bed for a closer look.

Blood. Blood, and hair. A few strands of dark hair, about the length of my finger.

"Julia Grace!"

I dropped Ada's hand with a gasp, backing up so quickly I knocked into the curtained divider. It toppled, crashing into the next bed so loudly I covered my ears instinctively.

"Julia, what on earth are you doing here?" Nurse Spencer said, tugging her dressing gown tighter. She stepped awkwardly over one corner of the divider, grabbing my elbow and pulling me away from the body.

"I came for a powder, and I thought…" I'd thought what? We had a flu victim in the infirmary?

I helped her right the divider, settling it around the bed where no one would be able to peer in.

"Come on. Have you gotten that powder yet?"

I shook my head.

"I'm going to give you a little something to help you sleep. What on earth were you thinking?" She seemed to be talking more to herself, so I didn't answer, merely let her lead me back to the other end of the room, to a seat opposite her desk.

"What's she doing here? Why is she here? I thought the police—"

"Shh. The ambulances…well, there's too much demand in town right now, and the police couldn't take her this morning. They're supposed to send someone tomorrow. One of the farmers has been making the rounds to the outlying areas to…to help the flu patients. Here. From my special stash."

I looked up. Nurse Spencer held out a tin of cookies. I stared at the cookies, then at her. Were cookies supposed to make me feel better that my closest friend was dead? That her rotting corpse was abandoned in the school because no one could be bothered to take her away for burial?

I took one of the cookies but didn't eat it. It was what she expected me to do, but I didn't think I could meet expectations at the moment.

Nurse Spencer smiled gently, eyes crinkling with pity. "You've had a shock. Both this morning and just now. There's nothing better for shock than a cookie, especially if it involves chocolate. And that's my expert medical opinion."

I managed a tiny smile and took a bite. It was crumbly but did have the promised chocolate. I wondered who had sent them to her, or if she'd talked the kitchen staff into making them. Surely there wasn't enough chocolate to make enough for the entire school.

The lump in my throat started to break up, thanks to the application of the cookie, but it threatened to come out as tears and I'd had far too many of those already.

I glanced back at the curtains. Ada would just be one more corpse loaded up with the rest. There was something terribly undignified about it all, but I couldn't think of the words to explain how. It wasn't just that she'd be stacked like firewood and carted away. It was the fact that she had to wait for the pleasure.

When she'd been assured I wouldn't go into hysterics, Nurse Spencer sent me back to bed with the headache powder, another cookie, and a pat on the shoulder.

My room was blessedly empty when I returned, with no sign of whomever—or whatever—had been there before. I closed Ada's wardrobe and put the clock back on the nightstand before crawling into bed.

Without the sound of Ada breathing beside me, it was the only thing to keep me company.

***

Though the teachers tried to make Sundays a somber day of reflection, most of the girls usually rebelled. It was the only day of the week we saw the boys, and there was usually a flurry of note passing. The other girls usually brought out their nicest hair ribbons, or the few small pieces of jewelry that would pass Headmistress Davenport's stern glare at morning inspection.

I didn't have any hair ribbons or jewelry, save the scuffed locket with a picture of my mother and grandmother inside. I usually wore it under my blouse, but on Sundays it was allowed to hang freely about my neck.

I wore the same thing I usually did on Sundays—a brown skirt and white blouse with a bit of lace down the front.

As I finished plaiting my hair, a part of me longed to open the wardrobe and take out Ada's case of contraband, to borrow one of her ribbons to wear in her honor. But at the same time, I couldn't shake the feeling that it was stealing from the dead.

I ran the back of my hand over my eyes, put on my glasses and put my mask in my pocket, and went down to breakfast.

Before we were allowed to eat our oatmeal, the headmistress said a long prayer about thankfulness and an even longer lecture about what a serious time it was, and how respectful we were all to be. She looked especially hard at the girls who had donned bright colors for the day, and I suspected at least a few would be sent to change before we left.

"Here at Mount Sinai, we are all God's children, made in his image, sinners and saints alike. That makes us a family, and our family has lost one of its own. This is a house of mourning."

I caught one of the maids shifting uncomfortably under the weight of the big bowl of porridge she was holding and felt instant sympathy.

At last, the headmistress sat down, leaving us to our breakfast. I still wasn't very hungry, but I managed to empty most of my bowl.

As we put on our coats and lined up by the door, Bernice

caught my eye. For a moment, I thought she would stand by me, but she looked away quickly and went to stand by her friends at the back of the line. Somehow, I wasn't surprised that even after her kindness the day before, she didn't want to be seen with me in public. My shoulders slumped and I stared at my shoes, trying to align the edges of my boots with the seams in the tile floor.

A cold rain fell as we walked across the lawn, down the muddy, wooded trail to the white clapboard church. On the other side of the building, a shorter line of boys meandered to the front doors. Most of the older students had enlisted as soon as they were able or been drafted. None of them came back. At least, none I knew of.

The gravel lot that was usually full of buggies and the odd automobile or two was empty. It had been empty ever since the order came through closing churches, movie theaters, and any place where there were large gatherings of people. I wondered if Pastor Brown was going to close the church to the public entirely.

With fewer than half the usual number, the sanctuary echoed with the shuffling boots and chatter. Sarah Brown greeted her older brother with a hug, her younger brother hanging back nearby. Even with masks covering the lower parts of their faces, the three of them were nearly identical, with mousy brown hair, pale blue eyes, and spectacles.

Over Sarah's head, I spotted Gloria and her twin brother saying hello, but he seemed more interested in Camille and the lace panel covering the deep V of her sailor blouse.

The few minutes of confusion before and after the service were the one time we could fraternize. I spotted more than one note exchanging hands. Headmistress Davenport cleared her throat menacingly when Charlie Johnson leaned against one of the pillars as he talked to Elvira, his eyes half closed. With his hair slicked back, he looked like one of the moving picture stars Ada pinned up on her side of the room, except for the bruise on the side of his face. At least half the girls were sweet on him, though personally I didn't see the appeal. He flirted with anything with legs, provided "anything" didn't include me or poor, mousy Sarah Brown. I supposed I was mousy, too, with my glasses and straight brown hair, but it never bothered me, much. I knew it bothered Sarah, though. I'd found her crying in the bathroom more than once after Elvira'd had her way.

Was it my imagination, or were an awful lot of boys sporting bruises? Andrew-with-the-spectacles had a bandage on his wrist, and both of Sarah's brothers had scrapes on their faces and hands.

I surveyed the room, wondering which of the boys Ada had been with the night she died. Or had it been someone else, entirely? A boy from town, perhaps? It was possible. It was a long walk, but doable if one was motivated. And it would be faster on a bicycle.

*What about an automobile?* No. Too loud. The roads around the school were usually deserted, and most people in the area still used horses. Someone would notice.

I took a seat in one of the pews in the back, near where everyone was talking. Close enough to hear snatches of most conversations, but not close enough to take part. I hung on the fringes, allowing my gaze to wander.

An acute pain in my chest reminded me once again of Ada. Usually I stood with her at these little social gatherings, waiting for her as she flirted with the boys or talked with the other girls before the service began.

The babble of voices battered me like a particularly rough stream now that I no longer had a mooring post to cling to.

I closed my eyes, rubbing my thumb along the patterned edge of my locket, allowing the texture of the metal, worn smooth through the practice, to dig into the pad of my thumb.

With my vision reduced to darkness, it was easier to concentrate on individual voices.

"…most horrible thing I've ever seen. Just left *lying* there like that." One of the ninth-grade girls, I thought.

"…practice last night. It was damn cold and wet, let me tell you!"

"Lucas! Don't swear in church!" the subsequent giggle was unmistakably Gloria, but I wasn't sure of the boy she was talking to.

"...team. Coach Howard made me run laps after." I had a vague recollection that Coach Howard was the tall man with the stern, angry face standing in the back of the church near Nurse Spencer. He had a scar over one side of his face and walked with a pronounced limp. He'd been injured in the war and sent home, and he was an angrier, coarser man because of it. Just the glower on his face on Sunday mornings was enough to make me give him wide a wide berth.

Unsurprisingly, Ada's name was on everyone's lips. It shouldn't have surprised me, but most of the conversations were less than flattering.

"She was fast, you know. I heard half the boys stepped out with her at one point or another," Elvira stage whispered, leaning closer to Charlie.

I clenched my fist around my locket, pulling on the chain as Charlie muttered something agreeable. He looked tired and not at all interested in their conversation, but Elvira just leaned in closer, batting her eyelashes at him.

"*You* never went with her, did you?"

"Of course not."

"Oh, I just knew it. I knew you had better taste than that."

"Good morning, good morning." The sound of Pastor Brown greeting everyone and the mass shuffling of feet announced the beginning of the service. His voice boomed over our heads. He was mostly deaf, and always spoke like he was addressing a crowd, even if he was just talking to one person.

Grandmother insisted I attend church with her every Sunday, but mostly I went from a sense of duty. There were too many inconsistencies in the Bible for me to be a believer, and even more inconsistencies when I listened to the sermons. I liked the routine, the ritual of it, though. When I was little, I liked the way the light came in through the round, colored glass window behind the pulpit. Mount Sinai didn't have the little round window with the dove, though. Instead, there was a big painting behind the altar.

We began with a hymn as always, and then there was a lot of recitations. I followed along from habit, my mouth forming words my mind no longer recognized. Instead it drifted over the heads of the other students. It was strange to see the pews so empty, so few adults. The teachers all sat in the two front rows, the main aisle dividing us by gender. I glanced at the other side of the church, absently trying to match a name to as many faces as I could, and regretting for the first time that I hadn't tried harder to get along with the other girls, or had an interest in the boys. If I needed to know a name before, I could always ask Ada. Honestly, most of the boys looked the same to me. A few stood out—like Charlie Johnson, and Andrew, and a few others, but mostly I couldn't tell them apart. I always had a hard time telling people apart until I got to know them. It was embarrassing, but I couldn't help it. Grandmother tried to train me to remember everyone's names, but mostly I just faked it until their face was sufficiently absorbed into my memory.

I knew love notes were always signed with initials, or perhaps a little symbol. The teachers were vicious if they caught a student with one. Last year, a twelfth grader had to stand up in front of the entire school before dinner and read hers out loud before everyone and wear a sign around her neck that said TROLLOP for a week. The headmistress wrote to her parents. I don't know what happened after she went home but knew there'd been another punishment waiting when she got off the train. I wasn't sure what the teachers did at the Academy, but I'd heard several of the boys had been caned for breaking rules.

Even of the "J" named boys I could identify, there were too many to narrow it down. I did find Andrew-with-the-spectacles, though, sitting two rows behind Anthony Black and within arm's reach of two more Andrews whose last names I didn't know. Not for the first time, I cursed the lack of creativity our mothers and fathers had displayed when using so many of the same names over and over again. It made it so much harder to find someone when all one knew was their initials, and even worse when most names had duplicates. There were three Andrews, for example, and Charlie, Charles, and Chuck.

It wasn't any better with the girls, but at least the other Julia was in the twelfth grade, so it wasn't as confusing during class.

Someone prodded me in the ribs, and I realized we were supposed to be singing again. I stood up, clutching my hymnal, still open to the song from the beginning of the service, and made a halfhearted attempt to follow along with the new number.

The clouds outside parted, and a thin beam of sunlight hit a velvet ribbon three rows ahead of me. I stared at it, wound in a petite ninth grader's dark hair, and had a sudden flash of the night before, the blood and hair clinging to Ada's fingertips.

"In this time of grief and sorrow, we must remember that the Lord forgives all sins, if only we ask for his mercy."

My attention turned suddenly back to Pastor Brown. Was he really saying what I thought he was saying? That god would forgive Ada's murderer?

The very thought made every muscle in my abdomen clench. Whomever had done that to her, left those bruises behind, wrapped his hands around her throat and held her under water, deserved to burn in whatever hell existed.

"I encourage all of you to search your hearts, your souls. To seek out the immorality and vice within yourselves before it is too late, and judgment is upon you. Though we all wander through the valley of the shadow of death, it is only through the light of our Lord, Jesus Christ, that we can find our way home again. Allow this to be a reminder of what comes to those who do not uphold the commandments of our Lord; to those who are given to lustful, covetous behavior."

Pastor Brown looked sternly at all of us, but he lingered on the girl's side of the church.

My hand clenched around my locket until I felt the chain straining, but he continued. "Let this serve as a warning to those to practice deceit, who do not honor their parents—or their teachers. For the Lord has commanded us to obey, and to break one of his commandments is certain death."

"And what about those who kill?"

I couldn't remember standing, but I was on my feet and everyone turned to stare at me.

Pastor Brown only blinked. "You stand up there, accusing Ada of her own death. You say it's her fault because she wasn't obedient or quiet or whatever it is you think a young lady should be. You've all but said it's her own fault she's dead. But what about the person who killed her? What about the person who hurt her? The one who strangled her and drowned her? The one who—who—" I couldn't bring myself to say the word "interfered," for what else could the purplish handprint on her thigh mean?

The girls on either side of me tugged on my arms, trying to make me regain my seat. Nurse Spencer was already out of her pew, coming around to the back of the church.

Shaking with rage and suppressed tears, I wrenched myself free and fled out the front doors of the church. The chain of my locket snapped as I pushed them open, and I felt a rush, as though a great tension suddenly released inside my chest.

The door banged shut. A moment later Nurse Spencer called after me, but I was already halfway down the lane to the churchyard gate, running for all I was worth.

# Chapter Four

*Dearest A,*

*For a long time now, I've been ~~wanting~~ longing to talk to you. I've admired you from afar, but did not think you would speak to me because you are the prettiest girl at school.*

*You have the prettiest hair. And I like that dimple on your chin. I know you probably have a lot of offers, but would you let me escort you to the Christmas dance?*

*Yours for always,*
*AB*

I didn't stop until I was back at the school, skidding to a stop on the stone patio in the courtyard. I barreled right past the place where Ada was found, crashing into the kitchen door and bouncing off again like a baseball. Jerking it open, I ran upstairs to my room, angry tears streaming down my face. Enid was chopping onions for lunch as I raced by, her knife frozen in confusion when she saw me. I pushed past the cook, ducked under the heavy frying pan in her hands and ignored any and all objections on my way to my room.

Sobs tore out of my chest. None of the dormitory doors had locks, but I gave it a good slam, hard enough it knocked my embroidery from the wall.

Pacing, hands on my hips, I strode the length of the room two or three times, until my breathing steadied enough for me to hear the clock. Grandmother had always encouraged me to listen to the ticking, to take comfort from it. It helped steady my nerves. Or she would set me to counting and organizing my button collection, or my embroidery threads, tasks I always found soothing and satisfying. Now though, I didn't want to be soothed or steadied. The reminder that I should control myself, be a lady, conform to expectations—

Enraged, I threw the clock on the floor, dashing it to pieces. Then I swept my book and the lamp and the pile of Ada's hairpins after it. Ripping my pillow from the bed, I threw it across the room, where it bounced off of Ada's wardrobe. The impact made the left-hand door open slightly.

I flipped the box of her belongings over, spilling them over the bed. Her books tumbled to the floor with heavy thuds.

I grabbed Ada's pillow next, hurling it as hard as I could.

It hit Nurse Spencer in the face, knocking her glasses askew.

"Julia Grace! What on earth is this display?"

55

Panting, I couldn't form words. The tears ran faster now. Even if I wanted to, I couldn't give voice to the anger and pain in my heart. There were no words for that kind of hurt. It beat itself against my ribs, throwing itself against bone like I'd thrown the pillows.

Nurse Spencer dropped the pillow, righting her glasses. I sank to the floor, curling myself around a sob. It felt like I was being split in two.

The shock drained from her face. The hem of her white apron and blue skirt appeared in front of me, and she knelt. She tried to pull me into her arms but I pulled away. My skin crawled; I wanted to tear it off. If I could just make it stop—

Another set of footsteps. Nurse Spencer was still trying to grab hold of me. Why couldn't she understand? Why couldn't she just leave me alone?

"Julia Grace, if you don't stop this now—"

"No, don't—"

The new voice stopped her. The white apron vanished. I didn't look up. I curled into such a tight ball, my nose touched my knees. I covered my ears, trying to shut out their voices. Dammit, why had I broken the clock?

Someone draped my heavy quilt over my shoulders, folded double, and pulled it tight.

"Julia?"

I didn't answer. I tasted blood; I was biting my lip and hadn't realized.

"Jules."

I blinked and looked up. Bernice sat down on the floor. She was still holding the blanket tight around me.

"A-Ada calls me that."

"Is it okay if I call you that?"

I pulled the blanket out of her grasp and shook my head, staring down into my lap.

"He shouldn't have said that. About Ada. It was an awful thing for anyone to say, but for a preacher it was especially bad."

I swallowed hard, dabbing at my eyes with the blanket. I was rocking again, but I couldn't stop.

Nurse Spencer puttered around the room, trying to right some of the damage I'd caused. I could feel one eye boring into me.

For her part, Bernice just propped herself against Ada's bed and sat there, seemingly content to wait for me to calm down, or…or what? Was she expecting me to sit here and pour my heart out to her?

I shuddered at the thought. My uncharacteristic outburst aside, I would much rather mourn in peace. Alone. Even with Ada, I hadn't confessed every thought and feeling. I wasn't about to start now with a relative stranger.

I wished they would just leave. Why couldn't they see I wanted to be alone? Why couldn't I shed my tears in privacy?

"Better now?"

I wasn't shaking or rocking anymore, at least. That was something.

Bernice started plucking hair pins from the floor, absently hooking them together. "You know, my brother has these fits sometimes. Spells. He doesn't talk, so sometimes it's very hard for him to make us understand what he needs or wants. Most days, Mother is about at her wit's end with him, though we've all gotten better at understanding his moods in the last few years. She nearly throttled him last summer when he took the Victrola apart. He put it back together again, but it took a few days and he left the pieces all over the parlor, and started screaming if anyone touched them."

I found a loose thread on the quilt and began to tug at it. Nurse Spencer finished packing up the things on the bed and came to sit beside us, leaning back against my bed.

"Julia?"

I didn't look up, but I nodded, getting stiffly to my feet. Now that the flood of emotion had passed, the remnants began to drain, down deep into the place they normally hid.

I licked my lips, tugging harder at the thread. "I'm sorry

for…for being rude," I said. It was the best compromise I could make. I would certainly *not* apologize for I'd said to Pastor Brown.

The nurse nodded. Her mouth was drawn into a thin white line. "Now. You must clean this up. And I know the headmistress will want a word after that outlandish display, but I think she understands…the circumstances. We all grieve in different ways, but we mustn't let our emotions get the better of us."

I nodded, fists clenched in the cotton quilt where she wouldn't be able to see them.

She checked the watch pinned her blouse. "Clean this up, then come down to lunch."

The two of them stood at the same time. Bernice put the little bundle of hair pins back on the nightstand. "I'll help you," she said, surveying the mess. The clock was beyond repair. Grandmother would be furious if I wrote home for a new one.

I shook my head, but Nurse Spencer was already guiding her out of the room. "No. She needs to clean up her own messes."

As she opened the door, I could hear the other girls coming back from church. That meant it was after eleven. I'd have about an hour to clean up before I was expected at lunch.

The door closed behind Bernice. It would take ages to clean it all up. I'd have to get a broom from the scullery downstairs to clean up the broken glass from the clock face. Outside, a dozen feet thudded down the hall, coming to a sudden stop as they neared my room. I couldn't hear the words, but I could hear the lowered voices.

Well, when *hadn't* I been a subject of gossip and ridicule?

I sighed, scuffing my toe on a bit of glass, and crunching a larger piece under my heel, grinding it into the floorboards.

***

I had another headache and decided to stop by the infirmary for a headache powder on my way down to lunch. As always, the door was partially open, but the sound of voices coming from inside made me hang back. Through the gap below the hinges, I saw Nurse Spencer and Miss Newton, the English teacher. The nurse leaned back against the counter by the sink, nibbling on one of the cookies from her secret stash. Miss Newton had perched herself on the edge of the desk and was gesturing with her cookie, the same way she gestured with the pointer in class when trying to pick out the parts of speech or accents on pronunciation.

"The girl belongs in a home," she was saying, flinging crumbs all over the tile floor. "*Not* in a decent school for young ladies. After that outburst this morning, I'll be surprised if Debra doesn't just send her home."

It took me a moment to realize Debra was Headmistress Davenport's given name. It was so strange to hear teachers calling each other by their first names.

"Beth, the poor thing's just had a massive shock. You know how close the two of them were. And to make matters worse, I found her in here last night, staring at the body."

A horrified look crossed Miss Newton's face. "What on earth was she doing that for?"

"I think it was an accident. How could she have even known the body was here? But it did rattle her something awful, I will say. The poor thing."

"Poor thing? The girl's a blank slate. I've never seen her smile, not once, since she came here. And now she goes telling off Pastor Brown? Who does she think she is?"

Nurse Spencer merely shrugged. "If you'd just died, and I had to listen to someone say those things about you, I can't say I wouldn't react the same."

Miss Newton sniffed, taking an unladylike bite out of her cookie. "It was the truth."

"We all have our flaws, but that doesn't mean no one loves us in spite of them. For example, you're rather judgmental and stuck in your ways, but we're still bosom friends."

Miss Newton glared at her, snapping off a piece of cookie and throwing it at Nurse Spencer, who giggled like a school girl and ducked.

I bit my lip, then backed away and headed for the stairs. The other girls were already gathered around the dining room table. I sank into my usual seat, ignoring the pointed stares and the way talk suddenly stopped.

Spreading my napkin over my lap, I stared down at the empty place setting.

Sarah scooted her seat a few inches away. The scraping of the chair against the floorboards seemed unearthly loud in the silence.

Miss Newton and Nurse Spencer came down a moment later, taking their seats at the staff table. Miss Newton had crumbs clinging to her sweater, but no one said anything.

Headmistress Davenport stood to address us all, saying a long prayer. It seemed to have a lot to do with asking for forgiveness. I kept my hands clenched tightly in my lap and tried to ignore the words, concentrating on the ticking of the mantle clock instead.

With every tick, I wished I could be anywhere but the Mount Sinai School for Young Ladies.

***

I woke with a start, heart pounding. I thought it was a footstep that woke me, but the room was dark and empty.

I hadn't pulled the curtains closed, and moonlight spilled down on me, pinning me in place like a moth on display until my heartbeat slowed.

The creak of hinges. I shot bolt upright in bed, spinning around just as the left side door of Ada's wardrobe swung open.

The lump was back. I tried to swallow it, croaking out her name.

Nothing happened. I was alone.

I squeezed my eyes shut and saw the attic window of Grandmother's house, the figure under the eaves. No one believed me when I said there was someone there, but for a moment the woman and I had made eye contact.

I shook my head, throwing my feet over the side of the bed and scattering papers to the floor. I'd fallen asleep in my clothes, re-reading Ada's letters, determined to glean any possible clue as to the identity of her suitors.

I'd made a list of everything I knew about them so far, which wasn't much. The only one I'd identified was Andrew-with-the-spectacles, but aside from his choice of eyewear (tortoise shell) I knew little about him.

Stacking the pages tidily, I set them on my desk. My embroidery project still lay face down where it had fallen.

I picked it up, brushing off some dust, and hung it back on the straight pin I'd forced into the plaster.

Now that I was awake, I didn't feel the least bit sleepy. Changing into my night clothes, I retrieved Ada's flashlight from the box at the foot of her bed and selected a book from my shelf. No longer in the mood for *The Yellow Wallpaper*, I chose *Little Women*. I always liked the cheerful coziness of the March household, and the closeness of the sisters. And if anyone understood loss, it was Jo March.

I climbed back into bed, kneeling on the mattress for a moment to adjust my pillows.

That was when I saw it.

The flash of red in the darkness was unmistakable. I lunged at the window for a better view. It *couldn't* be. It just *couldn't*!

The flashlight landed with a thump. I pressed my hands to the glass, hastily wiping away a cloud of condensation with my sleeve.

There! Running into the woods was the figure of a girl. Tall, picturesque. In the shadows it was hard to make out anything but the shape of her skirt and hair as they fanned out behind her, but then she passed a gap in the trees and silver moonlight bounced off waves of bright red, tied back with a pale ribbon.

I blinked, and she was gone. Not just vanished into the trees, but *gone*. There one moment, gone the next, like a stage performer.

Or a ghost.

I sank back onto my mattress, pulling the blanket up around my knees. I stared out at the woods and willed another flash of red hair to appear. A glimpse of a figure.

I stared until my eyes grew blurry. The last thing I remembered before my head simply became too heavy to hold up was a slight shift under the trees, like the billow of a calf-length skirt in the wind.

***

If there are words in the English language to describe my overwhelming dread of Monday morning, I am not in possession of them.

Seeing everyone back in uniform at the breakfast table made it feel, for a moment, like everything was back to normal. But no sooner had I buttered my toast than I caught a few words from the next table.

"I heard she was seeing Charlie Johnson."

"Don't be ridiculous, Camille. Charlie has better taste than that," Elvira said, tossing her blonde hair over her shoulder. "Besides, I asked him yesterday and he said no."

"Well, you can't deny she got around. She was probably with some townie. None of *our* boys would do anything like that," Camille shot back.

"You don't know that. And the boys from town aren't so bad," Gloria interjected.

"Well, it had to be someone, didn't it?" Camille turned suddenly to me. "You're her friend. Who was she seeing?"

I froze with my toast halfway to my mouth, appetite suddenly vanished. "I don't know. She didn't tell me."

"You're lying. You're just as lose as she was. I bet you're just trying to protect her," Elvira said hotly.

"I'm not!"

"Why else would a girl have silk underwear? Who do you think you are, princess?"

The other girls laughed, and I felt color rise in my cheeks. I let the toast drop to my plate and scratched under my collar. "My uniform itches."

Elvira rolled her eyes. "It's wool. Of course it does. But none of us go walking around in French lingerie."

My stomach turned. I stared at my plate, hands fisted in my lap. I waited for them to go back to their conversation and tried to ignore them, wishing Ada were still in her place beside me at the table. She would know what to say to make them leave me alone. Why did it feel like I was the only person who felt Ada's loss? She'd been so bright and vibrant. She talked to everyone, took part in every activity, and was kind to everyone—well, except Elvira, but Elvira wasn't kind to anyone, so I thought it evened out.

My shoes felt like they were made of lead as I followed the other eleventh graders to our first class. Usually math would be my favorite class. I took comfort from familiar formulas and predictable answers, but as I stared at the problems Miss Comstock scrawled on the board, I felt as if she were writing in Greek, or perhaps Chinese. The numbers refused to resolve themselves into something coherent.

I was saved the embarrassment of trying to solve one of these equations in front of the class when Mrs. Churchill, Headmistress Davenport's secretary, knocked lightly at the door.

"Excuse me, but I need to borrow Julia Grace for a few minutes," she said, handing a slip of paper to the teacher. The two of them bowed their heads by the door in whispered discussion. When Miss Comstock looked up, her lips were pursed. She nodded to me, gesturing out the door. I put down the chalk and hurried out.

"This is terrible business," Mrs. Churchill said, almost to herself as she guided me down the hall to the parlor where we took guests. A man in a trench coat sat uncomfortably in one of the pink wing chairs by the fireplace. On the sofa across from him was a uniformed policeman.

I glanced at Mrs. Churchill. She shooed me into the room. "Go on now."

I inched into the room. As soon as I was through the door, she closed it, pushing me a step further into the parlor.

The men both rose, nodding at me.

"You're Miss Grace?" asked the man in the trench coat.

I nodded.

"I'm Detective Buchanan. I've been assigned to your friend's case."

He smiled warmly, but he looked like he hadn't seen a warm bed or hot meal in at least a week, and a layer of stubble covered his chin.

When I didn't move, he gestured to the couch. "Have a seat."

"The other policeman interviewed me yesterday."

"Yes. I have Murphy's notes right here," he said, holding up a little black notebook. "But he's taken ill, and I've been handed the case. I like to make my own inquires. Just to make sure I have the facts straight."

I didn't want to sit, but I was aware I was expected to. It was what young ladies did when they were offered a seat, even though I hated the floral couch. The springs creaked, and unless you picked just the right spot before sitting, you'd get one right up the backside.

Once we were all seated, the detective opened his notebook and pulled out a pencil. "Why don't you tell me about Ada

Brooks?"

I blinked at him. "What do you want to know?"

"What was she like? Friendly?"

"She was my friend."

"Did the other girls like her?"

"I...I don't know." What kind of question was that?

"What do you mean, you don't know?"

"I mean, she was nice to everyone. But some of the girls didn't like her because she talked a lot. They thought she was...low."

"Low?"

"Low class. Her family has money, but she could be loud and unladylike."

"In what way?"

I ran my tongue along the inside of my teeth, trying to feel out the shape of the words to explain, but I wasn't sure they existed. "She liked to laugh. She made jokes. Some girls laughed, some glared at her. And she was friendly with the boys, so a lot of the girls disliked her for that, too."

"Anyone dislike her more than the others?"

I shrugged. "It depends. There's Elvira, but Elvira hates everyone. Sometimes girls are nice. Sometimes they're mean. I don't understand why they change like that, but it's just the way they are, I suppose."

He seemed more confused than ever by my response, but decided to move on, brows furrowing as he looked down at his notebook. "Any particular friends?"

"I was her friend."

"Anyone else?" His eyebrow began to twitch. I'd seen a lot of adults do that when they spoke to me, though I couldn't figure out why. The medical textbooks I'd borrowed from Nurse Spencer were less than clear on the subject.

I thought for a moment, then shook my head. "She spoke to the other girls about equally. We spent a lot of time together on account of being roommates. And friends."

"I see." He cleared his throat. "And what about Friday night? When was the last time you saw her?"

"Nine-fifty-four."

"That's very precise."

"As I told the other policeman, I had a headache. I get those sometimes. I went to the infirmary for a powder. The clock in the infirmary read nine-fifty-five when I got to the infirmary. The infirmary is just down the hall from our room; it only takes about a minute to walk that far."

"And what happened after that?"

"It was a very bad headache. Nurse Spencer told me to sleep in the infirmary."

"These headaches…you get them often?"

I shrugged. "Sometimes. My grandmother gets them, too. She says they're the plague of a heavy mind."

"The plague of a heavy mind?"

"She says both of us worry too much. It's one of the reasons she sent me here. So she could worry less."

"I see."

I wasn't really sure what he saw, since I didn't really understand it myself. I'd always done my best to stay out of her way, but adults sometimes seemed to find that more disturbing than if I were intentionally underfoot.

"What about that day? Did anything unusual happen?"

I thought very hard. "We had bacon with our breakfast."

The uniformed officer smothered a laugh, while his counterpart let out an exasperated sigh. "I mean, anything unusual with regard to Miss Brooks? Did she seem upset about anything? Maybe she received a letter, or had an unusual conversation?"

I could tell he was getting frustrated with me, but for the life of me I couldn't understand why.

"Well, I suppose it would depend on your definition of unusual. Our classes weren't out of the ordinary. I don't think there was anything strange about our conversations. But the other girls think I'm odd, so by that measure, everything was unusual."

He didn't bother to hide the sigh this time, sinking down into his chair. The constable's face was turning red. What was so funny?

"Miss Grace, did anything out of the ordinary in Ada's routine happen? Did you see any strangers hanging about? Did she mention any plans to leave the school? You told my colleague she mentioned meeting a boy."

"Oh, that. Well, yes. But that wasn't really unusual." I thought again of the other girls and their gossip.

"So she often snuck out to meet boys?"

"I'm not sure what you mean by often, but it wasn't the first time. She hadn't gone out after curfew since term started, though."

"So this boy—he was new in her life?"

I thought of the stack of letters. If my estimation was right, they'd been exchanging notes at church or some other place since January or February; one of J's early letters mentioned Valentine's Day.

"No, not especially."

Detective Buchanan covered his face with one hand. I'd said something wrong again, I was sure of it. I cleared my throat and tried again. "I wouldn't consider an acquaintance longer than six months to be new."

"So she'd been doing this for six months, though not lately?"

"Well, we were roommates last year, and she snuck out a few times then. But I don't know what she did during the summer. Her family lives in Lancaster. I don't know where the boy is from." Lancaster was a good hour away by train.

"And your family?"

"Chillicothe."

"I'm sorry to hear that. The flu's been bad in town."

I nodded, swallowing hard. Grandmother usually wrote every week, but I hadn't heard from her recently. Normally, this wouldn't bother me. Her many letters, filled to the brim with trivialities about the weather and what Mrs. So-and-so down the street was up to, and whether the raccoons had returned to ransack the garden and the garbage bins, and of course, her constant pleas for me to write more often. I usually ignored them after my initial read through. It wasn't that I didn't care, exactly. I just never had anything to say, and honestly couldn't understand why anyone not connected to the school would care about the daily goings on. I lived here, and I didn't care most of the time.

Well, at least not until Saturday morning.

"Were there any boys she seemed to be particularly interested in? I understand the schools are mostly segregated, but there are occasions when you intermingle."

I shook my head. "I've been trying to think for days if she paid special attention to anyone at church—that's when we usually see them—but I just can't think of anyone in particular she's spoken to recently. At least, no one she's paid special attention to."

"So she did talk to some of the boys at church?"

I shrugged. "Last Sunday she was talking to Charlie. Charlie Johnson. He flirts with almost all the girls. He and Ada like to tease each other, but I don't think she was sweet on him."

The detective raised an eyebrow. "I take it you don't like him very much?"

I schooled my features back into a neutral expression. I hadn't meant to make that face when I talked about Charlie, but I couldn't help it. He was just so...vile. He was like the human version of boiled onions.

"Not especially, no."

"Why not?"

"He isn't a very nice person. He tends to treat people like they're less than him."

"How did he treat Ada, then?"

"Like...like a toy or a game, there for his amusement. They would banter with each other, get a laugh out of some of the other boys, and then ignore each other."

"Anyone else she talked to? Last Sunday, maybe?"

I shook my head again. "We talked to Andrew...he makes a

point of saying good morning to us both every week. He was sweet on Ada, but it never went anywhere."

"Why not?"

"Well, Andrew is…" How could I put it politely? I didn't know him well, but I certainly knew why he was usually discounted when the girls were seeking beaus.

"He's not really what Ada looks for in a beau."

"And what's that?"

I shrugged. "Handsome."

At long last, the detective wrapped up his questions, after getting a detailed description of every boy Ada associated with over the past week. "You've a remarkably detailed recollection," he said, surveying the pad before flipping it closed.

"It's habit, I suppose. I spend a lot of time observing people."

"Do you?"

"Do you always answer questions with more questions?"

Slowly, a smile spread across his mouth. "I can't decide if you're unusually sharp, or unusually obtuse."

I shrugged. "Every obtuse angle is acute if you look at it from the right direction."

He smiled, chuckling a little. "True enough." Most people don't understand when I make a joke. It was one of the reasons Ada and I got to be friends. She understood my humor.

75

He gave me leave to go. I stood, smoothing down my skirt, thinking. He raised an eyebrow.

"I have—that is, I found…Wait here for a moment."

I darted out, rushing up to my room before I could change my mind. I'd already near memorized all of J's letters; handing over one or two wouldn't be a bother, though a tiny voice warned against giving him everything.

I took the top letter from the stack, checking to ensure it had the right signature, then shoved the rest of them back under the loose floorboard.

Detective Buchanan and his constable were waiting outside the parlor, looking bored and somewhat bemused.

Panting slightly, I held out the letter. "This is from her sweetheart."

# Chapter Five

**The Chillico**

Monday, October 21, 1918

## More Quarantine Measures

As influenza deaths continue to climb, city officials have placed the following additional restrictions on Chillicothe residents:

• Flu masks are to be worn in all public places.

• Spitting is punishable with a fine.

• All public gathering places (cinemas, theaters, restaurants, dance halls, etc) are to remain closed until further notice. In addition, all schools are now closed.

• While churches remain open for the time being, parishioners are strongly advised not to attend services. All funerals must be observed in private.

• Train travel should be avoided whenever possible.

• Shop owners are to discourage loitering.

Logic said giving the authorities all the information possible

increased the probability of Ada's killer being caught quickly and justly punished for his crime.

I had to have faith in those things, but blind faith was never my strong suit. I needed facts and evidence, not just the say-so of someone supposedly wiser just because they were most assuredly older.

I knew all too well how that sort of trust ended up. I faced it every day in English class, as Miss Newton tried to shame me during recitations. Her insistence I should be in an asylum alongside my mother was nothing new; she'd said as much to my face before.

But it didn't mean she was right.

Did it?

I stewed over these thoughts well into the evening. Cook must not have been able to get the requisite stock of onions with demand being so high, and our dinner of boiled chicken was mercifully light. Instead, she seemed to have compensated by using some sort of mustard sauce.

Bernice made a face. "I hate mustard. Is this supposed to be some sort of flu preventative? Because if it is, I'd rather have the onions."

"No, I don't think mustard does anything," Camille said, slicing off a large piece of chicken with her knife.

"There's no proof onion does anything, either. I was just

reading an article about it in one of Nurse Spencer's journals—"

Bernice groaned. "Do you mean we've been eating all these onions for nothing?"

"But the newspaper said last week that things were looking up. Fewer cases were reported, weren't there?"

I was about state the latest statistic when Gloria cut me off. "I hope so. I hate being held hostage here. I feel like Rapunzel in her tower," Gloria said with a dramatic sigh.

That made me think of something else I'd read. "In Norway, it's already too cold to bury the dead, so they're hanging them from trees."

"*What?!*" Camille dropped her fork with a clatter.

Gloria's face went ashen. "Julia, you're a ghoul! Why would you say something like that?"

I shrugged. "It's true. There was a newspaper in the infirmary, and I read a little—"

"Maybe not at the table," Bernice said quietly. I suddenly remembered the way Grandmother was always telling me what I could and couldn't talk about at dinner, and snapped my mouth shut.

"Well, things must be improving if Julia's not wearing her mask." Drawn by the shrieks of her friends, Elvira abandoned her conversation with the senior girls and turned to us.

Everyone looked at me. I touched my face. With everything going on, I'd forgotten to put it on. In fact, none of the girls at our table were wearing masks.

"Oh—" I started to get up, but Bernice grabbed my arm and pulled me back down.

"Leave it. You can't wear it while you eat, anyway. Besides. We're all in here, breathing the same air. If you were going to catch it, you would have by now."

"Yes, but—"

"You can go get it after dinner. But if you leave now, you'll be in trouble with Davenport, and she'll probably have your plate cleared while you're gone. Just wait."

I sat stiffly, pushing my food around on my plate. Suddenly, I wasn't hungry. I could feel the miasma all around us, closing in. With every breath, I knew it was there. It was coming for me. For all of us. I started twisting my braid around my finger again.

By the time dinner was over, I was a mess of nerves but tried not to show it. I wanted to peel off my skin and wash it in bleach. As soon as I was free I ran upstairs to my room and closed the door.

What should have been a refuge, however, left me exposed and open.

At first, I couldn't pick out why. But then I saw Ada's bed. The box of her belongings was gone, the wardrobe slightly open. The items on the nightstand were shifted slightly, as were the books sitting on my desk.

I opened the door, backing into the hall.

"Julia? Is something wrong?" Bernice and the other girls were just coming up the stairs.

"Someone's been in my room. Who was in my room?" I asked, whirling on them. What gave them the right? How could they?

She glanced at the others, but they all shook their heads. "No one's been in your room."

"Why would we want to go in there? It's not like you have anything worth stealing. None of us want your fancy underwear. We aren't hussies." Elvira sniffed, pushing past the cluster of bodies and into the common room. She threw herself down on a couch.

"Someone took Ada's things. They were supposed to go to her parents, but they're gone. Someone went through my things." My heart crashed against my ribcage, beating against it like a mallet.

"Are you sure? Maybe it was just one of the maids, come to collect it." Bernice held her hands up in what I knew was supposed to be a placating gesture. Grandmother did that a lot, when she thought I was being emotional. But someone had been *in my room*.

"No. They were in my things. They moved my books."

"What's going on here?" Miss Comstock asked, trying to peer over the heads of the students. I could just see the top of her blond hair at the back of the crowd.

Gloria explained while I tried to push Bernice away. Why did she insist on trying to calm me? Why couldn't they understand the invasion? What right did anyone have to even enter my room, let alone touch my belongings or take Ada's?

She took my wrists, but I jerked away. The anger was overwhelming now. "No. It's not right. It's against the rules. No one's allowed—"

Miss Comstock pushed her way to the front. "Julia! Stop it. The police came earlier. They wanted to look at Ada's things. They've taken them with them as part of the investigation."

"They just barged it, didn't even ask—"

"Does it matter? They're police. Were you hiding something?" Elvira sneered. The other girls, backing away from me, crowded around her. The implication hung heavily over the room, but I was too wound up to pay it any mind. I started rocking again.

"Julia Grace, stop that infernal rocking this instant!" Miss Comstock grabbed me roughly by the arm. Her hand burned. I shrieked and tried to tear myself free.

The next thing I knew, I was on my back on the floor, cheek stinging. Bernice stood between me and Miss Comstock, arms out and feet planted like a wall, like she could hold off the whole of the Kaiser's army if they invaded.

"Stop it! Can't you see you're only making it worse?" she cried.

"Bernice Loudon, you will step aside this instant!"

"No! You can't—"

"What on earth is going on here?" Cheeks flushed, Nurse Spencer and Miss Newton appeared at the stairs, panting slightly.

"Petunia, help me with her. Grace has just had a rather violent fit."

The two of them moved to pick me up. I scrambled away, still rocking, my jaw locked tight shut. I couldn't stand the feel of their hands on me, their breath so near. I suddenly remembered the germs, the flu miasma hanging over the dining room, and felt it creeping up the stairs toward us. I still didn't have my mask.

Bernice tried to reason with them. "Listen, you can't manhandle her like that. You'll just make it worse! Just let her sit quietly for a minute; she'll come out of it on her own." Her voice sounded like the scrape of iron nails against a glass pane. I covered my ears and closed my eyes to shut it out.

"Get out of the way!"

Miss Newton pulled Bernice aside while her colleagues grabbed me, hauling me to me feet and dragging me down the hall to the infirmary.

"Let me go! I haven't done anything!"

"This is completely out of hand!"

They pushed me down on a bed. I stood up again and tried to get away.

"Julia! That's enough now! Here, hold her." Nurse Spencer went to her desk, pulling out the key at her waist while Miss Comstock pushed me down on the mattress.

Her fingers dug into my arms. My skin crawled under her touch, but no matter how much I bucked or shouted she wouldn't let go.

By now word had spread. The girls from my floor were joined by the ones on the second floor. My vision swam. Headmistress Davenport's face appeared in the doorway.

"Don't you have anything to calm her down?"

"I'm not allowed to stock opium or chloroform. All I have is sodium bromide and laudanum. Those won't work fast enough."

"This is ridiculous."

For the second time, a hand struck my face. This time it was much harder. I shrank back into the thin mattress, as far from Headmistress Davenport as I could get—which wasn't far, with Miss Comstock on the other side of the bed.

"Listen to me young lady," she said, drawing herself up to her full height, her pearl necklace swinging over the edge of her full bosom, "*Ladies* do not behave in this manner. Not here. You will calm yourself immediately."

I held myself perfectly rigid, until I every muscle in my body stiffened like concrete. My teeth ground together. I stared at the pendulum swing of Headmistress Davenport's necklace. Every time it swung out, I named one of the bones of the hand in my head.

"There. Now you will be still." She snapped her fingers. Nurse Spencer appeared at her elbow with a glass of something.

"You will drink this in its entirety, and you will not move from this spot until someone comes to fetch you, do you understand? This is absolutely abominable behavior, and I *will* be speaking to your grandmother about it."

I continued to stare at her necklace. When I finished with the bones of the hand, I moved on to naming facial muscles.

"Look at me when I am speaking to you, young lady!"

With difficulty, I tore my eyes away and stared up into her face, which was pale with bright red patches covering her cheeks, as though she'd applied rouge with something the size of a broom. Her eyes bulged and I had to look away from the distortion. Suddenly all I could see was the formation of the muscles under her skin, my mind involuntarily peeling away her skin like an orange.

I was still holding my breath. My lungs strained, but I didn't trust myself to let it go.

"Answer me."

Very slowly, I nodded.

Nurse Spencer shoved the glass in my face. I jerked away from the sudden movement. Miss Comstock grabbed my shoulders and Headmistress Davenport latched onto my legs until I couldn't move. With an expression I could almost call regret, the nurse tilted back my head.

I couldn't hold my breath anymore. I came out in a woosh, right in her face. She recoiled. Miss Comstock shook me, clamping me against her chest. This time when she reached for my face, Nurse Spencer wasn't gentle. She poured the liquid down my throat. I coughed and struggled, but couldn't get away, couldn't make them stop. I inhaled almost as much as I swallowed, and lay there, too immobilized by coughing to struggle any more.

The other women let go. Nurse Spencer pounded on my back to help me cough up the funny tasting water, but the headmistress pulled her back. They spoke quietly for a moment, the rest of the school watching from the door of the infirmary. I put my face into the pillow and closed my eyes. If I could just ignore them, just forget they were there…

"She can't stay here."

"We can't send her home. Chillicothe is under quarantine."

"Is the asylum under quarantine?"

"If not with the rest of the city, surely on its own. You know how disease spreads in places like that."

"We could send her to Athens."

"That's over two hours by train. And Columbus is just as far."

"So she'll just have to stay here, then?" My eyelids twitched at Miss Newton's shrill objection.

"I don't see what choice we have. I'll telephone her grandmother and see if there's another relative who can take her in until the quarantine is lifted."

"Are you sure that's necessary, ma'am? Julia's usually such a quiet girl. The past few days have been such a strain, it would be enough to make any girl hysterical. We all know Julia is…different."

"I'm not sure if she's a lunatic, or an idiot," Miss Newton snapped. "But either way, she shouldn't be here."

Nurse Spencer's voice took on a pleading tone. "Please. I've given her something to calm her down. I'll give her another dose of the sodium bromide in the morning so she doesn't have another fit. I'm sure that with a good night's sleep, she'll be herself again."

One of them snorted. I wasn't sure if it was Miss Newton or the headmistress. "That's hardly much of an improvement. But very well. Seeing as there isn't much choice, give her whatever treatment you see fit. I do *not* want another display like this. Otherwise I'll be forced to send her to Athens, even if it means putting her on the train myself."

*** 

Despondent, I lay on the hard mattress without moving for the rest of the afternoon. The wild energy propelling me after lunch faded away into nothing after listening to the headmistress, my teachers, and Nurse Spencer.

Students were prohibited from entering the infirmary. Nurse Spencer moved me down to the last bed on the end, where there would be more privacy and put up the same rolling dividers she had used for Ada. I lay there, staring at the wall, shivering at the thought that just a day earlier, her body lay in the bed across from mine. The same curtains shielding me had shielded her from prying eyes.

I was still angry that someone searched my room and took Ada's things without asking, but it didn't seem to matter so much anymore. The medicine Nurse Spencer gave me made me drowsy, but didn't actually put me to sleep. I drifted lazily in and out, often with the feeling that I was floating somewhere above my bed, looking down on myself.

Light faded slowly from the room. Nurse Spencer brought a tray with my dinner, but I wasn't hungry. I asked for a book, or for my embroidery—I desperately wanted my embroidery—but she told me it was better if I just got some rest. I didn't have the energy to argue anymore.

At some point, the dinner tray was replaced with another glass of water mixed with the medicine. I had a vague recollection of Nurse Spencer ordering me to drink the whole thing, but that felt like hours ago.

I awoke suddenly and completely, unsure of what caused the rapid return to awareness. The air in the infirmary was still and cold, rising goose bumps on my arms and legs. I hadn't been given the chance to change into a night dress, and instead lay fully clothed except for my shoes.

I stared at the ceiling, waiting for my senses to tell me what the strange thing was that woke me. The only sounds were my breathing, my heartbeat, and the soft tick of the clock high on the wall by Nurse Spencer's desk, the face invisible from my current angle.

Slowly, the gooseflesh faded even if the feeling of unease didn't. Swinging my legs lightly over the edge of the bed, I rose and tip-toed to the window, looking down on the fountain.

There. Movement on the flagstones. At first just a whisper of shadow, but then it coalesced into Ada's figure, first her long red hair, then her shoulders and face and the rest of her body followed.

The wind seemed to carry her toward the woods. She looked over her shoulder once, back to the school as if searching for a light in the windows, a sign she'd been seen. Then she ran toward the trees.

Snatching my boots from beside the bed, I ran as quietly as I could after her, pausing at the infirmary door. I pushed it open slowly, hoping not to wake the nurse. She could be a light sleeper, tuned to the comings and goings of girls kept awake by the pain of their monthly flow, or hay fever, or an upset stomach after weeks of too much onion soup. She snorted slightly in her sleep and rolled over. I pushed open the door and darted out into the hall.

I raced down two flights of steps to the first floor and then the basement, sneaking through the kitchen, pulling on my boots as I went, hopping from one foot to the other and praying I didn't crash into anything in the dark. I found the slim pamphlet of household influenza precautions Cook kept on the counter, sliding it between the door and the jam so it wouldn't latch, then raced into the night.

The pearly moon that lit the way the past few nights was starting to fade. It washed the lawn in a bluish glow until I reached the edge of the woods, where it was abruptly cut off. Still, I thought I saw which way Ada was going, and took off after her, the loose tops of my untied boots flapping wildly against my ankles.

"Ada?" I called her name softly, the trees absorbing my words before they could travel far.

"Ada?" The further I got, the louder I called, but there was no response, no sign of her ghost.

I turned a circle and discovered another, larger problem.

I'd been born in the city. Every tree looked the same to me.

I had no idea where I was, and I'd lost sight of the school.

I took a few more steps, and the ground fell away suddenly. I caught myself on a nearby trunk, clinging tightly to the bark while my boots scrabbled for purchase in the grass and mud.

When I was finally able to stand, I stood there panting, leaning against the tree. Had I been traveling uphill or down as I left the school? I'd been so intent on following Ada, and the ground was so uneven, I hadn't noticed.

No longer moving, the cold seeped through my blouse. I took a few tentative steps away from the edge, squinting in the darkness and latching on to the shafts of moonlight cutting through the thinning canopy overhead. There was a fallen log; I remembered stepping over it. It was the same one, wasn't it? Yes, there was the sapling that had slapped my cheek.

I stood on the log and looked around for another landmark, but couldn't find one. A tree was a tree was a tree as far as I was concerned. Why couldn't they come with labels, the way the books in the library did?

A twig snapped, a sharp crack that made me jump and lose my balance. I landed hard on my backside, scraping my hand on a rock.

"Julia? Julia, can you hear me? Are you there?"

I jumped to my feet, about to call out, but then stopped myself. That was not Ada's voice. *Of course not. Ada is dead.*

"Julia? Julia!"

"Bernice?"

The shouts ended in a sigh and the crash of none-so-gentle feet through the underbrush. Bernice's stocky frame and her white nightdress materialized out of the darkness, wrapped in a blanket. "What are you doing out here?"

"Why are you here?"

"I saw you run out the kitchen door. I couldn't sleep. And you haven't answered my question."

*Should I lie?* Bernice, like the other girls, probably thought I was crazy already. After my fit in the common room, it would be a miracle if they didn't all agree with Headmistress Davenport that I be sent away to an asylum.

"I thought…" I couldn't bring myself to say it. Not now. Not after what I'd heard. "It's nothing."

Lightly, Bernice touched my elbow with two fingers. "Come on. You must be freezing out here."

"Do you know the way back to the school? I got turned around."

"It's this way." She nodded in a direction that seemed random to me, but soon I realized we were on a rough track. Here and there, ribbons hung from low-hanging branches.

"What are those?"

Bernice's lip twitched. "It's Rainbow Lane."

"What?"

"You've heard some of the girls at school. 'I'll meet so-and-so at the end of the rainbow.'"

I nodded, still not quite understanding.

"Like finding the pot of gold at the end of the rainbow?"

She sighed, pointing again to the ribbons. "They're all different colors, see? So you follow this path, and it comes out at the cemetery. That's where the girls meet their beaus."

I glanced over my shoulder, where the path faded into darkness. "Oh. Is that what they were talking about?"

"Obviously you've never gotten an invitation."

"I did once. Matthew Black. But I thought he was making fun of me."

Bernice looked like she didn't know if she should laugh or not. "Would you have said yes if you knew?"

"Knew what?"

"That he wasn't making fun of you?"

"I still don't know he wasn't. Why would he ask me to go to a cemetery? Especially when that's the only time we ever spoke?"

The sigh she heaved was strong enough to flutter the loose strands of dark hair framing her face. "You're something else, Jules. Anyone ever tell you that?"

I still wasn't sure I understood, but I tried to pretend I did. I also decided not to comment on the fact that she'd called me Jules. In the scheme of things, I supposed it didn't matter so much if Bernice used that nickname, too.

"Who is Marie, then? Why do they meet their beaus with another girl?"

"Marie is in the mausoleum. That's where they meet."

The mausoleum? And the girls thought *I* was a ghoul.

A cold chill blew down the back of my neck. I'd been too excited to pay attention to the cold before, but now I soaked it up like a sponge and shivered.

Bernice offered me part of her quilt, but I stopped, pinned in place by the sudden feeling of being watched. A shiver that had nothing to do with the cold ran down my back and all my hair stood on end.

A sudden high keening split the night air. Bernice whirled, staring upward at the branches in an attempted to divine the source.

At first I thought it was coming from the direction of the church, but then there was a loud crash from directly in front of us. I thought I heard sobbing.

"What on earth--?"

I ran toward the sound. It was Ada. I knew it. Just as I'd seen her ghost run out of the school, I knew it was her voice I heard.

The cold became a minor inconvenience as I raced down the narrow track. Nothing mattered except finding Ada.

The trees thinned suddenly, and I broke out into the rear lawn of the school, just a few dozen yards from where I'd entered the woods.

Ada's body lay face down in the fountain, her legs draped over the concrete side of the pool.

"Julia! What are you doing? You can't let anyone see you!"

I glanced at Bernice. When I turned back to the fountain, Ada was gone. The water splashed playfully, just as it always did, unperturbed by dead bodies or ghostly visions.

Together we tiptoed across the patio to the kitchen door. The pages of the flu pamphlet fluttered in the light breeze, beckoning us inside.

The kitchen felt eerily quiet as we stood there, trying to warm ourselves by the rapidly cooling cook stove before going back upstairs.

My mind swirled with the events of the past half hour. I knew without a doubt now that Ada was trying to send me a message. There must be something she wanted me to do, or else why would I continue to see her ghost running toward the woods?

"Bernice…when the girls go…when they go to the end of the rainbow, how do they make their…appointments? How do they know their beau will be there?"

She blushed a little. "Rainbow Lane goes past the mausoleum at the church. You know, so Pastor Brown doesn't see anyone walking up the lane to the church. It intersects with the path the boys take on Sunday. There's a little statue there, and the girls leave their messages inside. They call it the post office. One of the boys usually sneaks away on Sundays, taking the whole packet, and they hand them out when the teachers aren't looking. Their girl will tell them which hymnal is hers, and that's where they put the replies.

"The hymnals?"

"Yes. Before the epidemic, we always took the same three

rows of pews, right? So you might agree that the first hymnal in the second row on the right is where you'll sit, and then he'll leave his reply there."

She tilted her head. "You really don't pay attention to these things, do you?"

I shrugged. "I think I've seen it before—the notes going in and out, and I remember Gloria complaining when our In Town days were canceled that she wouldn't be able to go to the post office. I thought she meant the actual one in town."

She nodded at the stairs. "We should get to bed before someone catches us."

# Chapter Six

The next morning I woke up automatically. The clock on the infirmary wall read five minutes after seven.

*Why didn't the bell ring?* I wondered, wrapping my blanket around me and tiptoeing to the window.

On cue, Cook ran out, giving the bell three perfunctory rings before hurrying back inside.

Nurse Spencer's door was still closed, though I could hear her moving around inside. I waited by her desk and spotted the newspaper from the day before resting on the blotter.

The teachers tried to keep us away from the news. With so many fathers and brothers at war, they didn't want to upset us. Headmistress Davenport also seemed to think it was unnecessary for young ladies to be aware of current events, even though she herself—as an independent lady of business, I assumed—was always abreast of local and international events. I often heard her talking to the other teachers at the head table. These overheard conversations and letters from home were the only news from the world outside Mt. Sinai we got.

I picked it up, scanning news of the war, which recounted battles and the positions of Bulgaria and Russia, and a large advertisement calling for Red Cross volunteers.

I tried to absorb as much information from the headlines as I could before the nurse came out. Finally, on page three in the local section, I found two lines that made my blood turn cold.

*Police have ruled the suspicious death of Ada Brooks at a Chillicothe-area girl's school accidental. No charges will be filed.*

The notice was sandwiched between *Mrs. Gordon Freeman visited Columbus on October eighteen* and *Mr. and Mrs. Henry*

*Black have escorted their son, Henry Black Jr. to Camp Dix where he will train before going abroad to fight for our country.*

I didn't fly into a rage. For a moment, all I could do was stand there, holding the newspaper stupidly like some kind of statue.

Nurse Spencer's door creaked open. I dropped the newspaper as if burned, even though it was obvious she'd seen me reading it.

She pursed her lips, picking up the pages and refolding them neatly. "Anything of interest?"

I shook my head, unable to speak for a moment. I was saved the effort by a light knock on the door.

"Nurse?"

One of the maids stood in the doorway.

"Yes?"

"Cook sent me up. Our box of headache powders in the kitchen is empty. She hoped you might have a few you could spare?"

"Of course. Just a moment." She turned away to get one of the boxes down from the cupboard over the sink.

While they went about their business, I stood, unnoticed, stiff and unmoving as I tried to push down the rage engulfing my insides with a nearly physical effort.

*How could they? How could* he? *Anyone could see it wasn't an accident.*

"Julia?"

I blinked and looked up.

"Are you well? You look a little pale." She put a hand to my forehead to check for a fever.

"I'm fine." I took a deep breath, letting it out slowly. A cold sort of calm began to spread over me. A kind of detachment. It felt like I was floating above my body, which slowly responded to her command to sit down so she could examine me.

I couldn't feel the wood of the chair as I sat down, or the wool of my skirt against my legs, or her fingers on my chin as she had me look this way or that or checked my pulse.

"Well, there's nothing medically wrong with you. Do you think you can tell me what happened yesterday?"

"I'm very sorry. I just got very angry. I shouldn't have." It felt like a lie. Who wouldn't be angry about someone going through their things? Someone invading their private, personal space? Who wouldn't feel violated after being slapped and dragged away like an unruly dog?

But I'd learned a long time ago that the things I found upsetting did not upset other people. I had to bite my tongue.

"I need your assurance it won't happen again. Headmistress Davenport is very concerned. For your wellbeing, as well as the safety of the other students."

I knew what the expected answer was, but again, it felt like a lie. How could I promise to control my emotions forevermore, when I could already feel the rage bubbling inside of me? By lunchtime, I could get into a fight with Elvira and knock her teeth out. I wasn't planning on it, certainly, but if there was anyone in the school other than Miss Newton who would drive me into a fury, it would be Elvira Compton. And it would be just like her to make fun of me for my fit, and to draw the other girls into it as well.

Finally reassured, Nurse Spencer sent me back to my room to freshen up. I changed into a clean uniform and tried to scrape some of the mud off my boots over the waste bin. There wasn't time to re-braid my hair, but I tried to smooth it down with some water when I washed my face and hands. With my mask in my pocket, I went downstairs to eat.

The half-empty dining room felt strangely crowded with all those faces turned to look at me. I wished suddenly I'd put on my mask before coming down. Someone really needed to invent one that could be worn while eating. Maybe I would, after I left school and started my training to be a nurse.

I took an empty seat, one down from Sarah Brown. Once again, she scooted her chair away from me. I looked up. She stared at her plate.

My lips pressed together in annoyance. Apparently, my rage

hadn't yet fully subsisted.

Without looking up, I glanced at her out of the corner of my eye. "Madness isn't catching, you know."

She shrank back. Her voice was a bare whisper when she said, "I'm not allowed to talk to you."

I looked around the room, where everyone was either pointedly ignoring me, or whispering to their neighbor while sneaking glances in my direction.

"I'm sorry if I frightened you yesterday." That, at least, didn't have the taste of a lie when I said it. I really hadn't wanted to upset anyone else.

She shook her head slightly. "Pastor Brown is my great-uncle. He says you're a wicked, wicked girl and I'm not to speak to you."

"Well, you're not doing a very good job of it then, are you?" I snapped, not bothering to keep my voice down. I snatched up my napkin and spread it over my lap with a sharp *crack* of the linen.

Bernice sat on the other side of the room with some of the girls from the twelfth-grade class, but when she heard me she got up and sat in the chair between Sarah and me. "Well. Someone got up on the wrong side of the bed."

"I've never understood that phrase. Either both sides of the bed are serviceable, or one side is against a wall. There's no wrong side to get up from."

103

Bernice snorted, spreading out her own napkin. "You're something else."

"Something else of what?"

"You know, different."

"Something other than the norm."

"Yes."

"Good. Right now, I've had just about enough of pretending to be normal. I am angry and hurt and I've just lost the only person who really cared about me and I've had enough of being ridiculed and mocked for it." Tears sprang to my eyes. I wiped them away hastily, dropping my voice. "Did you know the police decided her death was an accident? 'Death by misadventure.' That's what it said in the newspaper. I saw it this morning."

Bernice put a hand briefly on my shoulder, but pulled it back quickly. Anything she might have said was cut off when the Headmistress took her place at the head table and began the morning prayer. I bowed my head like everyone else, but didn't close my eyes and kept my hands curled loosely in my lap.

We ate in silence. There were only ten of us at a table made for twenty. Islands of girls floated among the long white table clothes, held afloat by whispered conversations. At the head table, Nurse Spencer was deep in conversation with the headmistress. Her glanced flicked to me, and I knew I was the topic of debate.

When the plates were cleared away, she called my name, gesturing for me to follow her to her office.

Headmistress Davenport's office was the height of Victorian fashion, with heavy furniture and needlepoint cushions on all the chairs. No matter how closely I examined it, however, I couldn't find a single personal item anywhere in the room. The paintings were all generic landscapes, likely by former students. Her desk held a blotter, pen stand, and telephone. The books were all heavy tomes on educational theory or language or history.

She took her seat behind the desk. As soon as I was settled— perched uncomfortably on one of the needlepoint chairs—she launched into her lecture.

"I spoke to your grandmother last night. She agreed that were the situation less...unusual, you should be sent home immediately, at least in the short term. However, as Chillicothe is currently under quarantine, that is impossible. You have no other relatives in the area?"

"I don't have any other relatives at all. Just my grandparents and my mother."

"And your father's people?"

"I don't know anything of them." Well, nothing I was going to share with *her*.

The headmistress nodded. "She asked to speak with you this

morning, before I made my final decision."

I waited. She picked up the candlestick phone, holding the receiver to her ear. It took several moments before an operator picked up. I could only imagine the telephone company was as short staffed as everyplace else with the flu epidemic.

Finally, she was put through to my grandmother's house. They exchanged brief pleasantries, then she offered me the receiver. I had to come around to her side of the desk, sitting in the big leather chair, in order to take it.

"Don't touch anything. I'll speak with her again when you're done. I'll be just through there." She gestured to the door behind the desk, which lead to her room. "No more than five minutes," she said before vanishing inside.

I looked at the clock on the shelf, and put the receiver to my ear.

"Grandmother?"

"Julia, darling. Are you all right?"

"I'm fine, Grandmother."

"What happened?"

I sighed, and explained as briefly as I could about what happened. I had to go all the way back to the beginning, with Ada's death, as the news hadn't quite made it down into the city yet.

"This is appalling. Bad enough for the poor girl to be found dead—Are there any suspects?"

I'd already used nearly four minutes of my allotted time. "Not that I know of. Grandmother, how is Grandfather? Have you heard anything from the sanatorium?"

Her sigh crackled over the line. "No change. We had to take him to the hospital, but they're not permitting visitors. And there's been no word from the sanatorium, either. They've been quarantined for a week and a half. No word in or out. And of course, the mail is stopped, for fear it will spread infection. I've not had any word. But your mother's young and strong, for all her mental infirmity."

That was what worried me. According to the newspaper and the scraps I'd overheard, the flu was hitting the young and strong the hardest.

"I know it's awful, and even worse you can't come home, but you're feeling better now, yes?"

I stared into the mouthpiece of the telephone, the gaping black maw, as though I could stare straight through the metal grate covering the opening, down the line and into my grandmother's face. It hadn't struck me until just that moment how much I wanted to see her face and be assured that she was, indeed, alright. The strain came through when she spoke of grandfather. He'd taken ill at the beginning of the month, and it was several days before Grandmother realized it was something serious. Always one for the stiff upper lip, Grandfather was the type to suffer in silence and then cut off his own arm before seeing a doctor. It was a miracle Grandmother and none of the household staff caught it before he was taken away.

"I'm fine."

"Good, good. Be a good girl, darling. Put the headmistress back on. I'll see if I can't convince her you should stay. And I'll tell her what a miserable old biddy she is for even *thinking* of punishing you after what you've been through."

I smiled to think of my calm, stern grandmother taking on Headmistress Davenport. The headmistress might be strict, but for her to argue with my grandmother was rather like pitting rowboat against a submarine. The submarine might not make any waves, but it would surely destroy anything in its path.

I'd already exceeded my five minutes, so I hurriedly said my goodbyes. "I'll put Headmistress Davenport back on. Just a moment."

"Julia?"

"Yes?"

"Don't forget, your grandfather and I love you very much, no matter what. Your mother, too, though she isn't always able to show it."

My throat tightened. I hadn't seen Mother since July, when the first flu case showed up at the sanatorium. The last time I saw Grandmother and Grandfather, before taking the bus up to school, he'd been angry because the maid left my suitcases in the front hall, and he tripped over my carpet bag on his way into the dining room for breakfast.

I didn't think I believed in the things Pastor Brown said every Sunday from the pulpit, but years of Sundays ingrained a kind of habit into me. I reached up for my locket—newly hung from a spare bit of embroidery thread—and gave it a squeeze. *Please don't let that be the last time I see them.*

I put down the phone and knocked on the headmistress's door.

She emerged, reading spectacles balanced on her nose. "Go wait outside," she said, reaching for the phone.

I did as I was told, but just as I was about to reach for the door, it flew open, nearly hitting me in the face. I took two hurried steps back and crashed into one of the needlepoint chairs.

"Debra! We have to—Oh, goodness. Julia. What are you doing here? Nevermind," Nurse Spencer said when I started to answer. She smoothed down her blonde hair slightly, then shooed me out the door. "Go. Get to class. I must speak with the headmistress."

"I'm supposed to wait—"

"Go! This will take a while. Just go to class." She all but shoved me out the door, slamming it so quickly it tapped my backside as it latched.

Confused, I waited outside for a moment, trying to hear their conversation. While I could make out the murmur of voices behind the thick door, and the panic they both held, I could not make out the words.

I was already late for my first class, and still needed to go back to my room for my books, so I took my time going back to the third floor. Someone had pinned a note to my door. I recognized Elvira's handwriting immediately. It was all flourishes.

*Danger: Do not enter. Lunatic ward.*

I tore it down. The pin flew over my shoulder, vanishing into the common room carpet.

My room, at least, was just as it had been the day before. Disturbed, but at least it was the *same* disturbance, and not a new one.

All thoughts of class forgotten, I set about righting it— straightening the bedclothes, putting the books back in alphabetical order, tidying Ada's hairpins on the nightstand. Ada's flashlight was still on the floor by my bed. I tucked it under my pillow. If the police had asked, I would have told them the flashlight and the hairpins and the magazine were hers, but they didn't, and I was grateful to have the use of the flashlight for a few more days.

They'd gone through my embroidery basket, disarranging the colored threads. I had to go through and tidy them, sorting them all by color, and putting the needles, fabric, and other tools back in the right order.

Last, I walked around Ada's bed, crouching by the loose floorboard. It wiggled under my fingers, but when I pulled it up the opening was empty.

*Well, they did a thorough job of it, at least. If only he was this thorough in his investigation.* How could the detective possibly reach such a conclusion after only a few days?

If only I'd been able to figure out who J was.

Since my first class was English and I was in no hurry to see Miss Newton, I sat on the edge of my bed, brushed out my messy braids, and re-plaited them while I considered the possibilities.

Finally, I decided I couldn't put it off any longer. Tying on my mask, I gathered my books and began the long—but not long enough—trudge to English class and Miss Newton's certain vengeance.

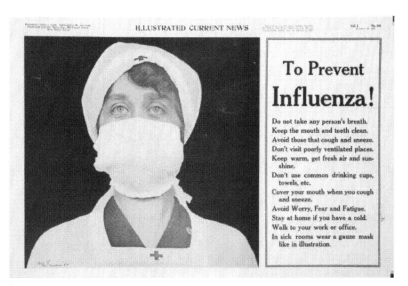

To Prevent Influenza, *Illustrated Current News*, October 18, 1918
*National Library of Medicine #A108877*

# Chapter Seven

I only got through the morning by keeping my head buried in my copy book. Not that I was working on the long essay Miss Newton assigned, or the problems Miss Comstock wrote on the board—I was done with those in ten minutes, anyway—but going over the list of what I knew about Ada, her suitors, and the mysterious J.

I made a list of all the J names I could think of. I'd done this exercise once before, but hoped revisiting it would yield better results.

It didn't.

If only the police hadn't found those letters. I wanted to re-read them again.

"Julia."

I looked up quickly, dropping my pencil. No one noticed, however. Miss Comstock was looking at Julia Watson, a senior girl who assisted her. Not that there was much to assist with, now that half the girls had gone home.

Suddenly, inspiration struck. I pictured the boys in church, in their dark blue sweaters and red ties, talking about football or the JROTC, flirting with the girls. Like us, there were many names that repeated—James, Thomas, Theodore. The boys didn't use first names with each other, though. They always called each other by surnames.

Flipping to a new page, I made another list, this one of all the last names I could think of from the Academy. Johnson, Jameson, James, Jewitt, Jones.

Charlie Johnson hadn't flirted with Ada, but they certainly made plenty of cutting remarks at one another.

J hadn't written to Ada for two weeks before she died. What if their romance soured?

In his last letter, he asked to meet her. Could they have been meeting "at the end of the rainbow?" It seemed likely. Ada's ghost *had* snuck off in that direction, and I saw her on the path as we returned.

The bell for lunch rang. I packed up my things quickly, following the others to the dining room.

I knew something was wrong as soon as I walked in. The three long tables weren't set, and no one was sitting. The girls all gathered around the head table, where Headmistress Davenport stood, wringing her hands.

"What's going on?" I whispered to Gloria, who was closest.

"I don't know."

"Girls! Girls, please, have a seat." The headmistress waved to the empty chairs.

The kitchen door banged open, and one of the maids—one of the younger girls who didn't usually work in the dining room— came out with a large stack of plates precariously balanced in her arms. Hastily she began laying them on the table, slapping down flatware from her apron pockets.

The headmistress cleared her throat, and the maid shrank back, setting the tables as quickly—and quietly—as she could.

Once we were all seated, the headmistress cleared her throat again. Her knuckles where white where her fingers latched on to each other.

"The influenza has come to Mount Sinai."

A collective gasp rose up from the gathered students. It sucked all the air from the room. Gloria and Camille clung to each other.

I bunched my fists in my skirts. My breath hitched and I closed my eyes, but the nightmare was already here. I'd ready every pamphlet, every news clipping I could find on the virulent disease, but this was one case where no amount of knowledge could forearm us against the danger. It struck the young and healthy in the morning, killing them by dinner, or lingered for weeks in the form of pneumonia, slowly filling the lungs until the victim drowned on dry land.

I'd read and studied, hoping to prepare myself. I knew it would come. It always came. It could wipe out an entire household in a week.

When it hit the sanatorium, it spread like wildfire, burning through patients like dry kindling. It started with a single case, the week after we last saw my mother. Usually we visited every Sunday when I was home from school, but by the next week they turned us away at the door.

"Just a bit of the grippe," said the orderly at the gate. "Nothing serious, but we don't want it to spread to the public."

But by August it was a full quarantine. No one in or out. The last I'd heard, the week before I left for school at the start of September, out of four hundred seventeen patients and one hundred seventy-eight staff, nearly two hundred fifty were ill and seventeen had already died. Because it was a home for the mentally unstable, the newspaper didn't print the list of names. There were already too many names to print, between the rolls of dead, wounded and missing coming from Europe, and those dying of the epidemic here—though in summer, it hadn't yet reached those proportions.

It started with the sanatorium, but by September the regular hospitals were filling up with civilians. By October, movie theaters, libraries, and any place people gathered in large numbers closed.

The thought of it, this unstoppable wave of death, the idea of suffocating in open air and being powerless to stop it, absolutely terrified me.

I could handle blood. The idea of stitching wounds or setting bones did not bother me. When we dissected small animals in biology, I was the only one who didn't turn green and run for the bathroom.

But a disease that couldn't be treated, couldn't be prevented— that was ghastlier than even the horrors of the battlefield reported every day in the newspapers.

The babble of voices around me rose to a fever pitch. Some of the girls were crying, others shouting angrily. Elvira placed the blame squarely on the servants and the "lower class" girls—by which she meant students like Sarah and me. Sarah, who attended only because of her great uncle's position, and me, the crazy one.

The noise pressed in. I needed quiet to think, but it was too much. I started rocking, clutching my locket, and couldn't stop.

"Silence!"

Forty or so girls froze in place. Except me. I tried to stop, but I couldn't. Dimly, I listened to the sobs of my distressed classmates.

Headmistress Davenport loomed over us, straightening her spine. "This is a terrible tragedy, to be sure. But we will carry on for as long as possible."

The unsaid hung in the air over the head table. We would carry on, until there were none left to do so.

"With that in mind, there will be some changes. To begin with, the infirmary is now under quarantine. No one is to enter without my permission, unless you suspect you have contracted the disease.

"Masks will be worn at all times. If you do not have one, I have some here. We will boil them every evening, and re-distribute them before breakfast.

"Whenever possible, windows should be opened and time

spent outdoors. Meals should be eaten quickly.

"Make sure to wash your hands often, and to cover your mouth if you cough or sneeze.

"There will be more illnesses, possibly even some deaths. We must prepare ourselves. I have reported our cases to the local authorities, and as of now the Mount Sinai School for Young Ladies is under quarantine. I spoke to Headmaster Cash this morning, and the Academy also has two cases.

"More will be required of you in the coming days. You may be asked to complete tasks you are unaccustomed to for the good of others. I implore you to show the gracious, caring spirit we have tried to instill in you here, to rise above your own discomfort as an individual in order to do what is necessary for the whole.

"By the grace of God, we will get through this. Please join me in prayer."

We bowed our heads as the headmistress began to recite the Psalms. "Yea, though I walk through the shadow of death…"

I squeezed my eyes shut and clutched my locket, praying that morning's phone call wouldn't be the last time I heard my grandmother's voice.

***

The adults tried to insist that things go on as usual, but after lunch—which no one ate—Mrs. Hodge, the history teacher, was peppered with so many questions and so many bouts of tears that she finally conceded defeat.

"Outside. All of you," she said, draping her shawl around her shoulders as she shooed us out the door.

We trooped out the front door to the wide, sloping lawn. This was much more decorative than the patio at the back of the school, with a fountain three times the size and little manicured flower beds. It was cold, but at least it wasn't raining. We took seats wherever we found them—benches, the edge of the fountain, the tiny brick walls bordering the beds.

There were just the seven of us left in the eleventh grade, now that Ada was dead. Many were sent home at the start of the outbreak, at the request of their parents, thinking their homes would be safer than a school where we were packed in cheek by jowl. They may have been right, to a point, but it hadn't stopped Mildred Temple from getting sick days before school started. She hadn't returned to school after summer break, and I hadn't heard if she recovered from her illness.

Girls sat in little clusters for comfort, clinging to friends but as far from others as they could get. Elvira, Gloria, and Camille huddled together on a bench while Mary Anne tried to sooth a sobbing Sarah. Bernice paused as she walked past them, then sat down next to me on the edge of one of the flower borders. Not too close, but within arm's reach.

I pulled my skirt down tight over my knees, tucking them up to my chin.

Mrs. Hodge paced up and down the path in front of us for several moments, then stopped, turned on her heel to face us like a general, and began.

"In the thirteen-forties, thirteen forty-seven to be exact, there was a terrible outbreak of plague that spread all through Europe. It was the most terrible disease known to man at the time, and killed with blinding efficiency. There was no treatment, no cure. Doctors could do nothing but pray.

"The plague was spread by rats—more precisely, the fleas on the rats—but at the time no one knew this. They only knew that people were dying with such speed the grave diggers couldn't keep up. What rudimentary hospitals there were filled quickly. Graveyards overflowed."

The other girls stared at her in horrified fascination, but I kept my eyes glued to the flagstone path, watching the little heels of Mrs. Hodge's black boots as she walked up and down the path as she spoke, somehow fascinated by the sway of the hem of her skirt.

"All told, between thirteen forty-seven and thirteen fifty-two, it killed twenty-five million people, nearly a third of the world's population."

She stopped abruptly, gazing at each of us in turn. "This disease, this flu, it's nothing. It is bad, yes. But it is merely a footnote in the pages of history. Mankind has been through much worse. It has survived the Black Death, it will survive the Great War, and it will survive the Spanish Influenza."

"That—that's a horrible thing to say!" wailed Gloria, burying her face in Camille's shoulder.

"She's saying we'll make it through, you ninny," Elvira snapped. Then her face softened and she patted Gloria's shoulder. "It's awful. It's the most awful thing to happen us. But we'll make it through."

"But a lot of us *won't!*"

It was a horrible time for petty, shallow Gloria to be right.

\*\*\*

The arrival of the flu temporarily drove my impotent anger from my mind, but it still simmered. I sat at my desk that evening, well after lights out, with Ada's flashlight propped up on a stack of books so I could see my list of boy's names, and everything I knew about J.

If the police wouldn't bring J to justice, then I would have to.

Of course, it was much more difficult for me, since I didn't know who he was. Maybe the police had matched the handwriting in the letters to the boys at the Academy. Maybe he'd confessed. I couldn't be sure. There was no way to know. Either the police decided it wasn't worth pursuing between the Bolsheviks and the flu and the war and the rising racial tensions in the area, or they'd found him and he'd spun some kind of elaborate story that put him in the clear.

There was only one way to find out, which was why I found myself sitting up an hour after I was supposed to be asleep, composing a letter to Detective Buchanan, imploring him to re-open the case.

I knew it would be days—weeks, even—before the letter could be mailed, especially now that the school was infected. But students weren't allowed to use the phone except in special circumstances, and I knew the headmistress wouldn't count this as such. The police had passed their judgment; I should take it with the grace of a lady.

Ladylike behavior be damned. My closest friend was dead, at someone else's hand, and I wanted to know what happened. Lack of a telephone wouldn't stop me.

Perhaps it was my own internal clock sensing the hour, but

something made me go to the window. Pulling back the curtain, I glimpsed movement at the edge of the trees.

*Ada!*

I threw on my sweater and snatched up my boots. Peering out into the hall, I listened to the sounds of ragged coughing from behind the closed door of the infirmary at the end of the hall. I swallowed down a tight lump of fear, fingers searching my face for a mask that had already been taken away to boil. I suppose the thought was that if we stayed to our rooms after lights out, it wouldn't matter if we didn't have masks. But I couldn't shake the feeling that we were all doomed, anyway.

Too afraid of passing the infection, I went down the back staircase, tiptoeing through the twelfth-grade dorm and down the dark, narrow staircase to the kitchen. Just as the night before, I slid the flu pamphlet into the door, pulled on my boots, and raced across the lawn after Ada's ghost.

This time, I knew what to look for and followed Rainbow Lane into the woods, checking every few yards for a tell-tale ribbon dangling from the branches. Some of them were hard to see in the dark, and I cursed myself for leaving Ada's flashlight on my desk. I hadn't even remembered to turn it off. The battery would be hopelessly worn down when I returned. At least the trees were bare, allowing some moonlight to filter through

Hardly used to running, I stopped to catch my breath, leaning on a rough, narrow trunk. Somewhere up ahead a twig snapped.

Quieter now, chills running down my back and arms, I crept forward. Through a gap in the trees, I could just make out a looming shape.

Voices.

"What were you thinking?" The male voice was indignant, angry. A girl objected, her voice high and plaintive. I thought I recognized it, but I couldn't make it out clearly. I thought she was calling his name.

"You idiot! What now? What if I get it? I'm supposed to go to training next week."

"Please, Johnny! I just had to see you one more time!"

I slipped through the shadows until I nearly impaled myself on the iron fence surrounding the graveyard. The parsonage and the church were huge lurking shadows in the distance, but between the trees and the dark and the slant of the hill, I couldn't see them clearly.

I found the path into the cemetery, following it back to the mausoleum, but instead of Ada I saw two figures, and automatically hid behind one of the taller gravestones. I peered around the corner just in time to see a boy, straddling a bicycle, give Gloria a hard shove. She stumbled, landing hard on her

124

backside. "Don't come near me!"

"Johnny!"

He backed away, pushing off as he turned the bike toward the road, pedaling as fast as he could. Gloria lay sobbing on the grass. I hesitated. Gloria was hardly someone I would call a friend, but I knew you were supposed to comfort people in situations like this. He had treated her very poorly.

I came out of my hiding place and went to sit beside her. I wasn't trying to be quiet, but when I crouched next to her, she jumped, flinging herself away.

"I'm sorry, I didn't mean to startle you."

"W-What are you doing here?"

"I...I saw something in the woods. I came to have a look."

"*Saw something?* What's that supposed to mean?"

I tilted my head, unsure why she was asking. "It means I looked out my window and saw something in the trees, and I didn't know what it was. So, I came to find out."

She stared at me, hiccupping away her sobs. "You're very strange."

"So I've been told. Are you all right?"

She looked back at the place Johnny had been standing. "Of course I'm not alright. The man I love just—just—" She dissolved into tears again. I sighed, stretching out my legs a bit. They were beginning to cramp, and it seemed we would be here a while.

"He doesn't seem like a very nice person."

Gloria glared at me. "You don't know him at all! He's very kind, and sweet!"

I didn't say that those usually meant the same thing. "I only mean, if a boy is going to yell at you and shove you, maybe you're better off without him."

She sniffed. "You don't know anything about boys," she said, addressing a tree.

I shrugged. "Obviously." I certainly wouldn't want to spend time with a boy who yelled at me and threw me on the ground. Come to think of it, it was why I didn't spend much time with the girls at school, either, if I could help it.

"I just wanted to see him one more time," she said quietly, to the grass.

I nodded, even though she wasn't looking at me. I would give anything to see Grandfather again.

# Chapter Eight

*January 20, 1918*

*Dear Mr. and Mrs. Grace,*

*I am writing to you today with regard to your granddaughter, Julia. Her teachers and I have some concerns about her that I think require your attention.*

*While she is very bright and excels in math and science and is an avid reader, she has been struggling in English and French. She has been very insubordinate and rude toward our English instructor, Miss Newton, and does not get along well with the other girls.*

*Her other teachers and the prefect for her year have raised similar concerns that Mt. Sinai may not be the right place for her. While I know she has only been with us a short time and has a unique background, I felt these concerns were grave enough to bring to your attention. I would like to discuss this further with you, either via letter, or if you would care to come in person I would be happy to meet with you. I can also be reached by telephone, if that is more convenient.*

*I remain committed to providing the best education for as many girls possible, and hope that we can find a way to better accommodate Julia's needs. This will, however, require some*

*assistance from you as she struggles to assimilate with the other*

*students.*

*Sincerely,*

*Deborah Davenport*

*Headmistress*

*Mt. Sinai School for Young Ladies*

"We should go back to the school. You'll catch a chill."

Gloria snorted. "It's hardly safer up there. Besides, you're the one in your night dress."

The thin cotton was already soaked through with dew. It would be frost by morning.

I stood up, brushing myself off the best I could and adjusting my sweater around my shoulders. I hesitated before offering Gloria a hand. She took it and I helped her up, then discretely wiped my palm on the hem of my cardigan when she looked away.

"Do you...do you come here often?" I asked, hesitantly.

Gloria gave me a wary look that quickly turned into a laugh. "Is that supposed to be some kind of line?"

When I didn't answer, only stared at her, confused, she shook her head the way Bernice sometimes did. "Nevermind. It's none of your business, anyway."

"I know. I only meant, did you ever see Ada here? Did you ever see her with anyone?"

That was enough to get her attention. She stopped and raised an eyebrow. "Why do you want to know?"

I wasn't sure how I could explain it, without telling her everything, so I did. I told her about seeing the body. Seeing the bruises. And my suspicion that whoever had been writing letters to Ada was the one she'd gone to meet that night. The one who killed her.

Gloria shook her head when I was done, face pale. "Gracious, I didn't know that. I never saw her after…after they found her. I only woke up when everyone started screaming and making a commotion. By the time Camille and I went out to the common room, there were too many people to get a good look. Not that I wanted one," she added hastily, looking away. "What a gruesome, awful business."

"I just want to know who she was with. The police chose not to press charges. They're saying it was just an accident. But it doesn't look like an accident. I just want to know why…"

My voice broke on the last word. The urge to cry snuck up on me, like a black cat in the night. I'd been calm, composed. But saying the words opened the lid on the well of tears that seemed to refill every time I put the lid back on.

Gloria shook her head. "You should just leave it. If the police say it was an accident, then it was an accident. How can you say it was different? She was so wild, she was practically asking for something to happen. And you know how she was with the boys. She'd flirt with anything with legs. She probably led on some townie, and he didn't like it and fought back. They can't control themselves, you know."

"When you came out here tonight, did you ask Johnny to push you? Did you ask him to yell at you?" The rage was bubbling up now. It seemed the internal kitchen where my emotions brewed only had one lid, and a growing number of pots. I could either control the anger or the tears, but I couldn't keep them both in check. Not at the same time.

"What do you know?" she snapped. "Of course I didn't *ask* him to hit me. What kind of question is that? He just lost his temper is all."

"So maybe, so did Ada's beau. Only he didn't stop with a shove."

"Then maybe she shouldn't have gone out with him in the first place!"

"Maybe you shouldn't have gone out with Johnny!"

130

The slap turned my head, but it wasn't nearly as hard as the blows from Miss Comstock. I stood there blinking away the bright spots in my vision as Gloria ran away, her sobs echoing through the trees as she raced back toward the school.

I sighed, following more slowly. I rubbed my cheek, once again considering how much I preferred books over people. Why did I always have to say the wrong thing? And a better question: Why were people always so damn unreasonable?

When I got back to the school, Ada's ghost was floating in the fountain again. I stared at it, no longer frightened by the apparition and too tired to muster up any other emotion.

"I know. I'm trying. I'll find out what happened," I told her.

The vision faded.

Gloria had made it back to the school. Unfortunately, she'd removed the pamphlet from the back door. I stood there, staring at the locked door for a moment before it flew open. One of the maids stood framed there, enraged. Over her shoulder was Headmistress Davenport, in her dressing gown, a thick braid of grey hair over her shoulder. Tucked in a corner, covered by shadow, Gloria sobbed into her hands.

The maid grabbed my ear and pulled me into the kitchen. I let out a yelp.

"Are there any more out there?" she asked, hands on her hips.

131

I shook my head. Headmistress Davenport grabbed my other ear, pulling me to her. She leaned down until our faces were mere inches apart. I recoiled from the heavy smell of her breath, whimpering slightly as she twisted the top of my ear.

"What do you think you're doing? I warned you. What do you have to say for yourself?"

At last, she let go. I rubbed my ear. I started to say that she'd only warned me not to have another fit like I had in the common room, but closed my mouth on it. *That is not the expected response, even if it's true.* Grandmother's voice drilled into my head. People always say things like, "Honesty is the best policy," or "Don't lie to me!" but adults, in particular, are not very fond of the truth. Not in the slightest. I'd already gotten one slap in the last quarter hour for telling the truth, and I wasn't eager to get another.

"I'm sorry, Headmistress," I lied.

Her nostrils flared as she looked down at me. I stared at the swinging sash of her robe, the tassel swaying irregularly back and forth with each of her movements. I wanted to stop it, to make it swing with the regular motion of the pendulum in a grandfather clock.

"Both of you will go back to your rooms. And since you seem so eager to be in the kitchen, you can both help out here while we're shorthanded. Miss Cartwright, you'll help with cooking—all three meals—tomorrow. And you, Julia Grace, will do whatever the staff tells you to do until I tell you otherwise. Cook and one of the kitchen maids are both ill, so Mary is going to need all the help she can get. Starting with serving the meals." She nodded to the tall, reedy maid behind me. I glanced up at her, and she glowered down at me.

"Yes, ma'am."

"Now both of you, back to bed before I decide to lock you in your rooms."

There weren't any locks on our doors, but I decided it was best not to say that, either, and instead followed Gloria's slumped shoulders back up to the third floor.

***

The next morning came far too soon. Someone knocked on my door shortly after the morning bell rang—I was trying to get an extra five minutes of sleep to make up for all the late-night wandering I'd been doing.

The knock came again, and then one of the younger maids, about the same age as one of the ninth or tenth grade girls, stuck her head in. "Miss? You'll get need to get up now. You're needed in the kitchen."

133

Sighing, I slid out of bed like some sort of boneless sea creature. The maid, clad in apron and mask, had a basket heaped with white gauze. She used a pair of tongs to select a mask from inside and hand it to me. "Fresh from the steam press in the laundry," she said, too cheerfully for the hour. I tied it on, then closed the door to get dressed.

Gloria was already in the kitchen, chopping vegetables for lunch and dinner when I arrived. "You're the one who's to help serve?" asked one of the maids. She was a head taller than me, with broad shoulders and frizzy reddish hair. A deep, freckled tan was visible above her mask.

I nodded.

She sighed, shaking her head. "I hope you're stronger than you look."

I understood the reason for this almost immediately. Waiting by the stairs to the first floor was a cart, laded with bowls and a large pot of oatmeal. The pot alone had to weight forty or fifty pounds, at least.

"We have to carry that upstairs?"

"Normally we'd just carry the pot up to the dining room and one of the little'uns would follow with the bowls, but we have to serve individually now. That means the whole kit and caboodle have to go all the way up the fourth floor where the staff rooms are, and we ain't got a dumbwaiter."

I stared from the cart to my companion. "That's insane. It will spill before we make it to the top of the stairs. And there can't possibly be enough there for everyone." Normally, Mt. Sinai housed about a hundred students, and another twenty-five or so teachers and staff. The rickety little cart probably only held enough to feed twenty or so people. We'd have to make at least three trips, even with the reduced numbers.

"That's orders." The maid glared at me.

"I'm only saying, it would make more sense if we set up a serving line in the dining room. If the girls came down one floor at a time to limit contact, then we could serve them, and they could take their bowls back to their rooms to eat. If they left the dishes in the common rooms, we could come to collect them after."

The maid glanced over my shoulder to Mary, who was listening intently from her post by the stove, stirring another pot of oatmeal.

"Do it. Take the headmistress her breakfast first and explain. We're too short staffed to waste time remaking meals or cleaning up broken china if that cart tips."

The redhead nodded, pulling down a tray and putting together the headmistress's breakfast. With the help of two of the "little'uns," I helped carry armload after armload of bowls and spoons up to the dining room on the first floor. It took two of us to move the pot of oatmeal, which was even heavier than I expected.

I was given the task of going door to door letting the girls know it was time to eat. Once all the ninth and tenth graders came down, I got to go back up to the third floor and repeat the process with my own classmates and the twelfth graders. While they ate, two of the maids and I went to collect the dirty dishes from the second floor.

Finally, after everything had been cleaned up, Mary handed me a bowl and pointed to a corner of the kitchen where I could eat. My skin crawled at the idea of taking off my mask in such a crowded area, but I was too tired and hungry to complain. I sat, gulping down oatmeal as fast as I could.

I was ten minutes late to my first class. Miss Newton made me stand at the front of the room with a sign that said, "Late girls don't make the grade." It was humiliating, and I could feel the seven sets of eyes belonging to my remaining classmates boring into me. My inner pot of rage boiled. I closed my eyes, trying to ignore it. Instead I concentrated on the lecture. I wasn't keen on Shakespeare but listening to Miss Newton dissect every aspect of Romeo and Juliet was better than listening to my heart race, or the imagined hum of fourteen eyes looking right through my skin. My arms began to droop, fingers slightly numb from holding up the sign.

"Miss Newton, I think Julia's fallen asleep," Elvira said.

My eyes snapped open at the same time Miss Newton's ruler came crashing down on her desk. I jumped.

"Are we boring you, Miss Grace?" she asked, acid dripping from every word.

"No, ma'am. I was listening."

"Then perhaps you can tell me the implications of the opening of act two."

I stared at her. She'd been lecturing on the end of act one, which we'd just finished reading in class the day before. We hadn't started act two yet. And I was standing at the front of the class, my book still at my desk.

"Well?"

"We haven't read act two yet."

"Miss Compton. What is your take on act two, scene one?"

I stared at the two of them, determined to keep my rage in check as Elvira explained the conversation between Mercutio and Benvolio. When she was done, Elvira flipped her blonde hair over her shoulder. I couldn't see her mouth behind the mask, but the way her eyes crinkled and narrowed made it clear she was smiling at me.

I wanted to stuff the stupid sign down her throat. It was all I could not to march down the aisle and do it. We were in the middle of an epidemic, there were three people in the infirmary who might die, and she and Miss Newton were busy playing games?

The longer I stood there, listening to Miss Newton drone on and on about a non-existent, ill-fated romance—between two people who honestly were absolute idiots in my opinion and shouldn't have gotten together in the first place—the less meaning it seemed to have. My best friend was dead, her murderer would go unpunished. At least one of the people upstairs would probably be dead by the end of the week. We were essentially trapped in a plague pit, too far from town for help to come. My grandfather and my mother might be near death, if they hadn't succumbed already. And my teacher wanted to torment me over a three-hundred-year-old play, just because I'd annoyed her by being late. I'd already been punished once for actually breaking the rules. I didn't need to be punished again for following them.

Before my brain caught up with my body, I was walking down the aisle, throwing the sign in the garbage on my way out.

"Julia Grace! Where do you think you're going! Get back here!" Miss Newton shouted. Her face was as red as her necktie.

I stopped. It was suddenly very hard to swallow. *I'm going to be in so much trouble*, I thought, turning slowly on the spot.

*It doesn't matter.* "I'm going to do something useful."

"You will sit down immediately!" Miss Newton's voice turned shrill. She came around the side of her desk with the ruler clutched in her fist.

"There are people dying in this very building—someone has *already* died, and you want me to stand here and pretend to care about some stupid play? You want me to stand here and let you punish me when I haven't done anything wrong?"

"Oh, you've done plenty. When I get through with you, you'll *wish* standing in front of the class was all you had to worry about!"

The other girls looked like they were watching a tennis match, eyes darting back and forth between us.

My whole body shook with anger and fear and I don't know what else. Part of me wished I'd just sat down when she told me to, but the greater part knew it wouldn't change anything. She'd just punish me more for being a willing victim.

I was already as good as expelled. What more could Headmistress Davenport do? Throw me out? Well, I supposed that was a possibility.

But it didn't stop me from opening the classroom door, sliding out into the hall, and slamming it in Miss Newton's face.

She shouted at me from behind the door, even swearing once. I leaned against it, eyes closed, trying to draw breath.

Down the hall, another door opened. Then another. Faces

139

peered out into the corridor, where I stood, heels braced on the tile. I didn't know what to do, so I stayed put, a human doorstop.

"Julia? What are you doing?"

Miss Comstock's face was concerned, her voice tinged with uncertainty. From where I stood slumped against the door, which wobbled at my back, the knob turning wildly, she seemed to tower over me, and I couldn't help but wonder if she planned to strike me again. I looked away.

"I just wanted her to stop," I said. And then from nowhere, I began to cry.

I lost my grip on the floor tiles. My feet slid out from under me and I landed on the floor. Miss Newton threw herself against the door with such force it knocked the back of my head and pushed me a few inches into the hall.

"Beth! Beth stop it!" Miss Comstock called to her. She pulled me up by my biceps and the door flew open. On the other side, Miss Newton's face was brick red. She brandished the ruler at me. "You! You troublesome little ingrate!"

The ruler came down hard. She was aiming for my cheek, but I turned my head into Miss Comstock's collar bone and it hit my shoulder instead. She drew back for another blow, but it didn't come.

I peered over my shoulder. Bernice held Miss Newton's wrist

in her iron grip.

"That's enough," she said. It was the same type of calm, firm voice Headmistress Davenport used when we were really, *really* in trouble.

The English teacher's face flashed from bright red to chalk white and back again. Tearing her hand away, she took a step back but the door of her room was blocked by a crowd of students.

More girls were out in the hall. This time it wasn't just the girls from my dorm, but the entire school—such that it was with our current numbers.

The shouting drew the attention of the headmistress. She came huffing and puffing, elbowing her way through the gathered crowd.

"What on earth is all this ruckus about?" she demanded. She'd come so quickly, her cheeks were pink with exertion.

"Grace was causing a disturbance in my class," Miss Newton spat.

"That's not true!" I snapped. I couldn't take it anymore. "I wasn't doing anything until you started picking on me. I didn't even complain when you punished me for being late, when I was in the kitchen the entire time! You can ask Mary! You didn't—"

"That is quite enough. Beth, I'll take it from here," Headmistress Davenport said, laying a gentle hand on the other woman's arm. In that moment, I knew exactly how things would turn out.

"Everyone, back to your classes. Now!" she clapped her hands, shooing everyone out of the hallway. Miss Comstock released my arms and trailed back after her own students to the math room, leaving me alone in the hall with Headmistress Davenport.

"You. My office. Now," she said, pointing the way.

# Chapter Nine

## FLUE EPIDEMIC IN OHIO

Recurrent Outbreaks—600,000 Cases—12,000 Deaths In Ohio—Caution on The Part of Local Health Officers Advised—Danger of Removing Quarantine too Soon.

---

Recurrent outbreaks of influenza attributed by state health officials to premature relaxation of local closing regulations, are continuing in various parts of Ohio, reports to the State Department of Health indicated today.

These outbreaks, returning in numerous communities after conditions had presumably been restored to normal, are delaying the final extraction of the epidemic which has caused an estimated total of 600,000 cases and 12,000 deaths in Ohio.

The responibility of these recurrences rests with the local communities, according to the State Dpeartment of Health. The action of the Public Health Council, conferring upon local health officials power to recind closing regulations when they should consider it advisable, strongly advised caution.

The danger in reopening as soon as a local outbreak appears to have died out, says the State Department of Health, rests in the fact that as soon as theatres, churches and other places are opened, visitors will come

[Fulton County tribune. (Wauseon, Ohio) November 29, 1918]

I trudged along the tile corridor and took the same seat I'd occupied the day before across from her desk.

"What will your grandmother say?" she asked, pulling the office door shut. She settled herself into her chair, hands clasped on the blotter. I went limp in my chair. All the fight was gone now. I was too tired to defend myself.

*I shouldn't have to defend myself. I didn't do anything wrong.* A tiny spark of indignation flared up but died again almost immediately.

"I shall have to call your grandmother about this incident, you know. Your behavior the past few days has been completely unacceptable. Do you have anything to say for yourself?"

I snorted a little. "Go ahead and call her. I know you're going to expel me, anyway. There was a girl found dead just a few days ago. There are more dying upstairs. But if my behavior *offends* you, then by all means, send me home."

I stared into the depths of the inkwell on her desk. Light from the windows reflected off the glass and the dark ink within, distorting the patch of light into a curved swirl.

"You know, a little remorse would go a long way to improving your case."

"I'm not sorry for what I did. I have no reason to be. Ada's killer is walking free, we have flu in the school, and Miss Newton is upset because I haven't read all of *Romeo and Juliet* yet. Which wasn't the assignment, by the way. We weren't supposed to finish the play until next week. But she decided to humiliate me instead, after I'd been in the kitchen all morning. I didn't even get to eat breakfast until after everyone else was done and the washing up was finished. But no, really. *Romeo and Juliet* is *far* more important than any of that."

I glared at her. I was being rude. Unladylike. The blank calm I was so good at cultivating in tense situations completely abandoned me. I didn't care if she was angry. I didn't care if she expelled me or called my grandmother or sent me home in the middle of an epidemic. There didn't seem any point in staying at Mt. Sinai anymore. I wasn't wanted, and I didn't want to be here.

Someone knocked on the door. I wondered if my meetings with the headmistress were destined to always be interrupted.

Without waiting for an answer, Bernice stuck her head in. "Headmistress? Miss Newton sent us to see you."

"Wait outside. I'm not finished here yet, Miss Loudon."

"That's why we've come. Miss Newton said I was being disruptive and insubordinate because I told her she shouldn't have spoken to Julia like that."

"And who is that with you?"

The door opened a little wider, and Mary Anne Flowers appeared. "Miss Flowers? What is your part in all of this?"

"I agreed with Bernice."

"And so Miss Newton sent you to me?"

"Well…"

Bernice hid her face behind her hand. Even with the mask I could see she was trying not to laugh.

Mary Anne tried again. "I may…I may have said she was a horrid cow for the way she treats people." She said this last very quickly. I gaped at her. Bernice snorted, then quickly tried to school her countenance back into something more suitable to begging the headmistress for mercy.

"You did *what*?"

"I know it was inexcusable, ma'am. And I'm very sorry. But you should see the way she is, especially with Julia. She's absolutely awful. She goes out of her way to embarrass us, especially if she thinks you're…different." Her glance flicked over to me, then down to the carpet.

"What on earth could have possessed you—*you*, Mary Anne! A prefect!—to say such a thing? And to a *teacher*?"

But the prefect merely looked down at the toes of her shoes.

Davenport shook her head, rising from her desk to face them.

146

"This is unacceptable behavior. From both of you. And you are both such exemplary students!"

Bernice wasn't laughing now. She wrung her hands in the fabric of her skirt.

"While I appreciate the situation might be perceived to be…unfair, we must all learn our place in this world, which is not always—in fact, it is *seldom*—fair. Especially for women. But that does not give us the right to lash out at our neighbors. You leave me no choice. You will both write letters of apology to Miss Newton. And since she is the one you have wronged, you will spend half an hour after lessons cleaning her classroom."

"If I may, ma'am?" Mary Anne raised her hand slightly, as though we were in class. "I was made prefect of the eleventh-grade dormitory because the girls see me as a leader, and I'm a good student. I know that makes what I did seem even worse, but it's also my job to represent the girls in my year. I'm their advocate to the staff. If there is something they need, it's my job to present it to you and Miss Comstock.

"We are also taught that a lady uses her privileges to help those who have none. It is our job to care for the sick and needy, to aid the downtrodden, and to be the pillar of support at home when there is trouble abroad." True. It was all in the school charter. A more poetic version was framed just above the teacher's table in

147

the dining room.

"In this instance, ma'am, we had a hostile foreign power—that is, someone from outside our dormitory—who took exception with one of our members and has routinely made her a target, just as the Kaiser has routinely made his intentions toward France and England known. This is a person who as all the power in the world, while we, as students, have none.

"We all know Julia is…a little different. Sometimes she doesn't understand things the way the rest of us do. But she's a good student, and in her way, she's kind. She has a very strong sense of what is fair and right.

"This week has been trying for all of us, but her especially, and she no longer has the comfort of a dear friend. Ada was always something of a buffer between her and the rest of us. An interpreter, if you will, just as one would need a translator in another country. I think in the same situation, any of us would lash out. Especially when faced with the targeted behavior of a superior.

"I submit readily to my punishment, ma'am. But I hold that while our methods might leave something to be desired, none of us are actually in the wrong."

For a moment, we all stared, dumbfounded at Mary Anne, who stared firmly back at the headmistress without blinking. I'd never heard her say so much together without a text book in front of her to read from.

Slowly, Davenport nodded. "That is…a compelling argument. I will take it into consideration," she said at last.

"Ma'am?" Bernice took a step forward. "Is it true what they're saying? About Ada?"

"Rumors are abundant, Miss Loudon. You will have to be more specific."

She swallowed hard, glancing in my direction. Her voice lowered slightly. "Is it true…they're saying the police think it was an accident. Is it really true no one will be arrested?"

"That is not something you need to concern yourself with. It's a matter for the police."

"But ma'am, how could Ada *accidentally* beat herself and drown herself in the fountain?"

"If you must know, the police *have* located the boy she was with that night, and I can assure you it was indeed an accident. Apparently, there was a quarrel of some sort and she slipped. The poor boy could do nothing for her. What would be the point in dragging his name through the mud?"

My hands clenched on the armrest. Bernice and Mary Anne both looked my way. The anger flared again suddenly. I sucked in a breath to try to quell it.

"But—"

"That is enough. Both of you, go back to class before I reconsider your punishments."

"But ma'am, what about Julia?"

The headmistress turned to me. "I will, for the time being, consider this to be extenuating circumstances. But one more incident like this—*one more*, and you will be expelled, quarantine or no. This is your *final* warning." She made a shooing motion. "Now get out of my sight, all three of you."

I followed Bernice and Mary Anne out to the hall. As soon as the door closed, Mary Anne leaned against the wall, panting. "Gracious. I thought she'd lay into me like a rabid dog," she gasped.

"Thank you," I said, sincerely. "Both of you. No one's ever stood up for me like that before." Not even Ada. Usually, if someone became focused on me the way Miss Newton or the headmistress did, she'd find some way to deflect their attention or lighten the mood, rather than challenging them directly.

"You're welcome. I just couldn't watch that anymore, especially after the scene in the dorm. It's one thing to get paddled for bad behavior, but that was something else entirely." Mary Anne's cheeks were pink, but she was breathing normally again.

I checked the clock in the hall. Only five minutes left before the bell. "Should we go back to class?" I asked more from duty than any actual desire. I would happily never set foot in the English room ever again.

"Not worth it."

"I should get my books, at least."

"Don't bother." Bernice shifted the stack of books on her hip. Both she and Mary Anne had time to gather their things before leaving class, and Bernice had taken mine, too. "I don't think Miss Newton is expecting you any time soon."

"Thanks." I tucked them under my arm as we dissolved into silence. I glanced at Bernice and Mary Anne, trying to decide if it was awkward and if I was supposed to say something. I didn't mind silence, even among other people, but others seemed incapable of abiding it, compelled to fill any lapses in conversation with annoying, useless chatter.

Mary Anne cleared her throat and adjusted her glasses. *Awkward, then*, I thought. Throat clearing was a distinct sign of discomfort. I sighed.

"Well, we should go to our next class, shouldn't we?" She led the way down the hall.

Still with some time to kill, they slid down the wall outside the math room, plunking down onto the floor. I couldn't stand the thought of sitting someplace that dirty, so I just leaned against the wall, listening to the murmur of Miss Comstock's voice.

"What are you going to do, Julia?" Bernice asked suddenly.

"About what?"

"Ada. The other night it seemed like you were trying to do something. Like you thought you knew who had done it."

I shook my head, staring at the black and white tiles. I lined the sides of my shoes up perfectly with the seams between two of them, frowning when the outer curve of my boots was an unsurprisingly poor match for the impeccably straight line. "I don't know. I think I know who she was with, but I'm not certain. And I don't know what to do about it. What can I do, when the police have already decided to let him go?"

My fingers squeezed around the edges of my books until my joints ached and the binding creaked. What *could* I do?

"Wait, how do you know who it was?" Mary Anne asked. She'd taken off her glasses and was wiping off the clouds of condensation worked up by her mask with a handkerchief.

"I found their letters. It's someone named 'J.' I think I know who it is, but I'm not positive. I thought maybe someone had seen them together, but the person I asked wouldn't answer the question."

"You know, when someone avoids a question, it usually means the worst," Mary Anne said, sliding her spectacles back into place.

152

"It says so in all the good detective novels."

Bernice smiled. "You read mystery novels?"

"Oh, all the time." She shifted her copy book out of the way, and picked up a thick tome from between *Romeo and Juliette* and our math book. "When in doubt, *Sherlock Holmes* usually has the answer."

I turned this over in my mind, thinking of Gloria and her refusal to answer the question. She'd been offended I'd asked, I was sure.

"You know, you remind me a bit of Sherlock Holmes," Mary Anne continued. It took me a moment to realize she was talking to me.

"Me?"

"Yes. He's a bit odd, too, but most people don't hold it against him. Well, except for criminals, of course. But he's very observant, and very smart. Well, he'd have to be, since he's the world's greatest detective."

"What would Sherlock Holmes do if someone murdered his best friend?"

Mary Anne didn't miss a beat. "He'd catch the killer, of course."

***

153

When it came time for me to report to the kitchen to help with dinner, I found the entire place in an uproar.

"What happened?" I asked the same freckled maid I'd worked with at breakfast and lunch.

"It's Mary. She's also down with the flu. She was fine this morning, but she just collapsed while she was mashing the potatoes. Then Annie and Cora both ran off. Said they couldn't stand working in a plague pit."

"Ladies!" Headmistress Davenport clapped her hands several times to get everyone's attention. I hadn't heard her come downstairs and jumped nearly out of my skin at the sound.

"Ladies, I understand this is a trying time, with both Cook and Mary ill. But we must have order!"

The banging of pots and the slap of knives against cutting boards stopped abruptly. The only sound in the kitchen was the pot of boiling water on the stove.

"Jenny, you've been here longest. You're in charge. From here we will go by length of tenure. If there are any disputes about that, you can bring them directly to me."

There was a mumble of assent from around the room, a mixture of relief and mutiny. With so many members of the kitchen staff now incapacitated or gone, the kitchen felt oddly empty.

"Ma'am, we need help down here. We're busy enough on a good day, but with the cook, assistant cook, and three of the kitchen maids gone, that leaves just me and Martha in the kitchen, plus the cleaning staff—" She cut herself off abruptly, but the unspoken words still lingered: *for however long they stay.*

Davenport nodded. "I understand. Gloria will not be down to help; she took ill this afternoon. I'll make sure someone comes down to assist."

Orders given, the headmistress turned and went back upstairs. I looked to Martha, the freckled maid. "Start taking the plates up and go get the little'uns. We'll be serving soon."

At first I thought she meant the two younger maids, but then I realized she meant the girls from the ninth-grade dormitory. The younger maids had run off.

After classes, we'd all been ordered back to our rooms. I pulled my sweater a little closer as I trudged up the stairs. All the windows had to be opened at least an inch, to let in fresh air, according to the headmistress. Unfortunately, it was late October and that made for some very chilly hallways.

"She should have closed the school two weeks ago, when the schools in town shut down."

I paused outside the first bedroom, my fingers barely brushing the knob.

155

"I can't believe we have to be stuck here. I—I want to go home," cried a second voice. A soft sob followed the statement.

"Oh, don't cry. I know it's awful. But at least we're together."

"But—But I want my mother. I don't want to be *here*, at school!"

I swallowed, fighting down the panic I'd been fighting against all day, wondering yet again how many of my family members were still alive. I wished I could call Grandmother again, little good though it would do.

I shifted my weight, and the floorboards creaked. The voices inside stopped, so I rapped lightly on the door. "Dinner's ready."

The sentiments of the two ninth graders were echoed throughout the school. In the third-floor common room, which we shared with the twelfth graders, I found three of the older girls lounging in the arm chairs, complaining about the unfairness of the situation. They seemed almost bored by the whole thing, like it was just an inconvenience, like a late train or the onion bin at the grocer being empty. One of them, brazenly, wasn't even wearing her mask.

"Dinner's ready," I said quickly, turning on my heel. I needed to wash my hands. I felt like I could see her breath in the air, a cloud of potential flu bacteria floating toward me. I backed away so fast I tripped on the rug.

"Hey, you're that weird girl. The one who had the fit the other day."

I paused, not sure how I should answer.

"I thought Davenport was sending you home. What are you still doing here?"

"We're under quarantine. No one can leave. And I can't go home, because Chillicothe is under quarantine, too."

"Well, aren't you lucky, then," she said, making a face.

"Lucky?"

"It's sarcasm, sweetie."

I still wasn't sure I understood, but she shooed me away. I hurried past them, holding my breath as my course took me past the infirmary. From behind the closed door came the sounds of the most wretched coughing I'd ever heard. At breakfast and lunch, Martha and I had left a stack of bowls and spoons and a pot of broth outside the door so Nurse could feed her patients. There were six beds in the infirmary.

It was only the first day of the outbreak at Mt. Sinai, and four of them were already full.

How many would there be tomorrow?

# Chapter Ten

[The Democratic Banner. (Mt. Vernon, Ohio) October 22, 1918]

After the incident that morning in math, our teachers seemed to decide teaching wasn't worth the effort. We were all too frightened, too distracted, to learn much, anyway. It was for the best. As soon as I'd collected the plates and brought them back down to the kitchen, I dragged myself back up to the third floor, half crawling up the stairs, and fell face first into bed.

When I woke sometime later, my room was dark. Clouds covered the moon and stars. Peering through the curtains, I saw that aside from the little lamp in the infirmary all the lights appeared to be off.

Fumbling in the dark, I found Ada's flashlight and turned it on. The bulb glowed orange with the dying battery. I used it to find grandfather's pocket watch. After he was taken to the hospital, Grandmother allowed me to take it with me to school. It made a nice ticking noise, and had his initials etched on the lid. I hadn't wound it in several days but risked slipping out into the deserted common room to check the time, winding the watch until it matched the clock on the bookcase in the corner. I drifted back to my room with it held to my ear and closed the door.

Laying down again, I put the watch on my pillow and timed my breathing to the ticking. Five ticks in, five ticks out.

Slowly, my jangled nerves began to relax. I pulled the covers up over my face. The same maid who had woken me up that morning came around just before lights out to collect our masks. I wished I had a second one, so I could sleep in it. I'd washed my hands so many times that afternoon that they were red and chapped.

A squeak of bedsprings made my eyes fly open.

159

Slowly, I turned my head. The linens on Ada's bed had been stripped at some point, the wool blanket folded at the foot with the pillow laid neatly on top.

There, on the edge of the mattress just across from me, was an indentation. In my mind, I could see Ada sitting there, putting on her shoes, or smiling as she told me about something in her magazine, or a moving picture she saw the last time she was home.

The bed squeaked again, and the depression vanished.

I blinked several times, pulling the blankets up a little higher. "Ada?"

The only reply was the faint aroma of attar of roses.

The bedroom door, which I remembered latching when I came back from the common room, clicked and opened half an inch. The door seemed to quiver slightly, as though nudged by an invisible breeze. It was an invitation if I ever saw one.

Slowly, I drew out my feet and placed them gently on the cold floorboards. The door opened a little further. Without pausing, I snatched up my boots and the flashlight, tossing my dressing gown over my arm as I tiptoed out into the hall.

I was faster this time. Ada's ghost appeared just a few yards ahead as I raced across the lawn. Her figure darted in and out of the shadows of the trees. Shivering, I followed as fast as I could.

When I reached the mausoleum, I stopped. There was no sound

160

from within, just the normal night noises of a forest gone to sleep.

There was no sign of Ada. I took a few steps closer to the building, expecting to see her there, but a movement at the corner of my eye drew my attention back to the trees. I turned just in time to see her long red hair vanish down another path.

This one wasn't marked with ribbons but was worn enough for me to follow it without trouble. My flashlight beam was so weak, it was useless. My boot—untied and flopping about my ankle—hit a rut in the path and I fell, sprawling in the dirt. The flashlight rolled out of reach and vanished in the bushes.

Ada was getting further away. I picked myself up and ran after her, ignoring the pins and needles sensation in my ankle. Low branches slapped me in the face. I tried to duck, but it was too dark. One of them slapped at my glasses, nearly pulling them off. I pushed through, limping until the path finally ended at the Academy.

It was the mirror image of the Mt. Sinai School for Young Ladies, but the Academy had a separate gymnasium and several storage sheds. The JROTC had targets set up on the back lawn for shooting practice.

I hovered at the edge of the woods, taking it all in. To the right, I saw the well-worn gravel track the boys followed to the church every Sunday.

161

There was no sign of Ada.

I whispered her name. "Are you there? Please, what do you want to show me?"

Silence. Not even a breeze to rattle the bare branches overhead.

Then…*something*. I leaned forward, trying to distinguish the soft sound from the pounding of my own blood in my ears. Was it a bird? Something high, not very loud. I thought it was coming from the school.

I crept forward, pulling off my smudged glasses, wiping them against my skirt.

A face appeared at one of the dark windows. A white figure in pajamas, framed by dark curtains.

I blinked, shoving my glasses back on. There, on the second floor, was a familiar face.

Below the window, Ada stood, silent. But this time, she faced me. She looked at me squarely, with a bruise on her neck and hatred in her eyes.

*That one.*

I don't know if I heard the words, or merely thought them. I blinked, and Ada disappeared. The boy at the window continued to stare at me.

I looked Charlie Johnson directly in the eye.

The next morning, I woke on my own. I hadn't gotten back to bed until after two o'clock because I'd been searching the underbrush for the burned-out flashlight. I'd wanted to storm directly into the academy and confront Charlie, but the kitchen door was locked. I wasn't sure what I would do if I got in. Talk to him? Unlikely. I wanted to beat him, to hurt him the way he'd hurt Ada, even if he was twice my size.

But I couldn't get in, and I'd been too afraid of waking anyone else. I was in enough trouble already. Somehow, the pragmatic part of my brain won out, and I backed away from the door slowly, my eyes glued to the second story window where I'd seen his face.

I couldn't doubt it anymore. Maybe the testimony of Ada herself wasn't enough to convince the police of his guilt, but it was enough for me.

I needed to find a way to talk to him. The question was, how? With the girls' school on lockdown, there was no way we'd be at church on Sunday. For all I knew, the academy could be laboring under its own outbreak by now.

Checking my watch, I saw it was quarter past seven. I sat bolt upright in bed. How could I have slept through the bell? Through the maid coming with our masks?

Stupidly, I turned to peer out the window. The patio and yard were deserted, a thick coat of white frost covering every available surface.

I rolled out of bed, throwing on my uniform with barely a pause to brush my hair. With one tail half braided, I answered the knock of the maid with the flu masks.

Except it wasn't a maid, this time. It was our French teacher, Miss Murphy.

"Here, take it. Everyone is to meet downstairs in the dining room in ten minutes. Hurry up," she said, pushing a mask into my hands.

A flutter of fear did strange things to my chest. Finishing my hair, I tied on the mask, stuffed the watch into my pocket and went out into the hall, following the other girls down to the first floor. The watch was a comforting weight against my thigh, banging lightly with each step.

"What's going on?" whispered one of the tenth graders to a friend as I passed them on the stairs. "Did someone die?"

"Don't say that!" snapped an older girl.

"Well, it's a possibility..."

The twelfth grader shooed us all down to the dining room. The tables weren't set. There was no vat of oatmeal, no teetering stack of bowls.

Headmistress Davenport stood in her usual place. Her face was pale, eyes shadowed and rimmed with red.

Our reduced numbers made the dining room seem larger than usual. As if for safety, we crowded together. I hung on the fringes, unwilling to let anyone touch me, even if standing in the open didn't feel safe, somehow.

The headmistress clapped her hands twice to get everyone's attention, but even her usual gesture of command was lacking in enthusiasm.

"Ladies, I'm afraid I have bad news."

The room held its collective breath. Friends and sisters reach for each other, further drawing in the small gathering. I stood alone, a cold chill rolling up and down my arms.

"Last night two students and three members of the staff took ill. That brings the total to twelve—too many for our infirmary.

"I had hoped we could avoid the epidemic status that has swept through the country—and the world—but due to the nature of the illness and its severity, we shall have to make accommodations.

"First, meals will continue to be served buffet style to limit contamination. All students must wash their hands before entering the dining hall, and masks must be worn any time you are outside your room.

"Second, as we have now outgrown the capacity of the

infirmary, the sick are to stay in their rooms. Most of you have your own rooms at the moment already, which is a blessing. Only the most severe cases will be moved to the infirmary from this point. All others will remain quarantined in their bedrooms.

"With the staff so reduced, I would like to ask for volunteers to aid in nursing the sick."

No one raised their hands.

At last, hesitantly, Maureen, the twelfth-grade prefect, raised her hand.

"Thank you, Maureen." The headmistress scanned the assembled crowed, looking each girl in the eye. Well, except for me. I was watching her pendant again as it swung back and forth.

"I need not remind you that in this time of difficulty, we must all pull together to aid one another. Anyone not helping with the sick will be given other duties. The details of those duties will be assigned to you by your dormitory supervisor. All hands will be needed for cooking, cleaning, and nursing. Until further notice, classes are canceled."

This last bit made me—and everyone else—look up.

"By His grace, we will all survive this trial, and be the stronger for it. Now please, join me in prayer."

We bowed our heads. My mind reeled. Who else was taken sick?

I peered around the room, counting. I wasn't the only one ignoring the prayer—there were several sets of darting eyes, each one counting the people around her, looking for missing faces. One girl from the tenth grade was missing. Other than Ada, she was the only red-head, and her absence was notable. I glanced at the cluster of twelfth graders, and only counted six.

When at last the *amen* was said, the headmistress sat down heavily in her chair.

Miss Newton, the dormitory supervisor for the twelfth grade, took her place. "Ladies, we have a lot of work to be done. Our kitchen and cleaning staff have been severely depleted, and we all need to work together to fill in the slack. I would like volunteers to help with cooking and serving this morning, and for washing up."

Several hands went in the air. As each chore was assigned, girls left the room to see to their tasks. I volunteered to help with serving and was sent down to the kitchen where those helping cook were already hard at work.

"Where are my servers?" The freckled maid, the only one left, had taken charge of the kitchen.

I raised my hand. Bernice had also volunteered to serve, as had a girl from ninth and one from tenth.

The maid looked Bernice up and down, taking in her stocky build. "You two, you'll be taking the broth to the infirmary, and any room with a ribbon around the doorknob. Those are the sick rooms. Don't forget the servant's quarters and the teacher's rooms, too," she said.

I nodded, suppressing a shudder. I didn't want to spent time in the sick rooms. I hadn't volunteered for nursing for a reason, but I also hadn't considered that serving would mean having close contact with the illness. Instead, she gave the job I'd thought to have—taking bowls and food to the dining room and ladling out—to the younger girls.

"Come on. This is going to take a while," Bernice said, nudging my arm. She went to the stove, hoisting a huge pot of vegetable broth and carrying it to the stairs. I took the basket we'd been using for the past few days to collect dirty dishes, filled it with clean bowls and stuffed several handfuls of spoons into my pockets, and followed her.

We searched the second floor for sick rooms but didn't find anything. "They must be in the infirmary," Bernice said at last, lugging the pot of broth up another flight of stairs. Sweat beaded her brow, and despite her best efforts not to spill, the front of her skirt was already damp.

"Do you want to trade?" I asked.

She glanced at my scrawny arms and shook her head. "No, I'm fine," she grunted, setting the pot down on the stairs for a moment to wipe her forehead.

"Where did you go last night?" she asked suddenly.

I blinked. "What?"

"I saw you run into the woods again. Where do you keep going? I know it's not to the end of the rainbow."

I shifted the basket of bowls to my other arm, biting my lip. "If I tell you, you'll think I really am crazy."

"Try me." She picked up the pot again, slowly making her way up the first flight of stairs.

I followed a few steps behind. "I think Ada is trying to tell me something."

Bernice stopped, broth sloshing over the edge of the pot. "What?"

I sighed. I knew I shouldn't have said anything. "Never mind."

"No, what is it? What do you mean?"

Finally, after much coaxing, she managed to tease out the story. I told her about the strange noises in my room, the sensation of being watched.

"And every night just before midnight, I see her run into the woods. Last night I followed her all the way to the academy." I told her about how last night's visit was different. For the first time, Ada had been perfectly aware I was there.

"I don't know if you're crazy, or just grieving," she said at last, continuing up to the third floor.

"I'm not crazy."

"My mother says that after Dad died, she used to dream of him all the time. Once, she thought she saw him standing in the kitchen and dropped an entire roast as she was putting it into the oven."

"I didn't imagine it. I'm not—"

"Crazy, I know. I heard you the first time." I thought she was done, but after a few panting breaths she spoke again. "I heard the girls talking. The younger ones. Some of them said they saw Ada's ghost in the courtyard. And Elvira is convinced she was in the common room. They're saying she put a curse on the school when she died, and that's why the flu is here now."

We came up on the side of the building with the twelfth-grade dormitory. The second door on the left had a white hair ribbon around the knob.

We stood outside the door, staring at the ribbon. It fluttered slightly in the draft from the stairwell.

"Ready?"

"No."

"Well, there isn't much choice. Could you get the door?"

I froze, eyes glued to the knob. I could see my distorted reflection in the brass.

"Julia?"

I shook my head. "I can't go in there. It'll get me."

I took a step back, squeezing the handle of the basket.

Carefully, Bernice put down the pot. "Jules?"

I glanced at her. "It'll get me."

Bernice put a hand on my shoulder. I pulled away, but it was enough to still the slight rocking motion that had begun.

"Give me one of the bowls," she said gently. I hesitated, then handed her one, and a spoon. She filled the bowl with broth, then knocked softly on the door and went in.

I waited for what felt like forever. Eventually, Bernice came out again, brows furrowed.

"Is…is she dead?" I whispered.

"What—? No!" A racking cough sounded from inside the room. Bernice looked over her shoulder at the closed door.

"We're going to need a lot more nurses."

> *Pleasant Valley Sanatorium*
>
> *For the treatment and care of the infirm of mind*
>
> *Providing long term care for those unable to care for*
>
> *themselves, including the old, infirm, and feeble minded*
>
> *of all kinds.*
>
> *Our modern, scientific treatments often provide*
>
> *permanent cures where other methods have failed.*
>
> *The largest, most up-to-date facility in tri-county area.*

# Chapter Eleven

With only one of the maids left, it was a good thing classes were canceled. Chores filled the rest of the morning. Some of the girls were so sick they couldn't feed themselves. When we finally arrived at the infirmary, Nurse Spencer looked ready to drop from exhaustion. "Oh, thank goodness," she said, pulling us inside before I could object.

"We need all the help we can get. The worst cases are in here. You'll want to start on the right. Cook and Miss Cartwright are the worst. They'll have to be fed by hand."

I peered around Bernice's shoulder. Gloria lay on one of the thin mattresses, her face pale and covered in red blotches. Her eyes were closed, but she moved restlessly, squirming under the blankets.

"Is there anything I can do?" Bernice asked, brows creasing with concern.

The nurse spared a tiny, exhausted smile. "For now, all we can do is make them as comfortable as possible." She nodded for us to get started.

"Jules?"

I stared at her. "I can't go in there," I whispered.

Bernice leaned so only I could hear her. "Julia, I know you think Ada needs you. But you can't help her if we don't get this under control. There are living people, right here, right now, that need you more."

I started to shake my head.

"Didn't you say once that you wanted to be a nurse?"

"I do. But I thought…I can handle blood. Blood isn't contagious."

"This is also part of nursing."

I forced myself to look on the two rows of beds and their miserable occupants.

173

"You can help them. I've seen the stuff you read. After Nurse Spencer, you probably know more about medicine and this flu than anyone else at Mount Sinai."

I looked at her, licking my lips. I made a face when my tongue touched the gauze. Just the thought of walking in there made my breath rattle with fear.

With one white-knuckled hand, I held on to the basket of bowls, following Bernice inside. She stopped at the desk, heaving the heavy pot onto a clear space.

"Start here. Fill the bowls, and I'll deliver them."

It was the best compromise. I nodded, setting down my own burden, and began filling the empty bowls. Bernice hurried away with the first two.

I wanted to cover my ears against the sounds of suffering and illness, but I couldn't do that and do my work at the same time. I tried humming under my breath to block out the noise, but it didn't help.

*One thing at a time,* Grandmother used to say when I felt overwhelmed.

*Just concentrate on one thing at a time.* Pick up a bowl. Fill it. Put it back down. I did it so quickly that I filled too many.

"We've got enough," Bernice said after her third trip.

I blinked and looked up. She handed me the last two bowls.

"Those two. There, on the end. They're both asleep. You can just put it on the night stand." She hurried off with servings for two more patients, then sat beside one of the ninth grade girls, too weak to lift her own spoon.

Just the thought of walking down the twin rows of beds made my chest tighten with fear. Miasma rolled off the patients, clouds of green, flu-infested air only I could see. I closed my eyes.

*Just a few steps. One thing at a time.* I could practically see Grandmother looking down at me, her face both encouraging and disapproving. She would be ashamed if she knew there were people in need that I could help, and I refused because of my own fear. I could hear her lecture now: *This is a time of sacrifice, and of great need. We must sometimes give up our own comforts and security so that others may have some small measure of it, who would otherwise have none.*

I took one step, and then another and another until I reached the foot of the first bed. Mary, from the kitchen, lay mostly covered by blankets. She cracked one eye open when I set down her bowl on the nightstand, but made no move to eat, pulling the quilt over her face and shivering.

I swallowed hard, backing away. For a split second, her blanket seemed more like a shroud.

*The first to die.*

I whipped around, splashing soup over my hand. Ada stood in the infirmary doorway, a dark look in her shadowed eyes. I opened my mouth to call to her, but then she was gone. With shaking hands I put the bowl on the night stand and wiped the broth off on my skirt; there were no towels. Ada was nowhere to be seen, but a cold chill raced up and down my spine and I shivered.

In the second bed, Gloria lay still except for her labored breathing.

She coughed so violently, her torso bounced on the mattress, pulling her from whatever restless sleep she'd managed to fall into.

Red rimmed, her brown eyes when she looked up at me, the dark shadows beneath giving her the appearance of a death's head.

"I'm being punished, aren't I?" she whispered through cracked lips.

I stared at her, too startled even to step back. "I—I don't know what you mean."

"For being a wicked girl. For sneaking out to see Johnny. I knew I shouldn't have." She turned her head into the pillow, coughing so hard, I thought she would turn inside out.

I reached for the jug and glass on the nightstand, pouring water for her, but when I held it out, she didn't take it. She glared at me instead. "The girls were right. Ada cursed us. She cursed me because I didn't say anything."

"Say anything about what?"

But then she started coughing again, even harder this time. The glass slipped from my hand and shattered on the floor.

"Out of the way!" one of the older girls snapped, pushing me aside. She helped Gloria to sit up so she could breath. I backed out of the way, crunching glass under my boots. I slipped in the water and backed into Mary's bed. It screeched, sliding a few inches across the tile floor and leaving deep gouges behind.

Gloria's eyes followed me, glowing embers starting out from her white face, the white of the sheets. I tried to blink away the image of her skull-like face, but she kept staring.

I turned and ran from the room.

As soon as I was outside, I felt silly. Running from a bedridden girl, just because she said mean things. And really, that was mild compared to what she and Elvira and the others usually came up with.

But the look on her face…that was a much harder terror to shake.

And what had she meant? Had she seen something the night Ada died after all?

Bernice found me a few minutes later, curled up on one of the couches in the common room, knees up to my chin, Grandfather's pocket watch pressed to my ear.

"Are you all right?" she asked, stopping at the edge of the rug. I glanced up at her, nodding slightly.

"I'm sorry. I didn't mean to run."

"I shouldn't have had you take care of Gloria, but I thought since she was asleep it would be okay. But she's mean as a snake even when she isn't sick. I don't think a fever has improved her disposition."

I shrugged. "I don't think it would improve mine, either."

Bernice smiled, but I hadn't meant to say anything amusing. "Can you help me get the stuff? I don't think I can carry the basket and the pot at the same time."

I nodded. We finished our rounds without incident, though it took over an hour.

When we finally reached the kitchen again, Bernice left the pot on the floor by the sink, unable to lift it again. Someone else had been assigned to collect the empty bowls, thank goodness. I didn't think I could go through it again. I sank down onto the bottom step, leaning my head against the wall.

"We're going to need more volunteers," Bernice sighed, dropping down next to me.

I could only nod. If every meal took nearly two hours just to serve…and then to clean up…and then to serve again… "By this time tomorrow, our entire day will be nothing but serving meals," I sighed. Already, I could smell the next pot of soup bubbling away on the stove, though the maids and kitchen helpers were nowhere to be seen for the moment.

"I'm telling you, that's what I saw!"

Bernice and I both looked up. Coming down the stairs were a pair of ninth grade girls, laden with baskets of dirty bowls and silverware. One of them, a tiny little thing with her blonde hair in tails, clutched her basket to her chest. "I'm not making it up! I really did see her!"

"Ruthie, there's no such thing as ghosts," her taller friend admonished. Her cheeks were pink with the effort of going up and down the stairs with their burdens, and she'd pulled down her mask to her chin.

"Emily! I'm serious!"

"What did you see?" Bernice asked, leaning back against the wall. We were sitting right in their path.

The girls stopped, neither looking pleased at being waylaid. "Ruth thinks she saw a ghost last night."

"I'm telling you, I did. It's that girl who died. She was on the stairs. I heard her footsteps. And someone moved my books."

"That's because you left them in the common room again. Of course someone moved them. They were in the way."

My empty stomach clenched in on itself like an icy fist. "You saw Ada?"

As though noticing me for the first time, they both turned. The one without a mask swept me up and down with her eyes, recognition dawning. "You're that girl."

I didn't have to ask what she meant. *That* girl. The crazy one. The one who had fits and yelled at teachers over nothing. The one who would be expelled when this was all over.

"Yes."

"I've seen you. You were her friend."

"We were roommates."

Ruth piped up again, bright patches appearing on her face. Her mask was too big, covering nearly everything except the slight blush around her temples. "I heard a rumor she was killed. I think her ghost is looking for justice."

Emily rolled her eyes. "Don't be ridiculous, Ruthie. Once you're dead, you're dead. You don't care about justice, and you certainly don't care about moving stuff obnoxious ninth graders leave behind."

"Where did you hear that rumor?" Bernice asked, pulling herself to her feet. She wasn't tall, but even with two steps between them, she was almost the same height as Ruth.

"It's all over the school. Please, can I put this down? It's really heavy," she said, arms shaking under the strain. Bernice and I moved out of the way so they could leave their baskets next to the giant soup pot.

"Where did you hear it?" Bernice asked again.

"I told you, it's all over. I heard some girls talking in geography. They're saying she was murdered. Someone else said she did it to herself, but I don't know how someone could murder themselves like that."

"Ruthie..." Emily rolled her eyes, opening her mouth to explain, but Ruthie was on a roll now.

"They said her beau did it. Or that it was some crazed flu patient from town, who was trying to find his family. But they're saying she wants to take vengeance on the school."

"Even if that made sense—which it doesn't—how would moving your books help her quest for vengeance?" Emily demanded, clearly out of patience with the conversation.

Ruthie sniffed. "Well, obviously she's trying to get our attention. Trying to create chaos and fear—that's what ghosts do."

I tilted my head a little at this statement, wondering how many ghosts she'd met. The spectral maid in Grandmother's attic certainly didn't seem to care about chaos or fear or even getting anyone's attention. She was simply *there*. And aside from the one incident outside the academy, Ada's spirit also seemed stuck in a loop. Her only form of communication was subconscious—as

181

though by replaying her murder over and over, she hoped someone would finally witness it, put a stop to it.

Punish the person responsible.

Ruthie continued, diving into a long tale of the ghosts at her old school, in Pennsylvania, and the ghosts of Civil War soldiers that roamed nearby. "The only way to communicate with them is through a séance. You have to call their spirits properly, or else they're too lost and confused."

Bernice finally lost her patience. "And what do you know about séances? Everyone knows they're a load of bunk."

Ruthie straightened up, summoning her full if unimpressive height. "I know plenty! My mother goes to séances every week to talk to my Papa."

"And she pays money for this? Sweetheart, your mother's a sap. Someone's fleecing her for all she's worth."

Ruthie's cherubic face contorted in anger. "How dare you! You can't say those things about Madame Marron!"

The tiny girl was ready to fly into a rage. I took a step back when it looked like she would throw herself on Bernice, but her friend pulled her back. "See? What have I been telling you? *Mrs. Brown* is just another table-tapping charlatan. She couldn't even come up with a decent *nom de guerre*."

Ruthie sniffed, clearly as annoyed with her friend as she was with us, but I couldn't help but wonder.

"Ruthie, have you ever spoken to a spirit?" I asked. My voice felt fragile and weak. I had to strain to make it heard.

She nodded gravely. "Oh, yes. When I was home in July, Madame Marron called up the spirit of my grandmother and my older brother." Her enthusiasm drained away. Very quietly, she said, "He died in France, back in January. They buried him in a mass grave over there. There were so many dead, they couldn't all be identified. But he told me not to worry. He told me he had my picture with him, and he'd always remember when we had it taken, in Philadelphia. Right before we moved here." She sniffled, dabbing at the corner of her eye with the edge of the over-sized mask.

Once dry, the fire in her eye kindled again. She turned back to Emily. "So there. How could Madame Marron know about that, unless Billy told her? How could she know which picture he took, or when it was taken?"

Emily opened her mouth, but if she had an answer, she swallowed it, instead offering a tiny smile of reconciliation.

"Why don't we just get our food, before we have to go back to work? I'm starving," she said.

Bernice grinned. "Here, here!"

My stomach gurgled in agreement, but no one else seemed to

notice. I chewed on the inside of my lip while scavenging for the few remaining bowls and utensils that were clean, and we each ladled out some of the leftover soup, which had cooled and turned to mush. Still, I was so hungry it hardly mattered.

Even if the soup wasn't appetizing, Ruthie's words had given me plenty to chew on.

***

I went back to my room after lunch, collapsing on the bed for a nap. It had been nearly a week since I'd had a decent night of rest, and I could feel it all over. I closed my eyes and was dead to the world for hours. When I finally woke up again, Bernice was pounding on my door.

"Go away," I mumbled into the pillow.

"Jules! Come on. We have to go serve dinner."

Reluctantly, I pulled myself out of bed. Once again, we went through the motions of that afternoon, hauling the big soup pot up to each floor for those too ill to go to the dining room. There was a new ribbon on the second floor, in the ninth-grade dormitory, and two more in the twelfth.

My stomach churned as we headed to the infirmary. I closed my eyes against the memory of Gloria and the vile things she'd said, and the little voice whispering in my ear as I stood over Mary—*The first to die.*

My hands shook as I knocked on the door. Bernice shifted the stew pot to her hip, shaking out one tired hand and sloshing beef broth down the front of her uniform. She muttered something unladylike and tried to brush it away.

The door swung open. Nurse Spencer, eyes red rimmed and face beaded with sweat, let us in. I patted my mask nervously as we crossed the threshold.

If the nurse's state of disarray was marked, it was nothing compared to the rest of the infirmary. Maureen had apparently convinced some of the other twelfth grade girls and the prefects to aide with the nursing. Mary Anne was bathing Cook's forehead, while our history teacher washed glasses at the sink.

Patients writhed in their beds, straining to find a position that was both comfortable, and would allow them to breathe. My eye went immediately to Mary's bed, but she was still bundled up in blankets, unmoving and completely invisible except as a lump on the mattress. Beside her, Gloria coughed miserably, her face as white as the pillowcase.

```
The Great Madam Marron
Recently of Paris, France.
Fortunes told, palms read (daily,
10am-6pm)
Spirit medium (by appointment only)
Receive knowledge from the beyond
from one of the most acclaimed
spiritualists in Europe!
Reasonable rates.
4 Oak Street, Chillicothe
```

# Chapter Twelve

"Same as before?" Bernice asked, hefting the pot onto the corner of the desk. I nodded, setting down my basket.

When everyone had a bowl, I spooned out three more servings for those on nursing duty. Nurse Spencer looked ready to drop as she sank down into the chair behind her desk, pulling out the little silver key to unlock one drawer. Mrs. Hodge stood next to her, speaking quietly, like they'd both forgotten I was there.

"There's almost nothing left," Nurse Spencer said, shaking her head at the drawer. "That supply was supposed to last the rest of the school year, but we've never had so many ill at once."

"We'll do what we can. There's more for fevers than just aspirin. And you know as well as I do, it's not helping much, anyway."

The nurse shook her head. "Neither is anything else."

"You need to go rest. You've been working since yesterday. We've got things under control for the moment. We'll wake you if anything changes."

"I can't. I'm the only one qualified..."

"Dearie, you might be the one with the fancy hat and title, but you're hardly the first person here to see epidemic or tragedy. I've served my time with the Red Cross. We'll manage."

She shook her head again. Her little white cap, barely holding on with a single bobby pin, flopped loosely. Her disheveled hair fell in curls around her face. "But on this scale? I can't--"

"Trust me, *nothing* could prepare *anyone* for this. We'll just have to do what the rest of the world is doing, and muddle through the best we can. Now go get some sleep before you take ill yourself. You won't do anyone any good then."

Reluctantly, she nodded, pushing back her chair. Her black

boots dragged all the way to her bedroom door, which closed softly behind her.

Mrs. Hodge looked up, as if noticing me for the first time. I quickly looked down into the soup pot, stirring the cooling broth.

Her eyes bored into me. Slowly, I looked up. She was, in fact, staring.

"Are you planning on just standing there, or are you going to do something?" she asked, her voice harsher than I'd ever heard it. I yelped, dropping the ladle and snatching up one of the bowls, hurrying to the nearest bedside.

I found myself standing between Mary and Gloria again. Gloria didn't even notice I was there. She stared at the ceiling, shaking with cold even as sweat poured down her face.

Someone had left a wash basin and rag on the nightstand. I put down the soup and reached for the rag, hesitantly dabbing it against her face. She turned her head away, but otherwise didn't acknowledge me. Once again, I was invisible.

I couldn't bring myself to touch her skin, instead packing the cool cloth around her neck and cheek, where it would hopefully help to bring her temperature down.

There was so little any of us could do. The Red Cross notices all said the same thing—all we could do was offer comfort. Give them food. Water. Replace their blankets. But medicine wasn't doing anything for the fevers, and now we were almost out. The influenza was a wildfire, consuming everything in its path.

Gloria's dry lips moved. They were cracked and pale, like her entire body was made of clay, cracking and flaking and falling apart. I leaned down, trying to catch the words, but over the noise of the infirmary, I couldn't make out her weak, breathless voice. I pulled back and she started coughing again, but despite the violence of it, she didn't open her eyes. Her breath wheezed in and out, and I backed away, suddenly overcome by the sense of the miasma. I wanted to vomit. To bathe. To get as far away from it as fast as I could.

I backed up until the back of my legs hit Mary's bed. She remained covered up, shielding her face from the sunlight and cold air flowing in from the window across the aisle.

I looked around, but all the bowls had been claimed. It was now just a matter of feeding the ones too weak to eat on their own. Bernice sat on the edge of one bed, gently spooning broth in Enid's mouth. A few beds over, Mrs. Hodge tried to comfort one of the students, who had begun to cry, but I couldn't tell who it was from my angle.

I couldn't go outside. I couldn't sit in the common room and wait for Bernice, not when there was work to do. I wanted to run, to hide, to get as far away from Mt. Sinai as I could, but I couldn't.

I couldn't let them think ill of me. They thought I was awful enough. How could I walk away now? There were so few of us able to help now. I couldn't turn my back on them.

I didn't want to. It wasn't that I didn't want to help. But the air in the room pressed down on me. Nervous sweat broke out on my brow despite the chill.

*I've already got a fever. It's got me,* I thought wildly. *It's got me, and I'm going to die.*

An inner voice—I couldn't tell if it was Ada or Grandmother at this point—snapped me back into focus. *If you're already sick, then it doesn't matter.*

Slowly, I sank down on the edge of Mary's bed. I touched her shoulder. "Mary, I've brought you some food. Would you like to eat?"

She didn't respond. I shook her shoulder a little, but she stayed silent.

*The first to die.*

Swallowing a hard lump of panic, I reached for the edge of the blanket, slowly peeling it back.

Her fingers, still clutching the blanket, were tipped in blue, as were her lips. Her eyelids fluttered slightly, but didn't open.

*Not dead.* My brain registered the fact before the rest of me, but I was already on my feet and halfway down the aisle.

190

"Mrs. Hodge?"

No response. I couldn't take my eyes off Mary. Her eyelids fluttered again, showing the whites of her eyes.

"Mrs. Hodge?" I said it louder this time. She finally looked up.

"Goodness. What is it, Julia?"

My mouth worked. I pointed to Mary. "I—I don't think she's well, ma'am."

It was a stupid, pointless thing to say. She had the influenza. But there was a big difference between *not well* and *that*.

Mrs. Hodge sprang up from the bed, moving faster than I'd ever seen her move before. For a white-haired woman of an age with my grandmother, she was surprisingly energetic.

She threw back the covers, revealing Mary, curled in a fetal position. Her fingers and toes were blue, the last stages of the disease as her lungs filled, depriving her entire body of oxygen.

"Mary Anne, get the nurse!"

The prefect jumped up, spilling soup on the floor in her hurry.

Everyone was looking now, the ones who were well enough sitting straight in their beds, straining to see what was going on.

Nurse Spencer came running with Mary Anne on her heels. She was in her stocking feet, hair unpinned for sleep, even though she hadn't changed out of her dress.

"Julia." Bernice touched my arm lightly and I jumped. "Jules, we should go. Let them work."

For the first time, she actually seemed afraid, her face ashen. I nodded mutely, but I couldn't pull my eyes away. I watched as Nurse and Mrs. Hodge tried to rouse the former kitchen maid. They rolled her onto her side, beating her back to try to get the fluid out. She coughed weakly, but even I could tell it was beyond hope.

I had the strangest sensation of time slowing down. Nurse Spencer brought her hand down, again and again on Mary's back, as though burping an infant. Mary's head lolled on her pillow, sometimes facing the wall, sometimes the ceiling. For a moment, though the gap under Nurse Spencer's arm, my eyes locked onto hers, and her face seemed to contort.

"You. This is you," she said accusingly, her white eyes open wide.

I could have sworn I heard the words spoken aloud, but when I blinked Mary's face was slack, her eyes unresponsive and glassy.

"Jules!" Bernice stood between me and Mary. She gripped my upper arms. I winced.

"Come on," she said, more gently this time.

I hesitated, but helped her gather up our things. We went out into the common room, where we'd be out of the way. A part of me wanted to stay to help, but there was nothing we could do. The infirmary had the medicines, or what was left of them. It's where Nurse Spencer was.

And if she and her appointed assistants couldn't help Mary...

Well, there was no one else we could go to.

***

After dinner, I sat in my room with my embroidery, the bedside lamp and an open window my only companions.

I was working on another wall hanging. It was intended for Ada; she'd seen the picture in a book, and I wanted to recreate it for her. It was a portion of a tapestry with a unicorn. I couldn't recreate the entire piece—it was huge—but I was nearly done with the center panel, which showed a young girl cradling the creature's head in her lap.

My limbs ached with exhaustion and tension. I couldn't even bear the thought of removing my mask, not with the disease so close. I stuffed my fear down deep inside, stabbing the fabric harshly. The needle burst through the other side, straight into my index finger.

I dropped the hoop with a little cry. Blood welled on the end of my finger. It was such little thing, a mistake I'd made a thousand times before. It didn't even hurt that badly, but my eyes welled up with tears anyway.

After the strain of the past few days, I didn't know how much more I could take. Between Ada and the police and Miss Newton, and now the influenza and the vision I'd had in the infirmary...I didn't want to leave my room. I wasn't sure I could. My room was still safe. It still felt clean, though I had to resist the urge to strip off my clothes and throw them out in the hall every time I entered. I wanted to bathe, to scrub every inch of myself so the influenza couldn't get a foothold, but that meant going into the contaminated hall, to the communal bathroom, then trudging all the way back to my room. It was pointless.

I hated the bathroom to begin with. There was no privacy. But, I thought, watching the single drop of blood drip down my finger and onto my lap, it was still relatively early. Our daily routines were completely off, now that classes were canceled. If I went now, would there be anyone else there?

Deciding it was worth a try, I gathered up my things and trudged down the long, shadowy corridor to the stairs. Most of the girls were keeping to their rooms, but there were a few subdued girls in the second-floor common room. They ignored me as I proceeded down the stairs to the first floor, then to the basement.

The bathroom was just next to the kitchen. I suppose because when they put in the running water, it was easier to send the pipes

194

to the same place. There were toilets on the second floor, and another on the fourth, but mostly if we wanted to bathe or relieve ourselves we had to go down the eerie basement hallway, past the kitchen. When they'd put in the electric lights, they'd only put in one for this corridor. It threw long shadows on the walls that reached and clawed for me. I shuddered.

Halfway to the door, I thought I heard sobs. I stopped, listening. Yes, there was definitely someone crying.

I pushed open the bathroom door, peering around the corner. Someone sat in one of the tubs—there were five, altogether, lined up along the wall—up to her neck in what passed for hot water, long dark hair spilling damply around her.

I started to back away, but dropped my bar of soap.

The sobs stopped abruptly. "Who's there?"

She turned around. It was Mary Anne. I hardly recognized her with her hair down, no spectacles, and her face red from crying.

"I—It's just me," I said. Too late to back away now. It would only be more awkward if I ran. I picked up my soap, clutching it and my bundle of night clothes to my chest. "I can go, if you want."

She wiped her face quickly with wet palms. "No. It's fine. I'm almost done." She reached for the linen towel draped over the neighboring tub and used it to dry her face. I looked away and went about the business of filling the furthest tub with lukewarm water as she climbed out, dried off, and reached for her dressing gown.

I bit my lip. Was I supposed to say something? Or was it more polite to ignore it? She obviously wanted time alone, or so it seemed. Damn it all, why were people so hard to read? Why couldn't I just open them up like a book and find the information in an index? This was why I always needed Ada. Geometry, chemistry, and calculus were a mystery to her, but people weren't. She understood them as well as I understood quadratic equations.

"Are—are you all right?" I asked at last. I wasn't sure if she could hear me over the falling water, but she paused, tying the sash of her robe.

She wiped her face again, this time with her sleeve, keeping her back to me.

"You'll hear it in the morning. But Mary died."

I swear, for a moment my heart stopped beating. I couldn't breathe. As though taking my silence for permission, Mary Anne turned around. "Just after dinner. We were able to get her breathing again, help her along a little, for a while after you left, but then...she just stopped. We couldn't do anything." Her voice cracked, completely dissolved by saltwater tears. She covered her face, sobbing into the hems of her sleeves.

I didn't know what to do. Ada would have hugged her; I didn't think I could. Instead I stood there with my sponge and one hand and the stupid bar of soap in the other, and stared at her like a lunatic.

"I—I'm sorry?" It was the only thing I could think of to say. What did one say in that situation? It wasn't as if Mary Anne and I were friends. I hardly knew her.

She took a deep breath, reaching for her towel. She blew her nose into it. "I'm sorry. I just—I've never—"

"I know." I put down the bath things and turned off the water, going around the tub to stand before her. There were still yards between us; I couldn't get any closer. I didn't think she'd want me to. But she looked up at me over the edge of the towel.

"It's hard. The first time. Knowing you can't do anything."

She nodded. "You lost someone?" Then she looked skyward and snorted. "Of course you did. Ada."

It was my turn to nod. "Yes. But before that. My aunt and my cousins. They died in August. Some of the first cases. We didn't know how bad it was, then." Grandmother and I went to help nurse them. Looking back, it was a miracle we'd both come out alive, after watching the three of them wither away. Aunt Helen's fever was so high, for so long, her hair fell out in clumps. My cousins, Amanda and Albert, followed within days. Albert contracted

197

pneumonia. Nothing we did had any effect. For a while it looked like Amanda would survive, but when she found out about her mother and brother, it was like it sapped out the last of her will to live. She suffocated slowly in her bed, while Grandmother and I looked on, powerless.

"My uncle was in France. There was no one else to take care of them. We tried to get Aunt Helen to a hospital, but she wouldn't go, and then suddenly it was too late. They were all gone." We'd called an ambulance for Amanda, but it took hours for them to arrive. Grandmother and I weren't strong enough to move her, and there was no automobile to take her in.

"When we came home, we thought it was over. We thought we could mourn. But then Grandfather..." My own throat felt suddenly tight. I tried to push it away. "He's been in the hospital ever since. Pneumonia. They're so crowded...we haven't been able to see him. There's no word..."

I blinked back the tears, wiping my own eyes with my sleeve. "I'm sorry. I was supposed to be making you feel better." That was what one was supposed to do, wasn't it?

Mary Anne nodded, her own eyes drying slowly. "It's all right. It's horrible. No, it's not all right. It's not all right that this is happening. That the world is on fire and falling down around us. But it's good to know that no matter how bad things are, we aren't alone in it."

"Is it?" I wasn't sure I understood. I'd always found comfort in being alone. Alone meant I wasn't being bullied, or tormented, or judged. It meant I was free to read, or embroider, or do whatever my heart desired. People meant chores and dirty looks and whispered comments and trying to find the right way to act in a dozen different situations and being wrong every single time.

"Yes. Don't you think so? We can make it through, if we work together."

My brows furrowed. I wasn't entirely sure how *working together* would defeat influenza. The Kaiser, maybe. But influenza? Well, at least it would keep us fed in the meantime. My aching arms could attest to that much, at least.

Though I didn't really agree with her, I bobbed my head anyway. It's what I was supposed to do. "We'll make it through."

# Chapter Thirteen

*Thursday, October 24, 1918*

*Dear Mother,*

*I hope one of the nurses is able to read this to you, and it's not horribly delayed by the epidemic.*

*I hope you are well. I think of you every day, and worry about your health. I've heard that some of the sanatoriums have been closing down, and had hundreds of deaths, but so far we've had no word from Pleasant Valley. I am trying to hope that means everything is well, but it leaves my mind open to worry.*

*So many bad things happened this week, I can't even begin to tell you about them. The girls at school say I am cold, but I don't think I shall ever be able to think of the past few days without crying. Maybe the next time I see you, I can tell you about it, but I don't think I can recount it all right now.*

*This morning made me think of the day Grandmother and Grandfather and I took you to the sanatorium. I was thirteen. It was just after the war started, and our butler, Wilson, enlisted, and Joanna the maid left to be an ambulance driver for the Red Cross, and so it was just us and cook and one maid who came to clean, and you had a fit in the evening, and nothing Grandmother or I* could do could calm you. There was nothing we could do to put the household as it was, and it bothered you, I know. This week, without Ada, I have wanted to have a fit of my own. I want to cry and scream and hide under my bed, but I can't. It's like when I dream about walking down a staircase, and suddenly the floor is gone and I'm falling, except I can't wake up, and I can't find the floor, and I just continue to fall because Ada isn't there to right me.

She would say I'm being silly. She would find a way to make me laugh. She could always do that, no matter how upset I was.

In any case, I tried to tell grandmother that sending you away wouldn't fix the problem. It would be a whole new place, with new people and nothing familiar. Breakfast would be at a different time, and your mattress would be different.

I tried to tell them they had to make the curtains extra dark for you to sleep, and you always sleep with three blankets, even in the summer. I know they didn't listen. That was why I brought you another blanket. I made sure it was one from your bed at home so it would be familiar.

I think Grandmother and Grandfather felt guilty for leaving you there. I know I did. But I understand their trouble. They are getting old. When you had that last fit at home, Grandmother had a black eye for a week, and Grandfather can no longer carry you to

201

*your room, and there's no Wilson to do it. Did you hear? He died in the trenches last year. I think I told you already, but I can't remember right now. My mind is a whirl, and I'm afraid I'm not making much sense now.*

*I shall end this letter before I make too much of a mess of it.*

*I love you, and I will see you when we pick you up for Thanksgiving dinner.*


*Love,*

*Julia*


After Mary Ann left, I sat in the bath for a long time, thinking about Mary and the flu and Ada. When I closed my eyes, I saw Ada standing at the end of the tub, just as she had outside the academy. Her brow creased in accusation, in anger. Why was I having a soak when her killer was still free?

I sank down, closing my eyes as the water lapped at my chin, careful not to get my face wet. I can't stand water in my eyes or in my ears. I never learned to swim because of it.

I bobbed back up, dipping my head back to wash my hair. After a week, it was greasy and heavy. It's a constant battle, trying to balance my need to be clean with my need to not bathe in front of a dozen prying eyes.

A pair of twelfth grade girls interrupted my brief solitude. They spoke quietly, the subdued atmosphere of the past few days filtering down even here, where we were—theoretically—at our most vulnerable.

I waited until they were occupied with running their own baths, then climbed out of mine, hurriedly drying off and wrapping myself in my ratty old dressing gown and scurrying off to my own room.

The bare bulb in the hall flickered as I passed under it. I paused, midstep, then kept going, faster than before as the hair on the back of my neck prickled, as though someone was watching me.

I swallowed hard. Electricity shot up and down my arms. I clutched my uniform tighter.

Something moved behind me, flitting from one pool of shadow to another. With a yelp, I took off and didn't stop running until I'd reached the third-floor landing.

Whatever had been there with me, it hadn't been Ada. I knew that much. Mary, maybe? Could her spirit still be attached to the school after such an unexpected demise? If that were so, then we were about to have a lot more ghosts roaming our halls.

The last two days, Mount Sinai had felt nearly deserted as girls stayed to their rooms, or their friend's rooms. No one studied or chatted or played chess or knit in the common rooms. No one lingered in the halls or in the dining room. We did our chores and we hid out of sight like it would stop the influenza from finding us.

It was just like the little poem the ninth-grade girls sang when they jumped rope.

*There was a little girl, and she had a little bird,*
*And she called it by the pretty name of Enza;*
*But one day it flew away, but it didn't go to stay,*
*For when she raised the window, in-flu-Enza.*

That bird, a skeletal crow, a carrion bird that watched us all with beady black eyes, was just waiting to swoop in through an open door or window. No one could understand how it spread so fast, how it killed so quickly.

I took a deep breath, reaching for grandfather's watch. Sinking down on the bed I cradled it to my ear, listing to the soft ticks and timing my breathing to it. I could almost hear his voice, feel his rough hands on top of my head. Grandmother always insisted I could do *better*, but Grandfather was the quiet sort. He would just pat my head—he didn't hug; Grandmother was the one who insisted on hugs—and tell me it was just fine.

I squeezed my eyes shut against the burn of tears. I couldn't tell anymore if they were for Ada, or Grandfather, or my aunt, or

204

my cousins, or my mother, or Mount Sinai, or for myself. Maybe they were for all of it. All of us.

The only hope I had was that outside these walls, Mother and Grandfather and Grandmother were still alive and well. I knew, deep in my bones, that if one of them died, I would *know*. Their spirits would come to me, the way Ada's had. Maybe it would just be a vision, like the maid in Grandmother's attic. Or maybe it would be like Ada, desperate for comfort. For answers. But I would know.

Lowering the watch, I stared into the face. It was plain glass, with no cover. In between the five and the six, just to the left, was a smaller dial that showed the day of the week.

The back of the watch was cast to look like a lily—Mother's name. It was a gift from his father when Mother was born. Back before they knew Mother was…different. Before they knew she didn't talk, or make eye contact. Back when they didn't know how much touching bothered her, when the only way to make her stop crying was to swaddle her.

Grandmother told me all of this when I was about nine. That was when Mother's care finally started to be too much for her. She'd always insisted she would never send Mother to an asylum—the treatment there was beastly—but hiring a trained nurse was expensive, and it was difficult to find one able to deal with Mother's…peculiarities. She was usually docile, happy to play her little games with flowers, or to embroider or draw. But sometimes, the strangest things made her angry, and she threw tantrums. Tantrums Grandmother and Grandfather couldn't control, and couldn't seem to calm her down from.

Grandmother tried to keep me away from her at times like that. Grandfather would push her into the coat closet in the hall and lock the door. It sounds cruel, but something about the small, dark space calmed her. Grandmother said she used to hide there when they had parties.

I climbed in once, after she'd been sent away. I was angry and scared that I'd be sent away, too. The dark little box blocked out the noise. There was only a small sliver of light coming through a crack at the bottom of the door. It smelled of wool and Grandfather's pipe tobacco, and Grandmother's perfume.

I understood the appeal immediately. My room—my retreat— was too big. Too open. Sometimes I hid under the bed to get away from my governess, or crawled under a pile of blankets. But I always got into trouble for that. *Young ladies don't hide. Young ladies don't crawl around with the dust bunnies.*

I wanted more than anything to crawl into that closet now. To have a safe place where the flu and the ghosts and Miss Newton and Headmistress Davenport couldn't reach me. A place where the war didn't exist, and I could finally breathe.

Laying down on my mattress, I covered my head with the pillow. Silence pressed in on me. Loud, screaming silence. I pulled the pillow tight until all I could hear was my own pulse, throbbing in my left ear.

I stayed like that until the throbbing went away. Until I could stand to be in an open room again, listening to the ambient sounds of the school around me. The clang of pipes. Subdued voices down the hall. Someone upstairs, striding from one end of the room to the other.

According to the watch, Ada's spirit would make her nightly appearance in just over two hours.

The empty side of the room mocked me, and for a moment I thought I smelled her perfume again. It would be just like Ada to lurk on her side of the room, waiting for me to notice she had something to say. She was like that, sometimes. She wanted others to *ask* what she was thinking, instead of just blurting it out the way she usually did. I'd learned it was a type of test. One I usually failed.

My theory was that sometimes, maybe when she was feeling particularly low, she like to make sure the people around her were still paying attention. That we still needed her in some way, I suppose. That we were still interested. So she would keep a secret, but make it known she had a secret, in her own subtle ways that I invariably missed, and wait for someone to notice.

"You're so thick sometimes," she'd say, when I eventually heard a rumor or asked her why she was annoyed with me. I'd learned a long time ago that *asking* why someone was annoyed violated the list of unspoken social rules I was so poor at learning, but it was too frustrating to waste time on such things when I had to share a room with someone. Besides, Ada never seemed to mind.

"Oh, Jules. It's not your fault, though. But don't you ever get curious?" she would sigh, and then pick up one of her magazines or change the subject.

I did get curious. I got curious an awful lot. But it was usually about things I wasn't supposed to ask about. Like where everyone else learned those silly, unspoken rules, and why no one bothered to teach them to me, and why wasn't there a handbook somewhere I could study? And when someone asked what I was doing, why did they always get annoyed when I answered them? Particularly when it was *obvious* I was reading, or embroidering, or what have you. Why did I need to explain it, when clearly no one wanted the answer?

*Oh, Jules…*

Ada's voice whispered past my ear, but I couldn't be sure if I'd imagined it, or if her spirit had returned to our room early.

Even though I wanted to hide, to stay away from everyone, I didn't think I would accomplish anything hiding under my pillow.

"Ada? Are you here? I need your help," I whispered to the room. My throat closed when I tried to speak louder. What if the other girls heard me? They already thought I was odd.

I thought back to my conversation with Emily and Ruthie. Ruthie was sure one could call up a spirit, to ask it questions and get an answer. Every spirit I'd ever met had simply...*been*. Like the maid in the attic, and the cold breeze in my great-uncle's former sick room, and Ada's spirit replaying her flight evening after evening. They were like records, playing themselves over and over again on a Victrola that never wound down.

But if what Ruthie said was true—if it was possible to pull them out of that endless loop, to bring them temporarily back into the natural flow of time, then maybe one *could* ask questions and get a proper answer. In theory, I thought it would work something like the slap Miss Comstock gave me during my fit. It would probably be painful, but I wasn't sure if it would be worse for me, or for Ada.

But either way, I had to try. I had to do something before her memory was lost forever, drowned out by the epidemic. If I could bring some new evidence to the police, then they would have to reopen the investigation, to prosecute the boy properly.

I didn't know what kind of evidence I would need, however.

Perhaps I should start by asking to borrow Mary Anne's Sherlock Holmes novel.

***

I found Ruthie and Emily in the first-floor common room, still in their uniforms. Emily sat with her knees tucked under her on the couch, her boots abandoned on the rug, while her smaller friend huddled in an old-fashioned wingback chair. They leaned over their armrests, whispering conspiratorially. The school was so quiet now, anything louder than a whisper felt wrong, like speaking aloud in the library, or laughing at a funeral.

That last thought made me shudder. I tried to push it away.

"What are you doing here?" Emily demanded, propping herself up on an elbow. Her mask was abandoned on a pillow beside her, like a lace doily. I tapped mine lightly, reassuring myself it was there, even though it covered half my face and the lower part of my glasses had tiny clouds of condensation on them.

"I wanted to ask you about the seances," I said, answering her question but directing it to Ruthie. She sat up a little straighter in her chair.

"I thought you didn't believe in seances," she said skeptically.

"I don't believe that every medium is honest," I corrected. "But I do believe in Ada and her ghost. I don't think she moved your books, but I do think she's here, with us."

Emily looked around as though expecting her to walk out of one of the closed doors lining the hall, or to appear behind me.

I licked my lips behind my mask, trying to keep my tongue from touching the cotton gauze. It occurred to me suddenly that I didn't know who would wash our masks overnight with the staff so depleted.

I forced the thought away, just as I had the one about the funeral, and turned my attention to the task at hand.

"I have some experience with...with spirits," I said, swallowing a tight knot in my throat. I'd never said the words out loud to anyone, though I'd hinted it to Ada. "I see them, sometimes. But all the ones I've seen...they're like watching a film in the cinema over and over again. They can't talk. They're stuck in the moments before they died. But maybe, if I had some help, I think I might be able to speak to Ada. To get some answers."

"Answers about what?" Emily scoffed, throwing herself back against the cushions.

"About the person who killed her."

"Are you serious? You want to hunt down a ghost, so you can find a murderer, while we're in the middle of a quarantine?"

"Yes."

The pair of them stared at me. What was so hard to understand about that answer?

I nodded, already wishing I hadn't come. "I'm sorry. That seems odd, doesn't it? But I have to. I have to do something."

"Aren't you paying attention?" Emily's bare feet dropped onto the floor. She sprang out of her seat. "Haven't you heard the rumors? Someone is already dead! More of us are going to get sick and die! There's nothing we can do to stop it! You shouldn't waste your time on someone that's already gone."

Even though she was only a ninth grader, she towered over me—no, that's not right. She loomed. The difference in height wasn't so much, it was the way she carried it and used it to her advantage, practically clubbing me over the head with her desire to be threatening. It was the same trick Miss Newton liked to use, leaning over me while I sat at my desk, trying to make me feel smaller.

I didn't like it from her, and I especially didn't like it from this girl. "You're right. More are going to die. There's nothing we can do to help them. We're powerless against the flu. The government and the doctors and nurses—they're all trying to push water uphill with a rake, as my grandfather says. We can't stop it. We can barely even comfort the sick.

"But the person who hurt Ada…he's still out there. He's walking free while we're quarantined. The police won't do anything. And unless I can find a way to convince them to arrest him, he'll continue to walk free. And who knows when he'll strike again. When he'll kill another girl. Maybe it'll be some girl from town. Maybe none of us will know her. Or maybe it'll be Elvira or Mary Anne, or one of you. There are still people we can help. There are still lives we can save. There are spirits we can put to rest."

"You're delusional. You're as delusional as your mother!"

"Emily!"

Ruthie's face was pale. She clung to the arms of her chair.

Emily, perhaps as shocked by her words as her friend, clapped her hands over her mouth.

"I—I'm sorry. I shouldn't have—"

I stared at her, hardly batting an eyelash. It was not the worst thing I'd heard my mother called, though it was one of the more inaccurate. "She's not delusional. She's feeble minded. There's a difference."

"I…I didn't mean—"

"If you want to insult me, at least get the terminology right."

Emily's face flamed. "I'm sorry," she said from behind her hands.

This was the part where I was supposed to say "It's all right," and absolve her of wrongdoing. I knew it, and yet I couldn't do it.

*These sorts of conversations are always such a bother,* I thought with a sigh. Finally, I settled on a response that was both socially acceptable and not a lie. "Don't trouble yourself."

Ruthie, perhaps feeling her friend had done enough, rose from her seat, coming to stand between us. "What do you want from me?"

"I need to know how the other mediums do it."

"But I thought you were a medium?"

My brows knit and I shook my head. "I don't think so. I don't talk to them, you see. I can see them, and sometimes from watching them I can gather what they want, but we don't converse, as such." The defiant glare from Ada at the academy was more than I'd ever gotten from a spirit in terms of interaction. Ada's spirit was incredibly active. Restless. It was like her murder played out every night in an attempt to show the truth. Like screaming into an empty room to get someone—anyone—to pay attention. But I was the only one who could hear. Or see, as the case may be.

"So you want to ask her questions."

"Yes. But it's almost as if she can't hear me. I…I think I know

214

who killed her. But I need her help if I'm going to prove it."

Ruthie and Emily studied me. I shifted uncomfortably in my slippers.

"I think I can help you. I can tell you what Madame Marron does when she wants to communicate with the spirit world…" Her voice trailed off suddenly. "Actually….I might be able to do better than that."

"What do you mean?

"Madame Marron lives just outside the city limits. Her house isn't part of the quarantine." She lowered her voice looking around as though she expected a teacher to come in at any moment. "Our classes are canceled, and no one is paying attention. We could sneak out tomorrow, and no one would even notice."

It was a long walk to town, but we made the trek once a month for our In Town days. It was about an hour and a half each way.

I quickly did the calculation. "I don't think there's time. Bernice and I are supposed to serve meals. We won't have time in between."

"Yes, you will. There are a lot of girls not doing anything to help. One of them will cover for you."

I shook my head. I wasn't the type of person people did favors for. "I don't think…"

"I'll make a bet with you. Tomorrow at breakfast—" It was the

215

only meal we still gathered for, so Headmistress Davenport could make her announcements "—Davenport will make it required that everyone help. The volunteers she already has are exhausted, and some are getting sick. It'll be all hands on deck, just watch."

There was a fair chance she was right. "And what are we betting?" I asked, eyebrow arched. I didn't have much of anything of value.

Ruthie thought for a moment, tapping a finger against her chin. "If I'm right, you have to let me help you."

My other eyebrow went up. "Let you help?"

"Yes. I want to help. I'm not good with the sick, but this sounds like an adventure. I want to see a real, actual ghost. Madame Marron has been able to channel my brother, but I haven't seen him. I want to see his spirit, so I can say a proper good-bye."

"And you think I can do that? That's not the way it works. I might be able to see them, but I can't just *call* a ghost. If I could, I wouldn't be asking for your help in the first place."

"You let me worry about that."

I shrugged. "Fine. And if I'm right?"

"Then Emily and I will help you with the serving. For two weeks."

"Ruthie!"

But Ruthie just waved her friend off, even though Emily's face was turning roughly the same shade of maroon as the Headmistress's wallpaper.

I pulled Grandfather's watch from the pocket of my robe. We still had about two hours before Ada made an appearance. "I think we should do it at night."

Ruthie raised an eyebrow. "Well, evening *is* the best time for contacting spirits. Midnight is, of course, the *best* time, but—"

"Not midnight. Five minutes past eleven. That's when Ada's ghost appears." Well, she didn't really appear at that point. That was when I heard her spectral form moving through our room, opening the wardrobe, spraying perfume, and then sneaking out the door. At eleven-fifteen, she ran into the woods. And at approximately ten minutes past midnight, her ghost reappeared, floating in the fountain.

I'd timed it all. I'd been watching her ghost for the past week, growing accustomed to the smell of attar of roses just after I got to bed; of waking in the night to see her on the patio. She had a routine.

But how long it would last was a mystery. None of the other ghosts I'd ever met had adhered to such a set schedule. The maid in grandmother's attic appeared, usually around dusk, but on different days. Sometimes a Monday. Sometimes a Saturday.

Different dates. Different seasons. Different times. I'd surmised it was because she'd been there for so long her ghost had been pulled out of time, so she no longer recognized it. Clocks have no meaning in eternity. How long would it be before Ada forgot time, too? Before her ghost lost all sense of herself, and was nothing more than a replay of a traumatic event? Over and over again, like a newsreel replaying itself for audiences over and over again?

"First thing's first. Madame Marron says we need to have guests in multiples of three at the table, and we need at least six. The three of us plus Madam Marron is only four."

"I never said I wanted any part of this," Emily objected, crossing her arms over her chest.

Ruthie ignored her. "Is there anyone else connected to Ada?"

I hesitated, then shook my head. Ada had been as unpopular as me, but for different reasons.

"What about that girl I saw you with earlier in the kitchen?"

"Bernice?" Frowning, I considered it. Bernice had been…supportive, at least. But I hadn't told her about the ghosts. And after the incidents in the infirmary… "I can ask."

I wasn't looking forward to it, but with Ruthie and Emily trailing behind—with varying degrees of enthusiasm—I made my way back to the third floor and knocked lightly on Bernice's door.

She answered it, bleary eyed with her brown hair tied up in

rags to curl, a book clutched in one hand with her finger marking her space. She'd forgotten her mask, and looked like she'd been dozing.

"What…"

"Bernice…I have a favor I need to ask."

> ## On the Rise of Spiritualism
>
> Since our great nation entered this bloody conflict, the grief-stricken have been all too willing to return to a darker period in their time of need, putting their trust in charlatans and confidence tricksters, rather than in their faith.
>
> While we all suffer from loss, we urge you not to follow the devil and his gilded path, for it leads only to more suffering and hell. These so-called "mediums" have no power over the dead, and cannot summon or communicate with those lost. Turn instead to God and the church.

# Chapter Fourteen

[From the Mt. Sinai Church Newsletter]

Bernice was surprisingly agreeable. She patted her curls. "Oh, but I just put my hair up."

"No time for that. We've got less than two hours. That will barely be enough time to get to Madame Marron's, and we still need to convince her to help us," Ruthie said, checking the small clock on the nightstand.

"Can't it wait until tomorrow?" Bernice asked, but she was already untying one of the curlers.

"We don't know if any of us will be able tomorrow," Ruthie replied ominously.

Mary Anne was harder to convince. "We shouldn't be going out of doors. At night. And with the quarantine! Do you know how much trouble we'll be in?"

"No one has to know. We're too far away. It's not like the police are standing guard outside." My respect for Ruthie's ability to argue only increased the more I saw her in action.

"Someone just died here. Can't you have a little more respect?"

"We're hoping to save people. And don't you think it's a little coincidental that the epidemic hit the school just after Ada's killer was set loose? We have a duty to bring her justice."

I wasn't the only one who raised an eyebrow at that statement, but Mary Anne seemed to consider it. "Fine. But I'm only doing this so the four of you don't kill yourselves wandering around in the dark."

A quarter of an hour later, we all met in the foyer. There was no sign of teachers or the headmistress. I hadn't even seen the Headmistress since breakfast, which was unusual. But now that everyone well enough was coming down to the kitchen to serve themselves whenever they had time, our meals—just like everything else—were completely out of order. I wanted to go back to my routine, but the threat of infection made it impossible.

Bernice found a lantern in the closet by the front door, and swiped a book of matches from the sideboard where we kept the extra candles. Mary Anne had a flashlight of her own. Then, quiet as mice, we slipped past the Headmistress's office and out the front door.

It was abysmally dark out, clouds covering the mood. The gravel lane leading to the school vanished into the shadow of trees just a few yards away. We waited until we reached the edge of the school grounds before using our lights, carefully shielding them from the windows as we hurried down the rutted path to town.

I was panting by the time we reached the bottom of the hill. We were walking quickly, faster than we usually did on In Town days, urgency pushing us forward.

"Where is this Madame Marron's house, anyway?" Emily

asked. She was panting a little herself. The hill was rather steep, and it took all my effort not to slide down loose gravel, all the way to the bottom. Climbing it again would be even worse.

"It's not far. Two streets over from the pharmacy," Ruthie said. She and Bernice, I decided, must be part mountain goat. The hill didn't seem to bother either of them a bit.

The road wound around, before finally coming to a paved street and the bridge.

Leaning on the railing, we stopped to catch our breath. I pulled out my watch, checking the time in the light of the lantern. "We don't have long. How much further is it?"

Ruthie pointed up ahead. "Other side of the bridge, then two streets south."

The light from Mary Anne's flashlight began to turn orange. She smacked it against the side of her hand, but it didn't help.

"Don't worry about it. There will be streetlamps soon," Ruthie said.

Emily peered over my shoulder to look at the watch. "Come on, we have to hurry."

"I can't walk any faster," Bernice said, holding up the lantern. Inside, kerosene sloshed every time she moved.

"Leave it. We can hide it here, in the bushes, and get it on the way back. If they've blocked the roads for the quarantine—and they probably have—then we don't want them to see our light, anyway," Ruthie said.

She sounded so authoritative, no one argued. Though I did catch Mary Anne grumbling about how ridiculous it all was— sneaking into town during a quarantine for a seance? It was completely mad.

Privately, I agreed, but I wasn't about to say anything. Not when I was the reason we were all here. But the further we walked, the more my doubts crept in. What if Ada wouldn't speak to us? What if she had nothing more to say?

What if Madame Marron was really just a fraud?

We ran across the bridge. It was a long way; Mary Anne and I staggering a few dozen yards behind the others.

"I—hate—calisthenics—" she gasped, stopping to brace her hands on her knees. I leaned against the railing to catch my breath, my parched throat closing in on itself and stinging with the cold, damp night air. I wished I could reach the river below and take a long, cool drink.

*Then again, maybe that's not a great idea,* I thought as the wind changed, blowing the scent of sewage and industrial waste directly into my sweating face.

Up ahead, lights waited at the end of the bridge, but I didn't think they were streetlights. A few flashes of movement confirmed—officers were blocking the road. The quarantine was still in full effect.

"What do we do?" I asked, finally catching up to the others.

Ruthie looked around. "This way." We veered off the road at the end of bridge. The officers, huddled in their car with a thermos full of coffee, masks hanging around their chins, were more intent on staying warm and not falling asleep from boredom than paying attention to half a dozen wayward girls sneaking through the brush.

As soon as we were off the road, I wished we had the lights again, even if they would have given us away. There was no way the police would have missed us.

"We're almost there," Ruthie panted, pushing her way through the underbrush. A branch snapped back, slapping me in the face. I yelped, putting a hand to my nose where the bridge of my glasses dug in.

"Are you sure you know where we're going?" Bernice's voice had a sharp edge. I wasn't sure if it was frustration or exhaustion. It could have been both. My entire body tingled with nerves, otherwise I might have been equally annoyed by our sudden detour. But I just kept pushing forward. One step after another, into the darkness. Into the void of the unknown.

"Of course. My parents live just over there."

I couldn't see where Ruthie gestured to, but it hardly mattered.

225

Mary Anne, lagging behind, slipped and grabbed a tree trunk to steady herself. I hesitated, but held out a hand. "It's not much further." I wasn't entirely sure about that—or rather, I was sure it was an extremely subjective statement, and I was not entirely convinced Ruthie and I had the same definition of *almost there*, but it seemed like the right thing to say in the moment.

Nodding, Mary Anne took my hand, and together we pulled each other forward. "I—really hope—that—this—is—worth it," she gasped.

Privately, I agreed. I squeezed her fingers, then dropped my hand quickly, wiping it off on my skirt.

Though the night air was cool, only a few degrees above freezing and dropping fast, we'd worked up such a sweat on the hike that we all had to pull our masks down, just so we could breathe. I stuffed my fists into my coat pockets. My hair, still wet when we left, had turned stiff with cold where it hung out beneath my hat.

As suddenly as we'd entered the woods, we came out on the other side. A residential street lay before us, street lamps every few yards gleaming in the night. I'd never been so happy to see a streetlamp in my entire life.

Sneaking through the dark gulf between two houses, we came out on the sidewalk, keeping a wary eye out for anyone working the epidemic—police enforcing the curfew, ambulances collecting the dead and dying.

Ruthie lead us to the next street, which was darker and a little shabbier than the one we'd left. Three doors up a yellow Queen Anne with brown and green trim sat hunched between two brick houses. It was hard to tell in the dark, but it seemed almost like the house was a jackrabbit, ready to spring if startled.

Candles burned in the downstairs windows, but on the second floor the steady light of electricity shone behind the curtains.

We pulled up our masks, exchanging a nervous glance before climbing the cracked front steps.

Barely visible in the doorway was a sign written in neat calligraphy:

*Madame Marron: Spirit medium*
*Seances, summonings, banishings.*

*Fortunes told, histories revealed. By appointment only.*

I swallowed the bitter taste of doubt. "Will she even see us?" I whispered, staring at the sign.

"She'll see us." But Ruthie's voice shook. I couldn't tell if it was fear, or cold, or doubt, but she raised her fist and knocked like she had all the confidence in the world.

For a long time, nothing happened. Despite the lights, I began to wonder if she was even at home. But then, it was very late, and we did not have an appointment.

Bernice sighed, throwing herself against the wall as though her strength had finally given out. Her half-curled hair had come free of her hasty pins, tumbling down around her shoulders.

Suddenly, the interior door jerked open. The woman standing in the door frame bore only a passing resemblance to the woman I'd pictured on the long walk.

She was tall and thin, the tips of a black bob peeking out from under a silk turban. It was made of many colors, though I could see none of them clearly in the dark, with the only light spilling over her shoulders.

A shawl, as multi-hued as the turban, was draped over her shoulders, but her dress was long and black. I couldn't tell if it was a mourning dress, or a going out dress, but something on it glittered slightly when it caught the light.

She narrowed khol-lined eyes at us as a curl of cigarette smoke wound around her face adding to the air of mystery.

"What in the name of…Ruth Key, what on earth are you doing here? Where's your mother? And who are all these?" She gestured at us with the cigarette.

My mouth compressed of its own will. It wasn't the cigarette,

228

or the heavy khol, or the fact that she smelled like a bottle of gin. It was the way her accent rapidly changed from New York to something vaguely Parisian as soon as she recognized one of her clients. I thought Ruthie heard it too; for the first time, her confidence seemed to waiver. She frowned, a little knot appearing between her brows. "I—These are my friends. May we come in?"

Madame Marron hesitated, then backed out of our way, holding the door open.

*"Cher*, your *maman*—"

"Drop the act, lady. We all heard you. If you're really from France, then I'm the Kaiser," Bernice snapped, once we were inside.

Madame Marron glared at her. I opened my mouth to point out the poor taste of her statement—after all, we were hardly here to kill her, the way the Kaiser had invaded France—but snapped it shut again, realizing it would be one of those unwelcome statements of fact no one was actually interested in.

She planted her hands on her hips. "Alright, fine. Have it your way. You wanna tell me what you're doin' here?" she shot back.

Ruthie looked close to tears. The psychic—or the fake, as the case may be—dropped her hands to her sides. "Look, I'm sorry. Really. But there ain't no one who's gonna pay Betsy Brown from Brooklyn to talk to the dead. But they will pay Elsie Marron, who

229

watched her entire village burn to the ground after the Germans invaded."

"So you take advantage of them?" Bright spots of color lit Emily's face, and I didn't think they were entirely from the cold.

"I ain't taken' advantage of no one! Not one of my readin's is fake! Well, most of the time. It's not like I can just turn it on and off like a lamp. Sometimes the spirits don't come, but that's none of my nevermind. You can send an invitation, but you can't make anyone sit down to dinner, as my mother used to say."

"You were lying to us the entire time!" Ruthie was near tears now, they were swimming at the corners of her eyes. The other girls jumped to her defense, until I couldn't keep track of who was shouting what.

Finally, Madame Marron—or Betsy Brown, as it were—put two fingers in her mouth and let out the sharpest whistle I'd ever heard in my life. We all covered our ears; I half expected mine to start bleeding.

"Listen here, you little scamps. I can't help where I was born. But I've got a very limited skill set, and this is the only way I know how to make a livin'. Now did you come here to throw accusations at me, or do you actually have some business?"

The other girls looked at me. I was the one who had brought them here; it would be my call to decide to stay. I stepped forward.

230

Bernice glared at Miss Brown, like she was trying to pin her to the rug with the force of her stare. On my other side, Emily wrapped an arm around her shorter friend, who was dabbing at her misty eyes with her gloves.

"My friend was murdered. I need to speak with her," I said, licking my lips.

Miss Brown's glare softened a little. "Hey...yeah, I think I read about that. You girls are from that school."

We nodded. Betsy Brown reached for an ash tray on the hall table, stubbing out her cigarette. She closed the door and turned off the porch light, supposedly so we wouldn't be disturbed.

"You got anythin' of hers?"

I reached into my pocket. The only thing left behind after our room was searched and her things boxed up were the magazine and hairpins on the nightstand, and the flashlight I'd accidentally stolen. Among the pile of pins, I'd found her favorite one, the one with the little enamel butterfly the size of my thumbnail. It was just small enough to hide in her hair, and the teachers didn't try to confiscate it as ornamentation. I held it out to her.

Betsy turned it over in her hands, closing her eyes for a moment. Her lips worked, but no sounds came out. "Yes. This will work. Come with me."

She led us down the long hallway to the back of the house,

stopping to light a candle at little table at the end of the hall, draped in black fabric.

"Are you sure about this?" Bernice whispered, taking my elbow.

I nodded, even though I wasn't, really. "I don't think she's lying"

"Well, one thing's for sure. No one *would* pay someone with an accent like that to talk to the dead," Emily whispered.

"I don't understand what her accent has to do with anything. The way a person speaks doesn't have anything to do with their talents."

Bernice smiled a little, squeezing my arm. "Well, you wouldn't. But that's what makes you special."

I didn't understand that statement, either, but by then we were inside a dark little parlor.

Madame Marron went around the room, lighting a handful of candles, just enough so we could see another black draped table in the middle of the floor, six chairs spaced around it. A few extra chairs were pushed into the corners, mostly hidden by shadow. On top of the table was a little box.

The medium took the seat opposite the door, cradling the hair pin in her palms. She closed her eyes, as though waiting for the little enamel butterfly to speak.

We took the seats around her, with me on her right. Ruthie, as though unable to stand touching her, took the seat opposite, as far from her as she could get, and the others spaced themselves around the table between us. Bernice took the space to my right. I got the feeling she had nominated herself my protector. She always seemed to put herself at my elbow when something was about to happen.

Betsy Brown raised her eyes to us again, holding out her hands, palms up. "Everyone join hands. I'm going to attempt to communicate with your friend. What's her name?"

"Ada," I whispered.

"Ada." She rolled it around on her tongue. "All right. I'm going to try to communicate with Ada. Inside this box, there's a bell, which she will use to communicate. One ring means yes, two means no. Three means she doesn't know or the answer is unclear."

I stared at the little wooden box. It was a little smaller than a loaf of bread, with brass trimmings and carvings I couldn't make out in the poor lighting. Across the table, Ruthie sniffed. Emily glared at the box, as though it was to blame for everything.

"Wait. How do we know this isn't all a ruse?" Mary Anne asked suddenly, looking from the box to Betsy.

The woman glared at her. Mary Anne glared right back. "Well, she's your friend, isn't she? So you should know. Now be quiet."

As if on cue, the candles around the room flickered. Hesitantly, I took the hands of the people next to me. I was still wearing my gloves, at least. I hate touching stranger's hands.

The medium sat straight in her chair, with posture even our headmistresses couldn't have faulted. Face lowered, her voice became deeper and throatier. "Close your eyes. Think of Ada. Think of the last time you saw her. Call her name with your mind."

Unbidden, the image of Ada's body in the infirmary filled my vision. I winced, trying to push it away. Tried to replace it with the memory of her on her bed with *Cosmopolitan*, reading aloud from that issue's short story. Ada, behind me in the mirror as she twisted my braids into something elegant and grown up. Dabbing on her mother's pilfered perfume, whispering about the boy she was going to meet, making me promise not to breathe a word to anyone, because she'd be expelled if Davenport found out.

Ada, face down in the fountain, with a bruise in the shape of a handprint on her thigh.

I squeezed my eyes shut, like I could close the shutters on the image, but it was there in my head.

"Are you okay? You're going to break my fingers!" Bernice whispered.

"Silence!"

We both jerked back. A low humming sound emanated from Betsy's throat, seeming to fill the entire space. I swear, it felt like my chair vibrated.

A cold breeze blew down the back of my neck, and half the candles stuttered and died. Mary Anne yelped. Someone kicked her under the table to make her be quiet. The bell in the box began to ring, chiming wildly.

"Ada Brooks! We seek your presence tonight! Are you with us?" Betsy's voice had an edge of command that completely masked her heavy, low-class accent.

Despite my long-sleeved blouse and my coat, chills raced up and down my arms and back. The hum grew louder. I flinched. Where was it coming from?

"Ada Brooks! We summon you to our circle!"

Beside me, Betsy was rigid as a board, her fingers clamped onto mine, at least as hard as I'd been holding Bernice's.

She exhaled so softly I almost didn't hear it. Then the bell rang again.

"Ada Brooks, are you with us? Please ring the bell again. Once for yes, twice for no."

*Ding.*

"Thank you. Ada, your friends have come here tonight to speak to you."

I could feel the others all turning to look at me, the defacto leader on this quest, but something didn't feel right. I couldn't put my finger on it, but something was…missing.

I looked around the little room, at the deep pools of shadows. Only one candle was left burning after the cold chill. I strained my eyes in the darkness, and then I saw it. Over Betsy's head, half hidden, was a small vent in the wall. The last remaining candle was in a corner, out of its path.

"Darlin', you gotta say something or she'll flee," the medium said.

I nodded, swallowing hard. I shifted in the hard wooden chair, stretching my legs out a little. They bumped into something, and inside the box the bell began to ring.

"Hurry, before she goes!"

I jerked my legs back, but my boots were stuck on something. The bell jingled wildly, and then the box slid an inch or two across the table, bunching up the black fabric as it moved.

Mary Anne screamed, throwing herself away from the table.

"You must not break the circle—"

I jerked my hands free and stood up. There was a soft *snap* as my boot pulled free of whatever it was caught on. The bell fell silent immediately.

"This was a waste of time. I'm sorry, everyone, for bringing you here. I thought—I thought it would help, but she's just a phony." I squeezed my eyes shut, trying to hold back my rage.

"Hey, now! Wait a minute! You can't go around making accusations! There was a ghost—"

"No, there was a thread under the table so you could ring the bell. It's attached to the floor just in front of your chair, isn't it? And isn't there a fan, hidden just up there? Don't mediums but bowls of water in front of fans, to generate a cold breeze? You placed the candles in such a way that they'd be effected by the air current."

Even in the dark, I could see the sickly pale cast on her face. Her khol-rimmed eyes looked like two bruises. Or the empty sockets of a skull.

"You were nothing but a phony from the beginning. What other tricks did you have planned? A rapping cabinet? Fake ectoplasm?" Ada's magazines were full of articles about mediums and charlatans, and the tricks they used.

I choked back the angry tears, staring into the death's head that was her face. "How dare you! We came here for help. To catch a killer. And you mocked her. You mocked Ada's murder, turning it into some...some side-show!"

"Jules!" Bernice grabbed my arms, pulling me away from the medium. I wasn't sure if she was trying to restrain me or comfort me, but she held me against her shoulder the way Miss Comstock had in the hall as my anger boiled over.

"She deserves better. Ada deserves better," I sobbed into her shoulder. Bernice squeezed tight, until I almost couldn't breathe. It grounded me, and I started to calm down.

Was I wrong? Why was I the only one who cared? Why did Ada's death only matter to me?

The cold breeze from the fan blew again, striking the bare back of my neck, just below my hat and in the open space between my braids. I shivered.

Bernice went rigid. Suddenly, the room was so quiet, it was like everyone in the room had stopped breathing. I sniffed, inhaling attar of roses.

"Jules…"

Dabbing at my eyes with my glove, I peered over her shoulder and froze.

The room was no longer lit by a single candle. A sheer specter floated over the table. From the waist down, she faded into nothing, her legs vanishing into the table.

But from the waist up, it was her. Ada. She looked around, taking us each in turn. Her long red hair, faded in death, seemed to float around her.

I recognized her blouse. It was the white one she'd been

wearing when they found her.

She looked at Mary Anne, and Emily, and Ruthie, then Bernice before turning to me.

# Chapter Fifteen

July 7, 1918

*Dear Jules,*

*Is your summer as dull as mine? There's nothing to do here, and no one to do it with. I miss seeing you every day. I swear, the most intelligent conversation I've had since school let out is talking to the cat.*

*Father and Mother have gone to San Francisco for two weeks, so it's just me and Jemmina, the maid. I'm not allowed to do anything. They left before I got back from school, and Mother forgot to leave me pocket money, so I can't even go shopping or to the nickelodian.*

*I know you said you're not very good at writing letters to people, but I have nothing else to do, so please write me back. Relieve me from my prison! This house is big and empty and Jemmina is busy and sour as a lemon, anyway, and not even the cat wants to keep me company right now, and it's so depressing. I know everyone at school thinks I'm the one who understands you, but really, I think you're the one who understands me. The people here are insufferable, and I miss the long talks we had before bed.*

*There is one boy in town. I don't like him much, but I'm so desperate for company, maybe we can get along well enough to make this summer bearable.*

*Tell me another of your ghost stories. It will give me something to think about until Mother and Father get back.*


*Your friend,*
*Ada*



Ada reached a translucent hand to me, eyes softening. Instinctively, I reached for her, too. Her lips moved, but I couldn't hear the words. I laced my fingers through hers, and the floor seemed to drop out from beneath me. I tried to brace myself on the table, but there was nothing to hang on to.

*I was running, darting through the shadows of the school basement with my favorite pair of shoes in one hand. Heart hammering, I stopped to put them on. The night was cold, and I wore a coat over my favorite dress.*

*No. Not my favorite dress. Ada's.*

*Ada's hands buckled Ada's shoes, and she swept an errant strand of red hair from her face.*

*Before I'd even had time to contemplate the concept, I was on my feet again, slipping through the kitchen door, leaving the flu*

*pamphlet in the latch, and then hurrying across the patio on tip-toe*
*to keep my heels from clacking on the flagstones. Once in the*
*grass, I took off running, breathing heavy with excitement as I*
*followed Rainbow Lane to the old mausoleum.*

*Tonight, I was the only one waiting. Sometimes others were*
*there, too, and we had to jockey for the best spaces. The*
*mausoleum was more private, but colder this time of year. Outside*
*was nice in fine weather, but anyone could see you and who you*
*were canoodling with.*

*I lit one of the lamps on the wall, claiming a hidden corner at*
*the back. As I passed the coffin, I kissed the first and second*
*fingers of my right hand and pressed them to the stone. I didn't*
*know who was inside, but the inscription read* Beloved Marie. *The*
*girls all called her Saint Marie, the patron of lovers.*

*The mausoleum was freezing, but I took off my coat, spreading*
*it on the hard ground and sitting down on top, neatly arranging my*
*skirt around me.*

*When I looked up, he was waiting in the doorway, leaning*
*against the open door.*

*"Well, look at this fine little filly," he said, a grin twisting one*
*corner of his mouth up. A curl of dark hair flopped over his*
*forehead rakishly.*

*I leaned back, bracing myself with my hands. "You sound like you want to go for a ride."*

*The grin broadened. In two steps he'd crossed the space between us, kneeling beside me. He leaned in, pressing his lips to mine. His fingers traced a line down my arm, and I shivered.*

*"Cold?" he whispered against my mouth.*

*"Mmhm. Warm me up?"*

*He started to take off his coat, but a sound made us both stop. Gooseflesh suddenly crawled from the top of my scalp all the way to the tips of my toes.*

*Charlie stood up. "Stay put for a minute."*

*I was on my feet in an instant. Two other boys, both grinning like devils, appeared in the doorway.*

*"What is this?"*

*"Just sit down, darling," said one, and I recognized the voice.*

*I looked from one face to another as they moved into the circle of light, fear and bile rising in my throat.*

*"Look what we have here. Johnson, tsk tsk. Really, I thought you had better taste. This one gets around, doesn't she?"*

*I looked from Charlie to the other two boys. "Why are they here?"*

*But an icy feeling of dread certainty was already coiling in my stomach.*

*The two of them crowded into the mausoleum with us. It wasn't a big building to begin with, and four was definitely a crowd.*

*"Get out of here, Lucas," I snapped. "I told you I don't want to see you anymore."*

*He pressed his hands to his heart, feigning hurt. "Aw, now. Come on, Ada. Don't be like that. See, I don't think you mean it. You were so...enthusiastic last time."*

*I was so angry, I wanted to spit in his face. "If by that you mean I nearly bit your tongue off when you put it where it wasn't wanted. I don't know what I ever saw in you." No, I knew. He was the only boy at school who lived near my parents' house. We saw each other over the summer, and there was no one else to talk to. But he gave Mildred Temple a black eye last year. She was a year older than me, but left school shortly after the incident. There were rumors she'd been in the family way, but of course it was all hushed up. No one heard from her after that.*

*The absolute boredom of a summer spent in Lancaster, home alone save for the maid, wasn't enough to make him that appealing.*

*Lucas was mean as they came; I'd steered clear of him myself, but not every girl was that smart. It was a shame. He didn't deserve a one of us.*

*He pushed his way forward, planting a hand against the wall behind me, trapping me. "You see, my friend Charlie here, he offered to help me out. Remember those letters I sent you? You never replied. I wanted to make sure you got them."*

*I shot an accusing look at my beau. He'd been in on this? "I threw them away." I kept all my letters from admirers. But he didn't admire me. He hated me. He wanted to tear me to pieces, and he hid it beneath the guise of a love-driven schoolboy. But what he felt was anything but love.*

*I turned to Charlie, my one chance. "Why did you bring them here? Why did you bring* him *here?"*

*Maybe realizing his mistake, Charlie tried to be the peacemaker. "Come on, Cash. You've had your fun. Now go away so I can have mine." The two of them squared off, leaving me trapped in the corner while Todd went around the other side of the coffin.*

*"This isn't funny. You can stop now," I said, my voice quivering. I tried to edge around them, but that only put me closer to Lucas.*

*"Aw, but the fun's just getting started." He grabbed my chin, kissing me so hard he slammed my head back against the wall. Stars danced in front of my eyes as he forced his tongue into my mouth.*

*I did the only thing that made sense—I bit down. Hard. I tasted blood as he screamed, tearing himself away from me.*

245

*I tried to run, but he grabbed my arm, throwing me back against the wall.*

*"Stop it!" Charlie ordered, grabbing my other arm.*

*I drew back and punched him as hard as I could in the nose.*

*"Bitch!"*

*But I was already pushing past them. When Todd tried to stop me, I ducked under his outstretched arms, stomping hard on his instep.*

*With all three boys howling in pain, I bolted for the door. Of all the nights to have the cemetery to ourselves! Where were the other girls?*

*I ran as fast as I could, but the ground was soft with recent rain. My heels sank into the mud, and my toes slipped on the wet grass. I wasn't fast enough. One of them caught my arm, nearly wrenching it from the socket. I had just enough time to register Lucas's face before he backhanded me. I would have gone sprawling if he wasn't latched onto my wrist.*

*The other boys were following now. Charlie shouted something at him. "Luke! Come on, stop it!"*

*"Shut up!" He turned back to me. "What kind of manners are they teaching you at that girls' school, huh? Is that any way to greet a friend?"*

*I spat in his face. "You're no friend of mine, Lucas Cash! Let*

*me go! I'll scream!" I tried to kick him, but he moved out of the*
*way, grabbing my leg. With his other hand, he shook me until my*
*teeth rattled.*

*"Go ahead! Who'll hear you out here, huh?"*

*"Luke—"*

*But Todd got between Charlie and us. I couldn't see what he*
*was doing with Lucas's broad shoulders between us, but could*
*hear them arguing.*

*I struck out again, and this time my toe caught Lucas in the*
*knee. It gave out and he stumbled. With my free hand, I beat him*
*around the head and ear. He tried to grab my arm, but I twisted*
*out of the way. My wrist popped painfully as I yanked it from his*
*grasp.*

*I staggered to the trees, my only hope of escape. He grabbed*
*my skirt, and the seam at the waist tore, one of the buttons flying*
*off. I landed on my hands and knees. He pinned my ankle into the*
*mud.*

*"Somebody help me!" I screamed, snatching up a stick and*
*whacking Lucas with it.*

*Todd joined in then, grabbing my arms. He pulled me halfway*
*to my feet, but I couldn't move with my shoulders twisted at such*
*an unnatural angle.*

*I screamed again, but Lucas reached into the pocket of his*

247

*blazer and produced a handkerchief. He stuffed it in my mouth. It tasted of lint, and something sour I couldn't place. "Hasn't anyone ever told you that little girls should be seen and not heard?" he hissed, an angry light in his eyes.*

*"Luke! Stop. Just let her go."*

*"Why? So she can go crying to Dragon Breath? No. We came out all this way just to see you, sweetie. I think we should get to spend some time together," Lucas replied, grabbing my jaw again and squeezing, like he meant to rearrange my teeth. "Come on, Johnson. Where's your sense of fun? Are you turning into a good boy, now? Or did this one steal your balls when you started stepping out together?"*

*Charlie's face clouded at that accusation. "It's not like that—"*

*"Yeah, I'm sure. She's just a little trollop, isn't she? She's been with half the boys at school."*

*I glared at him and tried to kick, but he planted himself on my legs, grabbing both thighs in his big, meaty hands, and clenching them until I thought his fingertips would burst right through my skin, like poking through the skin of rotten fruit. I screamed into the handkerchief, tried to spit it out, but he just grabbed my face again, the hand left on my thigh digging in even harder.*

*"Come on, Johnson. Why don't you have the first round, since you arranged this little party."*

248

*"No. I don't think—"*

*"What? Aren't you man enough?"*

*Todd dropped my arms suddenly and I went crashing to the ground. "If you won't do it, I will," he said. I couldn't see him, but I could hear the grin in his voice.*

*"Cash, I'm serious! Just knock it off!"*

*But Lucas didn't. I freed one hand, digging the nails into the exposed flesh on the side of his neck. He howled, slamming his fist into the side of my head.*

*The sky became mottled black and red, spots of light behind my eyes. I lay there half insensible, with my ears ringing while Lucas Cash pushed my skirt up over my thighs and fussed with my stockings. His weight pressed down on my chest. I couldn't breathe. I didn't think I wanted to breathe, if this was what he was after.*

*Suddenly the weight lifted. The ground shifted under me, and someone else was grabbing my wrist, pulling me away.*

*"Ada, get out of here!"*

*I looked up into Charlie's blurry face. His voice echoed, like he kept it stored in a tin can and had only partially peeled back the lid. The idea struck me as funny somehow, and I giggled.*

*"Ada, go on!"*

*He hauled me to my feet, but Lucas was already regaining his.*

*He clutched his stomach, shirt untucked and the first button of his trousers open. I sobered instantly. Todd lay on the ground behind him, but he was getting back up.*

*"You want to do this? You really want to do this? I can ruin you, Johnson. I can ruin you! You want to risk that, for some fast girl? Huh? Some no-count girl that'll go with anyone?"*

*I didn't stay long enough to hear Charlie's answer. With blood pounding in my ears, I stumbled back to the school. The ground still rolled beneath me, but with every step I regained my footing. I ran through the dark forest, skidding down hills and tripping over roots. Something startled and bounded out of the bushes to my right, but I couldn't stop to look. I had to get back to the school. If I could just put a door between us, a door between Lucas and me—*

*I practically fell into the clearing behind the school. The windows were all dark, but I could just see the flu pamphlet fluttering in the kitchen door. Almost there—*

*And then I wasn't. With only a few yards to go, my side about to split with a stitch like I'd never had before, panting, a strong hand grabbed the back of my neck, throwing me down. My head hit the edge of the fountain. The world went black, but I could still hear his footsteps, his panting breath, hot on my face in the cold night air.*

*I tried to fight, to struggle, but he just held my throat, and when*

*I didn't stop, he pushed my head down, into the water.*

*"That will teach you," Lucas growled.*


Around the table, the other girls all recoiled, startled by her sudden appearance. For the first time, I realized I wasn't the only person in the room who could see the spirit. But was I the only one who saw the vision?

Emily's jaw worked up and down, but she couldn't summon any words. Mary Anne was practically hiding behind her. Emily, in turn, had placed Ruthie between herself and the ghost.

"I'm so sorry. I'm trying to help," I said, tears rolling down my cheeks. Ada offered me a smile, and for once, I was able to make out her words: *I know.*

"I'm going to find him. I'll make him pay. I swear. The police won't do anything, but *I will.* I promise."

Ada nodded. Her fingers slipped through mine.

She was fading, her form slipping through to the other side as easily as her hand went through mine.

Her lips moved again, but I couldn't understand her words. I've never been good at reading lips. Her face began to dissipate, like steam over the vats of broth Bernice and I spent our days hauling up and down the stairs.

"Ada! Ada—wait!"

251

But she was gone. My shoulders slumped.

The disconnected "spirit bell" gave a single, soft chime inside the box.

I looked around. No one was touching the table. No one was within arm's reach of it. Even Betsy Brown had pushed her chair all the way back to the wall when the ghost appeared. I could hear her panting.

"Light! Someone find a light!"

I thought that was Bernice. After some fumbling, Emily found the light switch by the door. I winced as bright yellow light flooded the room.

In the harsh glare of the incandescent, I wondered if it had really happened at all. I closed my eyes, and when I looked around again at the pale faces around me, I knew it was true. Ada had been there. She'd come. She'd shown me who her killer was—and it wasn't Charlie. It wasn't the "J" from her letters.

"What—What was that? What kind of trick—"

"There! That wasn't a trick!" the medium was on her feet now, shaking but eager to defend herself. "You saw it! There was a ghost here! There was—she—"

Bernice shook her head. "No. It had to be...an illusion. That's it."

"Don't be daft, Bernice. How would she even know what Ada

looks like?" Ruthie's eyes shone, her faith restored, but Betsy's face, still pale, seemed more bravado than confidence to my eye.

"Looked," Mary Anne corrected. For the moment, we'd all forgotten that Ada was past tense.

I stared at the medium. I'd never had an experience that…strong before. Never had a ghost realize I was there, let alone try to speak with me.

Never had one show me how they died.

"What did she say?" I asked. "I couldn't hear her. But you could."

Betsy straightened up, adjusting her shawl and tossing the end over her shoulder, like a flyboy scarf. "She said 'thank you.'"

"Is that all?" I couldn't help but be disappointed.

"She knows you're trying to help her. And she appreciates it. And she…the one who killed her…" She swallowed, shook her head. "Whatever you girls did, whatever you're doing…You have to keep doing it."

"What are you talking about? We're not doing anything. We're just trying to survive," Mary Anne insisted. She sounded near tears.

"No. You've called up her spirit. Her spirit, which cries out for justice." She looked at each of us in turn, eyes darting around the room.

"You all saw it. I know you saw it."

We all looked away, staring at our shoes. A denial that was silent confirmation.

Betsy grabbed my arm. "She also said…she said she's sorry."

I nodded, staring down at the table, the little wooden box, and the space Ada had occupied over it.

The space she'd occupied inside me was much bigger. Massive. And empty. It threatened to collapse in on itself like a vacuum now that she was gone. I dabbed my tears away with my gloves.

"You all saw that. You can't go around tellin' people I'm a fake. I'd lose everything," Betsy was saying, slowly shooing us toward the front door. "The accent might be fake, but the ghosts ain't. You all saw it."

"Yes, we saw it," Ruthie confirmed, twisting the hem of her coat between her fingers.

"Good. Good. 'Cuz I'd be done if you started spreading rumors. *Unfounded* rumors."

Mary Anne narrowed her eyes quizzically behind her spectacles. "But I don't understand. If you're a real medium and can really call up the spirits, why go through the trouble of all the tricks? The bell, the fan?"

"It's like I said, you can send out an invitation, but you can't make anyone sit down to eat. I can call to the ghosts all I want, but sometimes, they just don't want to come." She looked sadly at Ruthie.

The little blonde's head snapped up. "But that not—My brother, he'd come—"

"He wants to rest, hon. Leave him be. He's been through a lot. You said your good-byes at the pier. Remember him whole, and happy and young. Let that be enough."

Ruthie nodded.

We were almost to the front door when Betsy stopped me. "Whatever you girls need, you come to me, you hear? Whatever you need."

I stared at her, not entirely sure I understood. But she nodded, shaking my arm a little. She leaned in close. "You have a gift. You can use it. And if you need help from me, just say the word."

I nodded, and she let go. I stepped back, unsure how I felt about her offer.

People don't offer to help me. Not usually.

Betsy turned her attention to the others. "Now. You girls be careful. Them pigs have been wandering all over the place, and they'll pick you up for sure if they catch you wandering around this late."

We nodded, slipping out her front door and onto the street. The cold air was a welcome relief, though I shivered more than usual as we retraced our steps back through the woods. At least Ruthie seemed to know where she was going. I had no choice but to trust her.

That was another new sensation. I didn't normally trust anyone. Not so soon after associating with them.

But sometimes, there's no choice.

And sometimes, you just *have to*.

\*\*\*

The walk back to the school seemed to take much longer than our hurried descent to town. We picked our way through the darkness, exhausted by the late hour and the excitement of the evening.

Bernice walked beside me the whole way, occasionally darting looks in my direction, but didn't say anything. I was glad. I needed to stew over the evening in my head before I could talk about it.

Ada had come. She'd come when I'd asked. Though I still had doubts about Madame Marron, I was sure she had some kind of ability. Maybe stronger than my own. Maybe just different, the way some people can paint and others can sculpt. Maybe her talents lay in getting messages from the dead, and mine lay in seeing them.

I shuddered. I'd rather have a talent for something else.

But we can only make do with what we have, as she'd said, and right now seeing the dead was the only tool I had at my disposal when it came to catching Ada's killer.

My suspicions about Charlie Johnson were half-right, at least. He'd been there when she died. He knew how it happened. Knew who took her life. We had a witness. From the way he'd tried to protect her, he might even be willing to speak out against Lucas Cash, if we could only convince him.

I shuddered, thinking of her horror, the blind terror propelling her through the woods. It was easy to see she'd fought back, but the ferocity of it…I felt a tiny note of pride at the way she'd fought. But it was quickly superseded by regret and loss. Whatever she'd done, it wasn't enough. Despite the violence of the act, the police hadn't done anything. Why? Why hadn't they done anything?

Lucas Cash might be the headmaster's nephew, but surely that wasn't enough to protect him from the law. Charlie Johnson must have kept the secret. Protected his friend, instead of his beau. Maybe Lucas threatened him. Or maybe Lucas as right, and the three boys had been conspiring from the beginning.

I wished I could talk to Detective Buchanan again. To ask why he'd allowed such a crime to go unpunished.

If not for the curfew, I'd insist on turning back, on marching right up the police station and asking for him. But it was after midnight. Even if we didn't get arrested ourselves for breaking curfew, the detective probably wouldn't even be there. And he probably wouldn't believe a ghost story from a bunch of schoolgirls, anyway.

A chill ran down my spine. The flu came to the school *after* the police. Which meant it had to come in with them. What if the detective was now delirious in some hospital? Or worse, dead? Then who would listen to my case?

"Will you go to the police?"

If my special talent was seeing ghosts, I was starting to think Bernice's might be seeing the inner workings of my mind.

"I don't know. I don't see how." Mail was stopped. Going in person would mean breaking the quarantine. And there was no way the headmistress would let me use the telephone. And what would I tell them? That my dead friend sent a vision to the six of us, to show us how she died?

Bernice looked thoughtful—and tired. We were all exhausted. My mind spun in erratic circles, like a slightly off-balance top.

We climbed the last hill to the school in silence, our feet dragging on the gravel. All the front windows were dark, the quarantine notice tacked to the front door. I wondered when someone could have had time to come all the way up to the school, just to paste that sheet in place. Couldn't they have done something more useful, like bringing us food or medicine?

The front door was locked now, so we slipped around to the back of the school. One window threw a square of illumination onto the patio—the infirmary. Someone was moving around, attending to the patients, but all I could see were shadows behind the curtains. The coughing was still audible, however, through the partially open windows.

As though everyone else was all thinking the same thing, we paused in that square of light.

Ada died on Friday. With a start, I realized she'd been dead exactly a week now, give or take an hour or so. Now Mary was dead, too. How many more would follow?

Mary Anne pulled the pamphlet out of the kitchen door, and we filed inside, doing our best to stay quiet as we tip-toed up the stairs, through the dining room, to the front hall, but someone was already there.

"Is that Nurse?" Emily whispered, peering around the doorway.

I leaned in closer for a better view. Sure enough, I could make out several dark shapes in the hallway, just near the front door. Had they realized we were missing?

"I think so," I whispered. They were too far away for me to hear the words, but it sounded like Nurse Spencer was talking to another teacher, just outside the headmistress's office.

"Sh! I can't hear anything! What are they saying?" Ruthie hissed, elbowing her way into the gap between Emily and me.

Someone turned on the light in the entry. Like cockroaches, we scattered, falling back into the darkness of the dining room. "…ambulance. I don't know what else to do," Nurse Spencer was saying. She sounded utterly exhausted.

"I tried calling. They said we're too far away. It could be hours before there's an ambulance available."

"How can they do that? There are people *dying* upstairs. Children! If they have to wait until morning, they'll be picking up *bodies*!"

"Shh! Keep your voice down." Miss Newton tried to quiet her friend, but even from our position, I could see the dark shadows under Nurse Spencer's eyes. There was something dark on the sleeve of her sweater, and smeared over her apron.

Ruthie noticed it, too. "Is that…blood?" Her voice turned high on the last note. Emily clapped a hand over her mouth, but neither staff member seemed to hear.

"Shh. Yes. I think it is."

The little ninth grader turned big eyes on the rest of us, as though we could make it go away, as the older, more experienced students.

"When my cousin was sick, he got a bloody nose. It was so bad. Blood everywhere. It was like…" Like someone had slit his throat. It was just like the medical books described arterial bleeding. I swallowed a hard lump. Ruthie's eyes were the size of dinner plates. She looked even more terrified.

I swallowed again, trying to clear the tightness from my throat. "It means their suffering will be over soon." That was what Grandmother said, at least.

Nurse Spencer spoke again. "Beth, we have to do something."

"I know. I just don't know what."

"Call again. Keep calling until we get someone here. A doctor. Another nurse. At this rate, there won't be enough healthy students and staff left to take care of the ill."

They shuffled back, out of our line of sight, and then the hall light switched off.

"I'll stay with her. You go get some rest," Miss Newton said in the darkness.

Nurse Spencer sighed. "I'll relieve you in the morning. Or send someone else down to do it. We're going to need a duty roster in the morning. Maybe I can get Hannah to do it. She's good at that sort of thing. She's been an absolute blessing." Hannah? Of course,

261

Mrs. Hodge. With her Red Cross experience, she would be taking charge, helping Nurse Spencer.

The nurse's shoes clicked over the tile floor, coming closer at a rapid click. Her path would take her right past our hiding place.

I shrank back into Bernice.

I closed my eyes. Not because I was afraid of being seen, but because I could *smell* it, the sharp iron tang.

When I opened my eyes again, the nurse was right in front of me, eyes straight ahead on her way back to the infirmary.

The entire lower half of her crisp white apron was stained with blood.

# Chapter Sixteen

*January 31, 2018*

*Dear Miss Davenport,*

*We have received your letter and are grateful for your concern.*

*As you said, Julia is a very bright girl, but sometimes has difficulty with people and unfamiliar situations. These can be very distressing to her, in ways that we do not fully understand. While your automatic response might be to force her to conform, this will only cause hardship for you both. She learns best with limited supervision, and will read voraciously, especially when a subject interests her. It distresses me to hear of her difficulty in English, as she has always loved to read.*

*With regard to her ability in French, I'm afraid I have no solution. We have tried to teach her both French and German from a young age, but she is very literal in her understanding, and this makes the differences in grammar and meaning very difficult for her.*

*Julia speaks very highly of her roommate, Ada Brooks, and I feel Ada has been a help to her in understanding her classmates. Given time and understanding, I think she will grow to make more friends and blend in more with her surroundings. In the meantime,*

263

*please do not force her into situations that make her*
*uncomfortable, as it will only distress her more. She needs time*
*and a quiet retreat more than anything else.*

*From her letters I can tell she has already improved, and beg*
*your patience a little longer. She has always been an exemplary*
*student, and I would hate for her education to be cut short due to a*
*lack of understanding.*

*If you have any additional questions or concerns, or would like*
*to discuss any necessary accommodations, please contact me. We*
*do have a telephone and can be reached in an emergency.*

*Sincerely,*
*Viola Grace*

The next morning, I slept late. It was a quarter past seven when
I rolled out of bed, desperately searching for my stockings.

I'd fallen into bed at some point just before three o'clock, too
exhausted to undress. I wasn't sure how long I'd lain awake in the
darkness, thinking of Ada's vision, staring at her empty bed, but
eventually, I drifted off. If not for the daylight streaming through
my window—and directly onto my face—I likely would have slept
until noon. But the last thing I wanted was for Bernice to do the

morning rounds without me, only to discover I was still asleep—
though not ill.

I rubbed my eyes, trying to banish the crust of sleep from them
as I lumbered down the stairs. I was still in yesterday's uniform,
wearing yesterday's braids. I wasn't certain, but there was every
possibility I'd grabbed yesterday's stockings, too, in my rush to get
downstairs.

The dining room was oddly silent as I slipped inside, but there
were so few healthy girls now—only about ten, total—that every
head turned in my direction.

I froze, and realized I'd forgotten my mask again in my rush.
*Drat!*

Mrs. Hodge, at the front of the room, gestured me forward.
"Come here, dear," she said, pointing to an empty space in the
group of girls. Behind her, Miss Newton rocked on her feet,
looking ready to drop.

"Ladies, it is with a heavy heart that I must tell you some very
hard truths this morning," the history teacher began. I swallowed a
lump of fear. The other girls all exchanged looks. The girl next to
me touched my elbow briefly, and I realized through the mask and
the black circles under her eyes that it was Bernice. Hesitantly, I
gave her hand a squeeze.

"The flu has struck, and struck hard, as you are all aware. I'm

265

afraid three girls left us in the night: Sarah Brown, Gloria Cartwright, and Marcie Parks." I didn't know who Marcie Parks was; judging by the looks the other girls were giving each other, neither did they. Mrs. Hodge sighed. "One of the maids."

A sigh of relief went through the small crowd. *At least it wasn't one of us*, it said. I closed my eyes and wished I could unthink it. Marcie Parks still had a family somewhere. She was still a person. The flu didn't care if you were a maid, or the richest girl in school.

"In addition, we have had a telephone call from the Academy. They are suffering under their own quarantine. I do not have a list of names, but as of this morning, seven are dead." Her voice cracked on the words. Bernice gripped my hand so tight, I thought my fingers would break.

She took a steadying breath. "What you see here now is the sum total of healthy students and staff, less those from the night shift getting rest. Miss Comstock has been kind enough to take over the evening round of nursing, along with Maureen and Camille, but I need more volunteers—at least two."

With another round of shifting looks, Mary Anne put up her hand, as well as Ruthie and Emily.

"Thank you. Mary Anne, you and Maureen are the only two prefects left in the school. I want to keep you on the day shift.

Ladies, thank you for volunteering."

One look at Emily and Ruthie, and it was clear they'd volunteered for night shift so they could go back to bed. I wondered if they'd gotten any sleep at all. Or maybe they were coming down ill, too?

"The rest of you, there is too much to do and not enough hands to do it. We need chamber pots, and we need them emptied. Not all the girls can make it to the washroom. We need food—I want a pot of broth on the stove at all times. Someone should stay in the kitchen to make sure there is always food and water ready for whomever needs it. Dishes need washed, and laundry—we need linens. Sheets, aprons, blankets.

"And most of all, we need nurses. We need girls who can go room to room, helping the girls eat or drink, keeping them comfortable.

"And lastly…I need girls who can help with those who have passed." Mrs. Hodge closed her eyes for a moment. "I can't carry the girls myself, even with help, and Miss Newton can't do it alone. We need to move them down to one of the classrooms, so when the ambulance comes, they can get to them quickly. This will allow us to move more severe cases closer to the infirmary, where we can tend to them better."

Slowly, Bernice raised a hand. Of the few of us left, she was the stoutest, the most athletic. Mary Anne raised her hand again as well. Mrs. Hodge nodded. "Thank you," she said, dabbing at her eyes.

"I also must inform you that our headmistress took to her bed yesterday afternoon, and her condition is…not promising."

This time, I was the one who looked at the other girls. Mary Anne, Emily, Ruthie, and Bernice all looked back at me. I remembered the blood on Nurse Spencer's apron. She must be in poor shape indeed; only the worse cases got nose bleeds—nose bleeds so strong, it was like a fountain of blood, spurting from the face as blood vessels burst.

Before I could stop myself, I raised a hand. "Mrs. Hodge? I volunteer to help the headmistress. I imagine she's in her room. So she's on a different floor from everyone else. And if she's doing poorly…"

Mrs. Hodge nodded. "Thank you, Julia. Nurse Spencer is with her now, but she's overdue for her rest. Get yourself some breakfast, then take some broth and another pitcher of water to her room as soon as you're done. Go now. The rest of you, come here and we'll try to create a duty roster."

There was a shuffling of feet as I wove through the crowd to the kitchen stairs. Once in the basement, the smell of plain vegetable broth permeated the air. It was so ever-present after the past few days, I didn't think I would ever get the smell of onions out of my hair.

No one had made porridge, however. After a little searching, I found the canister of oatmeal. There were barely two spoonfuls left in the bottom of the container.

I checked the bread box next—empty. The ice box was bare, too.

Beginning to panic, I ran to the pantry and tore it open. There were two crates of root vegetables, and some withered fruit on the shelf, as well as jars of flour, sugar, and salt, and some smaller containers of other spices.

"Julia? Julia, where are you?" Mary Anne called.

"I'm in here."

"What are you doing in here?" she asked.

"Trying to figure out how we're going to feed thirty people with a dozen potatoes, some parsnips, and three withered apples."

\*\*\*

Mrs. Hodge blanched when we told her the news. Apparently, no one had been keeping track of the food, and with the entire kitchen staff incapacitated, no one took note of the fact that the regular grocery delivery never came.

"We need—I'll have to find the phone number," Mrs. Hodge said, her cheeks turning flushed.

"I can do it," I said. "I'm going to help Headmistress Davenport, anyway. I can ask where she keeps the number, and make the call while she's resting."

"You know how to use a telephone?"

I nodded. "My grandparents have one."

Slowly, she nodded. "All right. But don't go snooping. Oh, but you won't do that, I know. You've always been so studious," she said, dismissing her own doubts before they could begin to take root.

I nodded again, crossing my fingers behind my back.

The lie—or maybe it was the fear of getting caught—left a bitter taste in the back of my mouth, too strong for me to consider boiling up the last of the oatmeal for my own breakfast. There wasn't a pitcher to be had in the kitchen, so I washed several bowls, spoons, and cups and left them on the drying rack, then took one of each and filled them for Headmistress Davenport. All the trays had migrated upstairs, so I had to balance them very carefully as I climbed the stairs to the first floor. Mrs. Hodge had set the day shift girls to collecting dirty dishes and linens, and I had to dodge past them on my way to the office. I hoped they would also be washing them.

I paused at the office door, trying to figure out how to balance the soup and the water without creating a mess. Even through the door, I could hear her heavy cough on the other side of the office.

It was about that time I remembered once again that I'd forgotten my mask. I'd been so distracted and tired, it had completely slipped my mind. But now I stood frozen, staring at the door knob, while disease waited on the other side and my only protection was two floors away.

"Do you need a hand?"

I nearly dropped the soup. Miss Newton reached in front of me, twisting the knob and holding the door open.

"I—th-thank you," I mumbled. I couldn't read her expression behind the mask. Part of me waited for her to make a cutting remark, but she just slammed the door behind me. I listened as her footsteps faded away.

The office was dark, a heavy cloud hanging over the room. It pressed down on me, threatening to push me straight into the floorboards.

The door behind the desk—always closed in the past—stood open now, the only light coming from a lamp on the other side.

"Headmistress?" I peered inside.

In contrast to the severe office with its heavy furniture, the Headmistress's bedroom was done up all in pastels. The wrought iron bed frame was painted white, and over it was a bedspread trimmed in about ten miles of white lace.

The personal effects missing from her office were all clustered on every available space. Photographs filled every horizontal surface. Landscape paintings and portraits of former classes hung on the walls. Above the bed was a beautiful sampler, far more intricate than my own work. I stepped closer for a better view. The letters were so precise, they could have been drawn on with a fountain pen. Below the alphabet were a few lines of poetry:

*The soul has moments of escape*
*When bursting all the doors*
*She dances like a Bomb, abroad*
*And swings upon the House*

A landscape with a cottage and a perfect little garden filled the bottom of the frame. Climbing roses wound their way up the sides, bursting into bloom at the top, just above the date—March, 1891. At the bottom right corner, I could just make out the initials *D.R.D.* hidden among daisies and lavender.

"The soul has bandaged moments/When too appalled to stir/She feels some ghastly fright come up/and stop to look at her. Salute her, with long fingers/Caress her freezing hair/Sip, Goblin, from the very lips/the lover—" the headmistress's raspy voice dissolved into a coughing fit. I still stood there, holding the water

272

and soup. Nearly dropping them, I hurried to help her.

She held a handkerchief to her face, and it came away bloody. Her upper lip was pink.

"I—I'm sorry." I wasn't even sure what I was apologizing for; it just seemed the thing to say. I was somewhere I didn't belong— the headmistress's *bedroom*—staring at her private things, unable to help her—"

She waved me away. Her long gray hair was down, braided messily and hanging over her shoulder. Spots of blood covered her nightgown.

"It's Emily Dickinson," she gasped at last, gesturing to the sampler with her handkerchief. "My mother said I should have used something from the Bible, but that was one I made for myself."

"I didn't know you liked to embroider." It felt like a stupid thing to say, but I didn't know what else I was supposed to say.

"I used to, quite a lot. But I can't see well enough anymore. Too many years staring at books, I suppose. My mother always said books were the ruin of a girl."

I looked from the sampler to the headmistress. "It's a good thing you didn't believe her."

Her bark of a laugh made me jump; not just because I thought it was another cough at first, and that she might be dying—but because I'd never heard the sound before.

"Well, something good ought to come of it. I suppose you're the one Petunia sent down." She wheezed, covering her mouth with the handkerchief.

"It was Mrs. Hodge, actually," I said, handing her the glass of water. She sipped it slowly, sinking back into the pillows. It was so strange to hear teachers referring to each other by their first names. The flu—and Ada's death—certainly seemed to have relaxed things around the school.

Davenport made a noise of assent in her throat and closed her eyes. Her hand shook slightly with the strain of holding the glass, so I put it back on the table.

"I—I brought soup. If you're hungry."

"Not right now," she wheezed, her voice barely audible as she tried not to cough.

Her cheeks were flushed, but the idea of checking the headmistress for a fever the way my grandmother used to put her hand to my forehead was unthinkable. My fingers twitched at the very idea, aborting it before they could even leave my lap.

"You aren't wearing a mask."

"I know. I forgot it this morning." My skin itched and I fought against the panic that had threatened to consume me for days.

She made the noise of agreement again. It was the type of thing she would have scolded us for just a week ago, but her voice was too weak now, her body to exhausted. "Useless, anyway. All our precautions, and look what they brought us…"

Eyes still closed, her words faded to nothing. If not for the way she wheezed audibly, a whistle accompanying every breath, I'd have been afraid she was dead, right there in front of me.

When I was sure she was really asleep, I turned off the lamp and slipped back into her office, closing the door behind me.

My heart raced with the thought of what I was about to do. The idea had been so sudden, so spur of the moment, I'd hardly taken time to think before volunteering. But the telephone was right there in front of me.

But first, I needed to find the number for the grocer, or we'd all starve if the flu didn't get us.

Thankfully, the Headmistress was an orderly woman. In the top drawer of her desk, I found a black leather book. Every page had a letter at the top, followed by a list of names, addresses, and phone numbers. The grocer was halfway through the book, under Martin's General Store. I passed their store every time we had In Town days, on my way to the streetcar stop. The nearest bookstore was ten stops and a transfer away. Ada used to make fun of me for getting books on our one day away from the school, but she always came with me, anyway.

"Someone has to keep you out of trouble," she would tease.

"But I never get into trouble, except when I'm with you," I would insist.

"*Exactly.*"

I'd never really gotten the joke, but she said it every time. Secretly, I think she just liked to come because the pharmacy near the bookstore sold lipstick, and the one by the bridge didn't. Ada loved lipstick, almost as much as she loved perfume. Headmistress Davenport would surely have had a fit if she ever found the box in the wardrobe.

Listening closely for any movement from the bedroom, I picked up the receiver and placed it to my ear, leaning in to reach the mouthpiece. It felt like ages before the operator finally picked up.

"P-Prospect 7268," I stuttered.

"One moment." The operator sounded more than a little frazzled as she connected me.

"Hello? Doctor?"

"N-no. I'm sorry. My name is Julia. I'm calling from the Mount Sinai School for Girls—"

"What the hell do you want?" asked the angry woman on the other end of the line.

"I-I'm sorry. I'm calling about our grocery delivery. It never came this week, and we're in desperate need—"

"We're all in desperate need, honey. My husband and both my boys are down sick, and I've been waiting since yesterday for that damn doctor, so quit tying up the line!"

The connection ended abruptly as she slammed down the telephone. I sat there, staring at the receiver and the soft electric crackle coming over the severed line, like it would somehow tell me where I would get enough food to feed everyone in the school for the rest of the epidemic.

I looked over my shoulder at the bedroom door, as though the headmistress, pained, ill, and sleeping, could provide guidance.

I took a deep breath and pressed down on the prongs on the side of the telephone, raising the earpiece again.

The same frazzled operator connected me a second time, to a different number.

After six rings, my grandmother's voice flooded the line. "Hello?"

I closed my eyes, afraid I'd cry with relief. It took me so long to compose myself, that she repeated the greeting.

"I'm here. Grandmother, I'm here. Hello."

"Julia? What are you doing? Are you in trouble again?"

I shook my head, forgetting for a moment that she couldn't see. "No. I'm not in trouble. Well, I am. A bit. But not that kind of trouble." My voice broke. I covered my eyes. "Grandmother, we've got the flu. I don't have it yet. But almost everyone else does. The headmistress is...very sick." I nearly said *dying*, but didn't want Davenport to hear me, if she happened to be awake. "And four people have already died, and we're almost out of food, and the grocer won't deliver to us, and I don't know what to do." The whole thing just spilled out. I dabbed at my eyes with the hem of my sleeve.

The only sound from the other end was Grandmother's deepest sigh. I could just picture her, sinking down onto the cane chair under the big telephone box mounted on the kitchen wall. She'd be wearing her long black dress, the one with the bands of embroidered flowers down the front. It was one of her favorite things to wear for staying at home, because it was loose and robe-like, comfortable for a day spent reading or doing needle work. She'd be wearing her slippers, because her knees ached in the cold, and any sort of heel made it worse.

"Grandmother?"

"I'm still here," she said quietly. "There's no one else at the school who can help?"

"Mrs. Hodge has taken charge. She used to be a Red Cross nurse, I suppose. And there's Miss Newton. But Nurse Spencer is completely exhausted. I think all the other adults are sick. All the staff. There's about ten or twelve of us left to do the nursing."

Grandmother asked more questions, about the school, the teachers, and a dozen other things. Finally, she seemed to come to some sort of conclusion. "I can't leave, not with the quarantine. Even if you'd convinced that grocer of the situation, she probably wouldn't have been able to do anything. I've got a friend who works at the Red Cross. I'll call and see if they can send someone to you. I know they're sending volunteers out with soups and things to the people who are too sick to care for themselves. They must have something they can do. You can care for yourselves for the time being, but you need the resources to do it."

I remembered the overheard conversation as we came sneaking back in. "They called last night, trying to get doctors and another nurse. But no one's come."

"I'll try again. Do you have the number for the Red Cross?"

I searched the desk again, and found a pamphlet like the one in the kitchen, though this one was slimmer, the message more urgent: COUGHS AND SNEEZES SPREAD DISEASES MORE DEADLY THAN POISON GAS SHELLS. Staring out from the center of the page was a monstrous face, I supposed meant to represent the disease itself, personified.

"Keep calling." She said it firmly, but I heard the doubt in her voice.

"Grandmother?"

"Yes, dear?"

"Are you all right?"

"I'm fine. Just tired. But I'm staying inside. I've sent the staff away. I'll be right as rain with some rest."

My throat constricted. "You should rest, then. I'll handle things here." I wasn't nearly as confident as I tried to sound, but Grandmother didn't point it out.

"Take care, dear. God bless you."

"I love you, Grandmother."

"And I love you."

Reluctantly, I hung up the phone. After taking a few moments to dab at my eyes, I picked it up and waited a third time for the operator. A different one answered this time, but she was even slower than when I made the first two calls. When I requested the number on the pamphlet, she apologized. "I'm sorry, the line is busy."

"Please, can you try? It's important."

She laughed. "Sweetheart, that's the number for the Red Cross. *All* their calls are important right now."

"Please. I'm calling from a school. Almost everyone is sick. Four people are already dead. There's been no one to pick up the bodies, and we're almost out of food—"

"Try again later."

And then she hung up, too.

Headmistress Davenport coughed loudly—too loudly for her to still be asleep. I put down the phone and went to check on her.

Her flushed cheeks stood out against the white bedding and her pearly hair. She turned toward me a little, pale eyes moving slowly. Beneath them, dark circles like bruises colored her face.

"Were you using the telephone?" she wheezed.

"I was trying to place the grocery order. Mrs. Hodge told me to. We—the kitchen's almost empty."

"They can't deliver it because of the quarantine." The next round of coughing shook her entire frame. She curled onto her side. I started to get another glass of water for her, but then the blood came.

It poured through her fingers, splattering onto the white coverlet like fireworks. I looked around, searching for handkerchief, a towel, anything—

Bracing one knee on the mattress, I pulled her into a sitting position, tilting her head back and trying to stem the flow. I found the handkerchief she'd used earlier tangled in the bedclothes. I snatched it up and pressed it to her face.

She coughed, choking on the blood. Panicked, I didn't know what to do. Her lungs were already filling.

I pushed her head forward. It was the only thing that made sense. At first the blood came faster. "Where are the handkerchiefs?" I asked. She pointed to a dresser in the corner. I sprang from the bed, yanking open the top drawer. In addition to several neatly folded underthings, a tidy row of handkerchiefs were rolled along the left hand side.

I snatched up several—as many as I could grab with one hand—and ran back to her. Belatedly, I realized I'd left bloody fingerprints all over the dresser, her underwear, and the bed.

I pressed a fresh cloth to her face. She swayed, her face turning a sickly shade of pale.

"It's all right. It's going to be okay," I said, tucking the pillows together into a large pile. Unable to hold her up myself, I laid her gently on her side on the pillows, so her head would still be propped up. "I'm going to go get the nurse. Or Mrs. Hodge. I'll be right back!"

The headmistress could only wheeze in response, her eyelids fluttering. I pressed her hand to her nose again when it started to slip. "Right back. I promise. I'll get help."

# Chapter Seventeen

*Monday, October 21, 1918*

*Dear Mr. Cash,*

*The police have just informed me of the result of their investigation, and that no charges will be filed.*

*I do not understand how they could claim Ada Brooks died of an accident, likely of her own making, but I hope that you will take at least some responsibility and ensure the perpetrators are disciplined. If the law has failed, then we as educators must ensure our students understand the consequences of their actions. As the one who pulled Ada from the fountain where she drowned, I can assure you no gentleman could ever "accidentally" inflict such harm on a lady. A life was needlessly taken from this world, and those left behind demand justice.*

*Sincerely,*

*Deborah Davenport*

I ran from the room. My hands, soaked with blood, slipped on the doorknob. I ran for the stairs, nearly crashing into Bernice and

Miss Newton. Between them they carried a body, wrapped in a shroud made of bedclothes. Bernice's face was stained with tears.

"For heaven's sake, don't run, child. What on earth—" Miss Newton took one look at me and stopped. "What happened?"

"It's the headmistress. I don't know what to do. She's bleeding and it won't stop—"

"Go get Nurse!" she ordered, setting down her end of the shroud on the landing. I tried not to think of who might be inside.

I ran up to the third floor.

The infirmary was a scene of chaos. Mary Anne and Miss Comstock were trying to change sheets stained with blood and bile while surrounded by the sounds of misery and pain.

"Julia! What—"

"Nurse! Where's Nurse Spencer? Where's Mrs. Hodge?" I asked, when I didn't see the nurse.

"I'm right here," Mrs. Hodge said, coming out of Nurse's bedroom. "What's the matter?"

"You have to come quick! Headmistress—!"

"Go on!" She shooed me out the door, following as quickly as her stiff hips and knees would allow.

"She was coughing, and then she was bleeding, and I couldn't make it stop, and I don't think she can breathe! I found Miss Newton, and she's with her now, but she told me to get Nurse—"

"Nurse Spencer isn't in any condition to help anyone, I'm afraid. I just put her to bed with a fever."

My stomach dropped down to my toes. How could Nurse Spencer be sick? What would we do without her to guide us?

The history teacher huffed and puffed behind me. We practically tumbled down the stairs, passing Bernice on the landing, still watching over the abandoned body.

Mrs. Hodge pulled me back. "Help her," she ordered. "I'll take care of the headmistresses."

"But—"

"Miss Newton and I will take care of it." She squeezed my shoulder as she pushed past. "We can't go leaving dead bodies on the stairs. It's unhygienic and very rude."

I stood there, a few steps below Bernice. Part of me wanted to follow, to help—but I knew it wouldn't do any good. I'd done what I could. *But there has to be another way...*

"Are you all right?" Bernice asked, sniffling. I glanced back at her. She wiped her nose with her sleeve. Her eyes were still red.

I looked down at my bloodied hands. "It's not my blood."

"I didn't think it was. You're shaking."

"Am I?" Sure enough my hands trembled. Come to think of it, my knees were also feeling a little unsteady.

I sank down onto one of the steps before they could give out completely.

Bernice sat beside me, wedging me in between her and the corpse. I pointedly didn't look at the shroud, resisting the urge to peel it back and see who was wrapped up inside.

We sat like that for several moments, listening to the sounds of the school. The constant sound of coughing echoed around us. It seemed to come from every room.

Footsteps raced back and forth across the floorboards as the few healthy girls fetched and carried, helping the ones that were well enough to the lavatory and emptying chamber pots for the ones that weren't.

"Do you think she'll make it?" Bernice asked quietly.

I stared at the black and white tiles below us. The sharp perpendicular lines seemed to waver before my vision. For the first time, I realized I must have stepped in some of the headmistress's blood; a red toe print exactly matching my right boot tracked my progress from her office, finally fading away on the third step.

"I should wash my hands," I said quietly. Suddenly, that seemed like the most important thing in the world. My skin itched all over. I bounced up from my seat and practically ran to the first floor lavatory, which had been shoe-horned under the stairs when the building got running water.

Inside was a single toilet and a sink. No one liked using that lav, because it was always dark and eerie, and it was unnerving to have to relieve yourself with the sounds of thundering feet right over your head. The bare bulb cast strange shadows over my face. I tried not to look at the mirror, instead concentrating on scrubbing my hands with the harsh soap. I rolled up my bloody sleeves as high as they would go, washing all the way to the elbow. Blood clung to the undersides of my nails, no matter how hard I scrubbed. I dug them into the soap, gouging out claw marks and tearing the nail on my left index finger, but still it wouldn't come out.

The light flickered. It did that sometimes, probably because of all the bouncing up and down from the stairs.

Something cold ran down my spine, and the cloying sweet smell of attar of roses filled the bathroom.

The soap slipped from my hands, sliding around the bottom of the sink. My fingertips ached from scrubbing.

I looked up.

Another set of eyes looked back at me in the mirror.

Gloria's face was hollow and angry. Her gaze burned into me the way it had in the infirmary, full of hatred. She hadn't been bruised when she died, but there was a mark on her cheek to match the handprint on Ada's thigh.

Horrified, I stared, mouth open. The handprint hadn't been there when she died, but I remembered it from last spring. Gloria came to church one morning with a red mark on her cheek. When Camille asked about it, she said it was nothing. Elvira didn't speak to her all day; I thought they'd quarreled, but why would Gloria's ghost show up now with the same mark?

Unless it came from the same place.

Someone knocked on the bathroom door. I jumped, and Gloria vanished. "Are you all right?" Bernice asked.

I swallowed hard, turning off the water and drying my hands. I pushed the door open before Ada had a chance to come back.

"I'm fine. Come on, let's move…whoever that is."

"Sarah Brown. She's small, at least. Miss Newton and I moved Marci, the maid, first, and she was nothing but muscle. I thought for sure we'd drop her and she'd slide down the stairs head first."

She showed me how to twist the corners of the sheet around my hands to make it easier to carry, but it was still impossible to get her down the stairs without bumping every step. By the time we got the first floor, we walked with her backside dragging on the ground between us. Neither of us was what you might consider tall, and I'd never been particularly strong. The past few days of hauling baskets of dishes up and down the stairs was more physical labor than I'd had in my entire life.

"In there. The French room." Bernice jerked her head toward the first classroom, where the door stood ajar. The desks had been pushed back to make room. Four bodies lay wrapped in sheets; Sarah made five.

Once we'd laid her down, I looked again, to make sure I'd counted right. "I thought there were only four…"

"Hannah Marks. She died right after breakfast. She was one of the twelfth graders."

The door of the office opened and closed. Bernice and I peered hesitantly into the entry hall.

Miss Newton leaned against the wall, her cheeks damp with sweat. She covered her eyes with a forearm, her hands as bloodied as mine had been. Her shoulders shook and she slid slowly down to the floor, a single harsh sob ricocheting off the tile floor.

Bernice and I exchanged a look. So that was it, then. Headmistress Davenport was dead.

Mrs. Hodge shuffled slowly out of the office, wiping her hands on her apron. Already our oldest teacher, she looked positively ancient, hunched over as she was.

When she spotted us, she shook her head. "I'm sorry, girls." She said it like there was something that could have been done. Like she'd failed us somehow.

She reached down and patted Miss Newton on the shoulder. "Come on. It will take all four of us to move her. We'd better do it now."

Slowly, we followed her back into the bedroom. There was so much blood on the bedspread and on her nightgown, it looked like a scene from a penny dreadful. Bernice gasped, covering her mouth.

"Come on, girls. Be brave. We all need our strength right now," Mrs. Hodge said gently, patting her shoulder.

The headmistress was far stouter than any of the students or the cleaning staff. We had to peel the ruined coverlet back, laying it on the floor, then Mrs. Hodge and I rolled the body to the edge of the bed. Miss Newton and Bernice tried to catch it, to lower her gently onto the commandeered shroud, but she was too heavy and moved too fast once she reached the edge of the mattress. Her head bounced off the nightstand, and she landed face down with a thud that rattled the matching lamps on either side of the bed.

The four of us let out a collective wince. Miss Newton quickly rolled the headmistress onto her back, patting down her bloodied, tangled hair. Her eyes stared blankly at the ceiling, one eye wide open, the other half closed. Miss Newton closed them, leaving bloody streaks like war paint over her eyelids.

"Let's just hurry and get this done, before any of the other girls see."

We gathered around, each taking a corner. There were so many frills and ruffles, it was hard to get a good grip. My hands were already sticky and stained with blood again.

Waddling like penguins, we half carried, and half dragged her through the office and front hall to the French room, lining her up with the others and folding the edges of the blanket around her, a giant red stain amid the comparatively tidy line of white figures.

I stared at them, just a moment longer than was necessary as the others filed solemnly out of the room.

The hair on the back of my neck prickled, and I knew that soon—very soon—Ada's wouldn't be the only restless spirit haunting Mount Sinai.

***

After the bodies had been secured, Miss Newton seemed to take pity on the pair of us. "Take a few minutes rest to gather yourselves. Get something to eat."

I remembered that I hadn't had breakfast. Despite the scene in the headmistress's room, my stomach grumbled. Blood was never something to turn my stomach. Grandmother said it was a good quality in women. "We spend enough time around it, no sense in losing your head. Blood is one thing we all have in abundance."

My boots clumped heavily down the stairs to the basement. Someone had thrown together our scraps of food, peeling the potatoes and frying them into a hash and putting the skins in with the rest of the vegetables for broth.

We had to wash some of the mountain of dishes before we could eat. Bernice and I did the task in silence. She stared at the floor as she dried, the last slow tears dripping down her cheeks.

I had cried for Ada—repeatedly, but couldn't bring myself to do the same for the headmistress. Maybe because she'd been so cold most of the time. There were a few bursts of kindness, a glimpse at the woman beneath the title, but I couldn't seem to summon enough emotion to cry.

"It doesn't seem to bother you at all," Bernice said, squeezing one last bowl into the drying rack. There were still more dishes—mounds and mounds of them—but we could do them later.

"What?"

"Davenport."

I shrugged. "She was bleeding last night when we came in. Who else could Nurse have been with, to get all that blood on her apron? Honestly…I was more surprised this morning when I went in, and she talked to me."

"What do you mean?"

"She wasn't delirious. She was quoting poetry. She talked to me about embroidery. She does lovely work. Or she did."

Bernice nodded, still staring at the damp towel in her hands.

"How do you do it?"

"Do what?"

"Stay so calm all the time. It's like none of this even bothers you at all. I wish I could do that. I think I'm ready to fall apart."

I didn't answer at first. "I don't know. Sometimes, I think…I think everyone is right, and there's something wrong with my head. I don't see things the way other people do. I don't know why. Maybe it's because of my mother. Or maybe it's just me. But most of the time, I feel like I'm coming apart at the seams. There's nothing for it, though, but to stitch yourself back together."

She glanced up finally, looking at me through long, thick eyelashes. For all Elvira made fun of her for being built like a boy, with thick limbs, big hands, and a square jaw, Bernice had the thickest eyelashes I'd ever seen on a girl. I wondered if it was because she was so boyish—everyone knows boys always get better eyelashes. At least, that was what Ada always said.

"That's it? You just…stitch yourself together?"

"Getting upset…throwing fits…it doesn't help." I colored, remember I'd had two such fits in the past week, despite myself. I reached up for my locket, rubbing my thumb against the back. "Things that upset other people, making them angry or sad…it's not that I don't feel it. I do. Sometimes not as intensely, but the only way to fix it is to work through it."

"You can't fix death." Bernice's voice was sharp, but her face softened slightly. "Sorry."

I shook my head. "I know. But it's all I can do. All I know how to do. I have to fix it." With both Ada and the flu, that meant we needed to keep more people from dying.

We sat down with our potatoes, eating in silence. On the list of problems that needed solving, our food supply was high on the list. At least most of the flu patients were eating only broth. We probably had enough scraps to make it for a few more days. But there was no meat, and we wouldn't even have vegetables for the healthy students and staff to eat once dinner was over. With nothing to feed the nurses, none of us would last very long.

While we ate, Mary Anne and one of the tenth graders came down with big baskets laden with dirty sheets, towels and uniforms. The laundry was down the same hallway as the bathroom, a dark and dingy place prone to housing spiders in neglected corners. The hall light flickered as they passed through the kitchen to the hall. I shuddered, my hackles rising at the memory of Ada's most recent appearance, and the image of Gloria in the mirror.

I took my dirty bowl to the sink. Bernice, apparently once again in possession of a stiff upper lip, set to work washing the remainder of the dishes. I went back to the pantry to check our stock.

The baskets of vegetables were half empty now. I searched high and low in the kitchen, but couldn't find anything else edible. Someone had turned the apples and oats into a porridge, and the remains of it clung to a pot Bernice had to leave soaking in the bottom of the sink while she scrubbed the bowls and flatware clean.

"Do you know if there are any grocers or farms outside the city?" I asked, picking up a towel to dry the growing stack on the counter.

"I don't think so. But I'm from Richmond Dale."

I blinked at her. "Where's that?"

"It's a crossroads south of here. We have a post office and not much else. My father owns a sawmill."

"Oh." I studied our plain white china, scrubbing at the drops of water my dish towel refused to absorb.

"What about the farms around here? There's plenty of them. Maybe we could talk to one of them."

"We're in the middle of a quarantine, and even if they had telephones, I wouldn't know how to find the numbers. Anyway, it's October. Harvest is done. How much do you think there is to spare?" I could just see it now, if I tried going in person to one of the nearby farms, explaining why we needed bushels of food. I'd get run off with a hunting rifle for bringing the flu to their front door, if they didn't just shoot on sight because I was a stranger.

"I'll try the Red Cross again. Maybe I'll be able to get through this time. Maybe Pastor Brown can help."

Honestly, I wasn't sure the pastor was any more likely to talk to me than the farms. I wasn't exactly popular, and there had been my outburst on Sunday. Had it really been less than a week?

Once the dishes were clean, we began the arduous task of carrying meals to everyone.

When I came to Mount Sinai, there were roughly a hundred students, and another twenty-five or so teachers and staff. But as we moved through the halls, slowly climbing higher and higher in the building, the dwindling number of students on each floor made the school feel abandoned. Haunted, even. Haunted by the living as they slowly faded.

The ninth graders still had about ten students left, but four of them were ill. The tenth graders only had three healthy students of the five left at the school. And the twelfth wasn't much better.

The eleventh grade was the worst, however. Bernice, Mary Anne, and myself were the only students still standing. Ada was dead, and Sarah and Gloria. Camille and Elvira weren't doing well at all, if rumor was to be believed.

Instead of waiting in the hall, I took a bowl and spoon into one room while Bernice did another. There wasn't time to be dawdling. After the horror of seeing the headmistress's death, giving broth to a sick girl hardly seemed a challenge. The inevitability of the disease hung over me like a cloak. It would only be a matter of time before I contracted it. Bernice allowed her mask to hang around her chin as we climbed one staircase after another. On the landing, we had to move to the side so Mary Anne, Miss Newton, and two little ninth graders could carry down another shrouded body.

"Who is it?" Bernice asked, her voice barely above a whisper.

"Camille," Mary Anne replied. She paused long enough to wipe the sweat from her forehead, then they continued their slow shuffle down the stairs.

"It's like it's after our year," Bernice said as we watched them walk away. "Like it wants to wipe out the eleventh grade, specifically."

As we watched Camille's body sway like a hammock in a storm, it was hard not to agree with her.

***

With everyone concentrating their efforts on the sick, no one was on the first floor when I snuck down after lunch to use the telephone again.

I paused outside the office door. The iron tang of blood lingered, even through the closed door. Or maybe it came from the French room, just a few yards away. I swallowed, fighting back the image of Headmistress Davenport's body, prostrate on the bed, soaking in blood.

The office was just as I'd left it, save for a streak of blood the blanket had left behind when we moved her body. I stepped over it carefully, closing the door to the bedroom.

I searched the telephone register again, for any familiar names that might be helpful. Most of the names—J. Andrews, Oak Street; Mr. & Mrs. Lowry, Prescott Avenue—were completely unfamiliar to me.

I started with the Red Cross number, but the line was busy, so I asked the operator to try the church. The phone number for that, at least was listed on the first page of the book, followed by Pastor Brown's number. The headmistress—*former* headmistress—liked to keep school-related numbers together, at least.

If anyone could intercede for us with the Red Cross, or act as in intermediary with the local farmers, anyone who might help us, it would be the pastor, so I asked for his number first.

"I'm sorry, Miss, there's no answer."

I closed my eyes. Wouldn't anyone answer their phone?

"Alright. I have one more number to try," I said, giving her the number for the Academy.

Once again, it rang endlessly, until the operator disconnected. I thanked her and put the earpiece back on the hook.

The book couldn't tell me anything else. I didn't know who most of those people were. Part of me wondered if one of the teachers, or a prefect, should be doing this job instead, but everyone else was occupied, and I'd volunteered for the task. It wasn't their fault it was harder than I'd anticipated.

I checked the rest of the desk, not really expecting to find anything, but hoping for something, some name—perhaps a handy, numbered list of things to do when everything fell apart and there was no one left to help.

Instead, I found stamps, a letter opener, a neat row of pens and pencils in the center drawer, and a little pearl-handled knife for sharpening them. The bottom drawer held files with labels like *grocery receipts* and *bills, unpaid*. All of the receipts were for Martin's General Store, which I already knew was a waste of time. I wondered if the doctor ever came for Mr. Martin and his sons, or if they were still waiting.

The top right drawer was full of stationery and notebooks. The one on top, a slim black leather volume I'd seen the headmistress carry many times, was pocket sized with a tiny pen clipped to it.

Inside it was full of lists, most of them with items crossed off. The last entry was dated Wednesday, and included a note to call about the grocery order, another to update the grade book, and one to call someone named Marcus. The last item was the only one not crossed off.

There were ledgers and a checkbook in the top left-hand drawer. I checked the first one, which was accounts for the school. The second one listed all the current students and our exam grades for the last half. There were a disturbing number of names marked off with a black line and the word *withdrawn*.

I put the books back and closed the drawer. The surface of the desk was no more interesting than it had been when the headmistress called my grandmother. The same clean blotter. Same pen stand. Same telephone. A small rack on one corner of the desk held letters. The section closest to the door had several envelopes crammed into it, while the rest only had one each. I pulled them out.

The first envelope was thin, addressed to the electric company, followed by one for the telephone company, and another to Martin's.

The last two, however, made me pause.

One was on thick, creamy stationary with a slight pinkish tint. Davenport's elegant calligraphy stood out sharply on the page. *Mr.*

*and Mrs. Reginald Brooks.* Ada's parents.

The headmistress would have called them, of course. But it was only courteous for her write, as well. After all, Ada had been in her charge when she died.

The second, on plain school stationary, was addressed to Detective Buchanan.

Without pausing to think, I pulled out the paper knife and slit the envelope open.

Inside was a sheet bearing the school crest, dated Tuesday, the same day the article in the paper about Ada's death was printed.

*Dear Detective Buchanan,*

*I have seen this morning the article in the Register, which lists the death of my student, Ada Brooks, as "death by misadventure." After our conversation on Saturday, I cannot help but wonder how you came to this conclusion, when a girl of sixteen was so obviously beaten, violated, and drowned. A girl hardly comes upon such injuries by "accident" or "mistake."*

*Ada Brooks may not have been a shining example of Christian values, but she was a young girl in my charge, and as her parents are not in a position to speak for her at the moment, I will.*

*If you can excuse the actions of whomever did this to her, you have no business carrying a badge.*

*Perhaps she should have chosen better company, but that company should have chosen a better pastime than rape and murder.*

*I insist the case be reopened, and a full examination of the facts made. I have spoken with Mr. and Mrs. Brooks, and their lawyer will be contacting you shortly, if he has not done so already.*

*For the sake of all of my girls, I want this case resolved, fully and completely.*

She signed it forcefully. Though the hand was neat, I could see places where the pen dug into the page, leaving behind a deep indentation.

The letter to Ada's parents was on her personal stationary, which was the palest shade of pink with flowers and swirls printed on the corners of the page. It was a heavy stock, and as soon as I tore open the envelope, I could smell her perfume.

No. Not her perfume. Ada's.

I bolted up from the chair and looked around, but there was no sign of Ada, or any other ghosts for that matter.

Slowly, I sat back down, turning my attention to the letters. Within a few sentences, I was dabbing at my eyes as the headmistress apologized for failing the Brooks's and their daughter.

*She was left in my care, and I failed her. I will do my utmost to ensure justice is done,* she wrote. Judging by her forceful words to the detective, she'd tried to do just that—but then the mail stopped, the outbreak happened, and neither letter got sent.

I folded them up and stuffed them back in their envelopes, turning back to the address book. I combed through every page, but couldn't find anyone named Marcus. Who was he, and why was he important enough to merit a telephone call? Was he a parent? A relative of hers, maybe?

Footsteps in the hall. I froze, unsure if I was really supposed to be in the headmistress's office. I might be able to excuse my presence with the telephone calls to the grocers and the Red Cross, but I didn't think even Mrs. Hodge would understand why I was riffling through the headmistress's desk and reading her mail.

The footsteps made a sharp turn, toward the dining room instead of the classrooms and office. I breathed a sigh of relief, stuffing the letters into my pocket. Then, on second thought, I pulled out two envelopes—one of the school stationary, and one in the pale pink—two stamps, and the little notebook, cramming them all into my pocket.

I tidied the desk, so it hardly even looked like I'd been there. I left the address book out, however. We'd need it later.

I was about to go leave when the smell of roses hit me again, this time so powerful it nearly knocked me over. I came to an abrupt stop, looking around.

Ada was nowhere to be seen, but I did spy something I hadn't noticed before. Under one of the little round tables in a corner was a box—the box filled with Ada's things.

I crept closer. Her uniforms were folded neatly on top. Underneath was the train case full of contraband. I wondered if anyone had opened it.

With a glance over my shoulder to make sure no one was coming, I lifted it out.

Her cosmetics were just as she'd left them. The pale pink lipstick she'd picked up at our last In Town day was still inside the little cardboard box, next to two more tubes, a little pot of rouge, and a few pieces of jewelry. One necklace still had a price tag looped through the chain, but I couldn't remember when she bought it.

Under the tray were the little bottles of perfume from her mother's dressing table. I wondered how rich someone would have to be to not notice six bottles of perfume missing. How many did her mother have?

Wrapped up in a scarf, I found what I was looking for: a handful of batteries.

# Chapter Eighteen

*August 23, 2018*

*Lucas,*

*Yes, I got your note. It wasn't funny. Leave me alone. I thought we could have some fun at the beginning of summer, but we have very different ideas of fun.*

*Don't talk to me. Don't write to me.*

*I'm burning your letters.*

*Leave me alone.*

*Ada*

Mary Anne and Bernice caught me as I was leaving my room with my coat.

"Where are you going?" the prefect asked, brows knitting.

"I'm going to see if the Academy will give us some food. I tried calling the Red Cross, but can't get through to them. My grandmother said she'll do what she can, but with the quarantine, that may not be much. She's all alone, now." The worried knot in my stomach twisted painfully.

Mary Anne nodded. "We should check the garden. Maybe there are still some vegetables left that haven't been harvested."

"See if you can get some meat from the boys. The JROTC has been hunting in the woods to practice shooting."

I nodded, buttoning my coat. I'd replaced the battery in Ada's flashlight and tucked it in my pocket, even though it was still afternoon. I felt better with its weight against my thigh.

I looked around the deserted hall, then leaned in slightly. "I want to talk to Charlie Johnson while I'm there. To see if I can get him to go to the police. He must be the one covering it up. The police think Ada just met one boy, but if they found out they were attacked—*ambushed*—"

Mary Anne's face turned pale as milk. "Julia, you can't. If the police think Charlie had something to do with it—"

"He did have something to do with it," Bernice said, hands fisted in her skirt. "At the very least, he's covering up for his friends. They should be in jail."

For a moment, I thought Mary Anne would make the same argument as the detective, that his—and his friends'—futures would all be ruined if they paid for their crimes. That somehow, they were more valuable to society as free men, despite the horrible nature of what they'd done.

My throat constricted, and for a moment I could feel Lucas's hands around my neck, the way he'd squeezed the life out of Ada.

Mary Anne grabbed my wrist. "Julia, if they find out you know what they did, they might hurt you, too."

I blinked, not quite understanding her point. "I'm still going." Jerking my arm free, I started down the stairs.

Bernice ran after me. "Jules, wait. You can't go down there alone."

"I'll be fine. If I'm not back in two hours, call the police." *If you can get through.*

I left through the kitchen door, stuffing the flu pamphlet in the door. The cover was tearing, and the pages were starting to come out.

Armed with the big basket we used for taking meals to the girls upstairs, I strode across the lawn and into the woods.

Even though it was only three o'clock, heavy clouds made it feel gloomier, and I was grateful for the flashlight, even if it wasn't dark enough to use it yet, since I did have a small detour in mind.

I followed Rainbow Lane to the cemetery. It was a rougher walk, but more direct than taking the gravel road to the church. The mausoleum door was closed, but the broken lock was hardly a challenge.

I shone the flashlight around the little room, but it didn't appear much different than it had in Ada's memory. There was a box of matches on a little ledge by the door, right next to a dusty oil lamp. More kerosene lamps were mounted on the walls. Mood lighting, I supposed. Not enough to clearly see anything.

Descending the stairs, I peeked into the dusty corners, shuddering at the cobwebs and dust. A part of me wanted to give everything a thorough washing down, but the greater part of me didn't think I could stomach having that much dirt on my hands. Our science teacher had gotten rather annoyed with me during the spring term for being slow and contrary, as she put it, when we were supposed to be working in the school garden. The truth of it was I couldn't stand the grit of the dirt on my skin or under my fingernails. It made me want to peel my skin off like gloves. She'd called me fussy and fastidious, and made me stay late to finish planting the pea plants we were supposed to be studying. When I finally came indoors to bathe, Elvira, Camille, and Gloria put worms in my bathwater while I was at the sink, scrubbing my hands and brushing out my hair. Miss Newton made me do lines for all the screaming.

The memory made me want to vomit. The smell of dust and mold was suddenly so overpowering, I couldn't breathe. I hurried out of the mausoleum, closing the door behind me and wiping my hands on my coat.

If there was any evidence of Lucas and Todd in the

mausoleum the night Ada was killed, it was gone now. I was
certain I wouldn't find it.

I glanced toward the pastor's house, a little stone building near
the church. The house was turned in just such a way that none of
the windows had a direct line of sight on the graveyard. I supposed
the person who built it thought the sight was too gloomy to wake
up to every morning.

No one appeared to be home. The windows were dark and
blank, though Pastor Brown's car was still parked in front of the
church. Maybe he'd taken his bicycle to see some of the more local
families?

I trekked onward, moving past the neat lines of gravestones. In
the back corner of the graveyard, four new plots, marked only by
freshly turned earth, were laid out, and there were seven more open
graves lined up, shovels abandoned by the holes. I wondered where
the gravediggers were. Surely their day couldn't be done already.
Not with so much demand.

Walking a little faster, I pushed through the back gate and
found the path the boys took to church every Sunday. It was
marked by gravel from the church to the cemetery, but that petered
away to nothing but dirt and grass as it vanished into the woods.
Panting, I followed the steep incline up to the academy.

It was a little disorienting, walking up to a mirror image of the girls' school, but with just a few differences. There was an extra wing to accommodate the extra students. The kitchen garden was on the opposite side of the lawn, to make room for their sports field and the shed with the equipment.

The academy, at least, seemed more lively. Figures passed back and forth behind the windows. Judging by the windows on the first floor, classes were still in session.

Their kitchen door was a little to the left of where ours was. I walked up to it, raising my hand to knock—

Then panicked and backed away. What would I say? They would think I was some kind of idiot.

No. It was an emergency. I just needed to knock, and ask to speak to the cook, and explain what happened.

It took two more tries for me to get up the nerve. By then, I realized some of the boys were staring at me through their classroom window as I walked back and forth, talking myself up to the task.

Blushing, I knocked twice. After several moments when no one answered, I raised my hand to try again, but then the door opened. The woman on the other side was thin, angular and bony, and had a sour look on her face, visible even with the mask.

"What are you doing here?" she demanded, coming up short.

"I—I came from the school. The girls' school. I—that is, our groceries weren't delivered this week. I was hoping, maybe, if you had something to spare—"

"You came here looking for a handout?" She scoffed, pushing past me.

Their bell was just like ours, but they didn't have a fountain on the patio. Instead there were benches and tables; it looked like the boys sometimes studied outside.

The maid rang the bell, and instantly the sound of scuffling and the scrape of chairs being pushed back could be heard from every room on the ground floor as the boys left their last classes of the day.

"Please. We've only got enough for one or two meals left, and the girls are sick, and the headmistress—"

"Get out! You come here with that flu? Can't you see we've got our own problems here? The boys probably got it from you lot, knowing how they like to sneak out. They think they're so sly, but we all know what goes on down there." She gestured vaguely toward the mausoleum, pushing past me again, back to the kitchen.

"Please! I've already tried everywhere else! We need help!" dropping the basket, I grabbed her arm. If I could just get her to *listen*—

She shook me off with such force I landed on my backside on the flagstones. She slammed the door shut before I could get to my feet.

I reached for the basket, swallowing a panicked lump that welled suddenly in my throat. From nearly every window on the first floor, faces stared out at me. I saw Charlie at the third window on the right. We stared at each other for several moments.

Rubbing the hem of my coat sleeve over my face, I gathered up the basket and bushed off my skirt. My right stocking was torn where it caught on the stones. I tried to hide it under the hem of my skirt and coat as I hurried around to the front of the building. If I couldn't talk to the cook, I'd talk to the headmaster.

While the front of the girls' school still looked like a rather large house, the front of the academy was imposing, with brick and stone and concrete all piled on top of each other, and a big sign over the front door. There was a covered porch with a swing, and a wicker table and chairs. Instead of our ornamental flower beds, they had a line of evergreen bushes under the windows and running down the drive. Two motor cars were parked out front, probably belonging to the teachers who didn't live at the school.

Their front door was a heavy dark wood, with a big iron knocker. Ours was just a plain little front door, painted green.

I reached for the knocker, slamming it home firmly three or four times, my anger at being rebuffed overshadowing my hesitation. Still, it was several moments before anyone answered. I could still hear dozens of footsteps and voices inside as the boys went back to their rooms, or to clubs, or to whatever it was the boys did when they were done with their classes.

The door swung open, and I caught my breath. Lucas Cash leaned an elbow against the door frame, looming over me. His eyes crinkled maliciously above his flu mask. "Well, look at the little mouse. Did Dragon Breath send you down here? Or don't you know you're not allowed to play with the boys?" he leered. He reached out, pinching my upper arm. "Or maybe you *want* to play with the boys, and that's why you came."

"Cash!"

The voice made us both jump. The scarred face of Coach Howard appeared over Lucas's shoulder. "What do you want?" he asked, addressing me.

"I—I need to speak to the headmaster. It's urgent."

He glowered, but gestured for me to follow. Lucas moved to let me pass, but when the coach wasn't looking, he gave one of my braids a hard yank and I yelped.

"What was that?" Coach Howard demanded.

"I—it was nothing," I said.

"Hurry up."

I trotted after him. Their entryway was much grander than ours, with carved woodwork and a big chandelier. Where our staircases were narrow, and hidden at the ends of each hallway, the academy had a grand staircase with carved finials and a burgundy runner.

The headmaster's office was larger, too. A Persian carpet covered the floor, and the shelves were filled with books and trophies and all sorts of things.

Headmaster Cash looked up from his desk. "Who's this?"

"She was out front, sir. Asked to speak with you."

"I'm Julia Grace. I go to the girls' school." I licked my lips, tasting onion and cotton gauze. "We need your help, sir." I quickly outlined the problem at the school. "Please. We only have enough left to get us through the morning. Only three of the teachers are well, and none of the staff. Our nurse is sick, and the headmistress died this morning."

That, at least, got his attention. "Go down to the kitchen. Take what you need. I'll send some boys by this afternoon with more."

I bobbed a little curtsy and thanked him.

My eye landed on one of the certificates hanging behind his desk. The name at the top was *Marcus Cash.*

I paused at the door and pulled the headmistress's notebook from my pocket. *Call Marcus*, the last item undone on her list.

"Did the headmistress call you?" I asked.

"You just said she…she passed," he replied, blinking at me in confusion.

"I know. She is. She did. I found a list on her desk. I think she intended to call you yesterday, but didn't have the time."

He shook his head. "I don't know why. Though we've been trying to keep an eye on things, with the outbreak. I told her we would help if we could."

I looked at him. He was a stern man, but not mean, the way the coach was.

The way his nephew was.

"Did she…did she ask about your nephew?"

At that he pushed back his chair. "What about Lucas?"

"I—It's nothing. Just…I heard he might have been…he might have been with a friend of mine. Ada Brooks."

"That is absolutely ridiculous. You know there is no fraternizing outside of church and official functions. Besides. From what I hear, that girl ran with the wrong crowd. You should learn to choose your friends better."

I squeezed the notebook in my fist. The binding creaked in protest, but I managed not to let the lid on my boiling pot of anger blow completely off.

I ran down to the kitchen before I could say something that would get me thrown out. As I rounded the corner to the stairs, I crashed into someone and nearly dropped my basket.

"Are you all right?" the boy asked, catching my arm to stop me from falling.

All the air went out of me, and something cold took up residence in my stomach.

It was Charlie Johnson.

"Charlie."

"Do you know you?"

"Julia. Julia Grace. Ada's roommate."

At that, his face turned pale. He backed up a step. "Oh. I heard what happened to her."

"You saw what happened to her."

His head snapped around, pallor vanishing in an instant.

"Who told you that?"

"Ada."

"So you're the reason the police came to me." His jaw tightened, but then relaxed. He ran a hand through his heavily pomaded hair, mussing it. "Listen, it's not what you think."

My grip on the basket was so tight the twisted texture bit into my palms and it creaked under the pressure. "You don't know what I think."

"I didn't—I didn't hurt her!" he hissed, dropping his voice at the last moment. He grabbed my elbow and pulled me into an empty classroom, closing the door.

I shook myself free. I was getting really sick of people

grabbing on to me. "I know you didn't kill her. But you know who did, and you're protecting him."

Aghast, he stared at me. "You can't—that's not—"

I reached into my coat pocket and pulled out a button. "It was Lucas. He and Todd were there. Ada isn't the first girl they've hurt, but she is the first one they've killed."

His back went rigid. "You don't know that. Lucas said she tripped."

"He held her under. I saw the bruises on her neck."

He yanked the classroom door open. "Lucas wouldn't hurt anyone. You should leave now."

I stared at the muscle flexing in his jaw, the way his brows were drawn down and his spine had straightened.

"I thought you could help me get justice for Ada. You cared about her."

He turned away. "She was a loose girl who got herself into trouble."

I put the button away. "Right. That's what everyone says. But you helped her get into trouble. You're the one who brought Todd and Lucas there."

Charlie closed the door again, leaning in so his face was inches from mine. "You want me to go to the cops? Are you crazy? Todd's in the infirmary right now. They're saying he probably

318

won't make it. Do you know who Lucas's dad is?" He laughed, a dry sound with no humor. "He's gotten him out of worse trouble than this."

My teeth clenched painfully. He jerked the door opened again, and this time, I stepped through it without looking back.

So that was the way it was. Charlie would stand by his friends, even though they were murderers.

My feet carried me without my knowledge. Thankfully, the academy had the same basic floor plan as the school, so it wasn't hard to find the stairs to the basement and kitchen. The angry maid was at the stove. I took a deep breath, hoping she wouldn't see me as I side stepped the main worktable and went directly to the cook with my instructions from the headmaster. She was reluctant, but led me through to the pantry.

"I'll set aside some of the tinned food for the boys to take over," she said, huffing and puffing as she started to push jars and cans of vegetables, beans, and meat to one side. Easily as wide as she was tall, she filled the doorway. I backed out of her way.

"We have a few vegetables left to make broth, but not much. And we'll need something more substantial for the healthy girls."

She nodded. Bags of flour, sugar, and oats were left in one corner. "Is your cook still up? Any of the kitchen staff?"

I shook my head. "The kitchen staff were the first to get sick."

Come to think of it, it was rather odd. The flu had to come in with the police, but the teachers had been the first people they spoke to. I wasn't certain they'd spoken to Cook or any of the maids at all. But if Ada had cursed the school…she'd been leaving through the kitchen door. Had one of the staff seen something, and failed to report it?

"Utter shame. Now. You take this—" She dropped a giant bag of oats into my basket. I staggered under the sudden weight. It was at least twenty pounds. "This is your breakfast, it'll last you a while. And these. Make sure you get some fruit every day, it helps ward off illness." She picked up a basket of apples and poured half of it into mine.

"Make the food for the healthy ones first. Save the scraps to make broth. Vegetable peelings, beef bones, boil it all up. You can strain it, and it'll be easier for the sick ones to drink. Add mustard and onion, and it'll help keep the flu at bay." She added a bundle of carrots, a bag of dried beans, and three onions. My arms threatened to pop right out of their sockets. "I'll fill some crates and send the boys over with more, but that'll get your dinner started. I suppose it's a good thing we're both infected now; it means we can help each other."

"Thank you, ma'am," I said. If I tried to curtsy, I knew my knees would buckle, but I bobbed my head to her just the same.

Her eyes softened. "Poor thing. Go home, then. We'll be thinking of you."

I thanked her again, shuffling back out to the kitchen. I looked up at the ceiling. In this very building were the last three people to see Ada alive. Her killer was so close, but I didn't see how I could get a moment to speak to any of them.

My toe caught on an uneven floorboard and I tumbled forward, dropping the basket and scattering apples and onions all over. The maid at the stove danced out of the way, shouting about clumsy girls who had no business in the kitchen.

"Oh, dear. Let me help you," the cook puffed some more as she gathered up the fallen produce, ordering the other kitchen girls to help.

"I'm sorry. So sorry," I said, scrambling to gather up the carrots. The bag of oats had split, and they were slowly leaking out like sand through an hourglass. Inspiration struck. "It's just so heavy. If I could get some help carrying it…"

"Well, none of us have time," snapped the angry maid, dropping half a dozen bruised apples back into the basket from her apron without much care for their condition. If they got jostled around anymore, they wouldn't be apples so much as applesauce by the time I got them back to the school.

"I know. And I wouldn't ask. But I know classes are over…I

321

thought maybe one of the students might help?"

The cook raised an eyebrow at me. "If you're up to something, missy…there won't be any hanky-panky here."

I stared at her, then looked down at the basket, which probably weighed at least half of what I did. I pointed to the bags of oats and beans. "It's nearly a mile back to the school. I just want someone to help me carry this."

"Mabel, go find one of the boys," she snapped, nodding at one of the kitchen maids. She hurried out of the kitchen, leaving us to do the cleanup.

She helped me hoist the basket onto the counter.

"Honestly. I don't know why I have to be the errand boy. If my uncle wasn't right there…"

Lucas stopped just inside the kitchen door, tugging his mask down around his chin, like he couldn't stand the feel of it on his face. That, at least, I could relate to. I scratched my chin, just under the edge of the gauze.

My jaw ached. I made a conscious effort to unclench it, but I couldn't help the way my brows knit and my eyes narrowed.

"What's the matter with you, mouse?" he scoffed, stuffing his hand in his pockets.

"Mr. Cash, if you could please help the young lady. She's come to get some food for her classmates."

322

"So we're feeding the poor now, are we?"

"Mr. Cash, if your uncle heard you—"

"Yeah, yeah. I know. He'd be disappointed in me. What else is new?" He swaggered toward me, looming like had at the front door. "All right, mouse. Let's take the scraps back to your nest, shall we?"

***

I followed Lucas outside. The basket beat against his thigh with every step. I trailed behind him, the pot full of rage I'd been nursing for days bubbling over. I could feel the lid vibrating. Any moment it would fly off and the contents would catch fire.

Should I come out and say it? Tell him that I knew what happened the night Ada died? That he was there?

No. As I watched his shoulders shift to accommodate the basket as we followed the path downhill, I knew he would kill me. I was smaller, slower, and weaker than Ada. It would take less than five minutes for him to strangle me with his bare hands. I could see it now. He could just turn, hitting me with the basket. A well-placed blow might even knock me senseless. I wouldn't be able to fight. Or he could drop it and do the task himself. He'd enjoyed beating Ada. He liked hearing her scream, knowing he had power over her.

That was what he wanted most: control. To control the people around him, or at least the girls. The people he thought were below his notice.

And they didn't get much lower than me.

"Where are you going?" I asked when he veered away from the path.

He rolled his eyes. "It's a shortcut. You can't really think I'm going to walk all the way down to the church, and then back to your school. It's out of the way. But it's a straight line if we go this way."

"Well, I know that. But it's easier to walk on the path."

"What are you complaining for? You're not the one carrying this." He hefted the basket, then turned and kept walking, muttering something I couldn't hear under his breath.

I moved the bag of beans to my other hip. My arms and back ached, and so did my knees. I tried to breathe slowly through my mask, but it felt like I wasn't getting enough air. I tugged it down around my chin, gasping.

"Come on. What's taking you so long?" Lucas turned back and saw me struggling. I put a hand out, leaning against a tree while I caught my breath.

"Don't tell me you're sick, too? Dammit!" he swore so

colorfully, I covered my ears. Dropping the basket, he tugged his own mask over his face. "You stay away from me. You're a danger."

A light breeze ruffled the few leaves still clinging to the branches. They rattled like bones, or the laboring chest of someone with pneumonia. "Not as dangerous as you."

That made him stop. He looked at me suspiciously, as though seeing me for the first time. I let the bag of beans fall to the ground and dragged my aching legs toward him.

"You thought it was fun. Do Todd and Charlie think it was an accident? That Ada just slipped and hit her head on the fountain? Or do they know you wrapped your hands around her throat and held her under the water?"

Lucas's face turned white, then red in quick succession. "What are you talking about? You're delusional."

"Maybe." The ground was starting to spin a little. I really wanted to lay down on the fallen leaves and close my eyes.

But not as much as I wanted to wrap my hands around *his* neck and hold *him* under water.

"Ada showed me what you did. How you came on her and Charlie in the mausoleum." I reached into my pocket where I found the button. "Did you know one of your epaulets is torn?"

He stared at me, blue eyes burning. "That's it? A button? You found a button? That doesn't prove anything."

I smiled a little. "That's right. I'm just the little mouse. I'm not surprised you forgot. You see, I collect buttons. They're always handy to have around, because you never know when you're going to lose one. And last fall, you lost a button playing football. I remember, because you were bragging in church about how you convinced your mother to replace the buttons on your coat with the buttons from your grandfather's army uniform. He was a sharpshooter, wasn't he? I can tell, because they had black rubber buttons just like this one. They wouldn't reflect, you see, and give away their position. Look, it's got the eagle crest right here, and the date on the back. Very distinctive. I'd love to have one like it in my collection."

The ground was definitely rolling now. Lucas's face had turned an odd shade of puce that I was pretty sure wasn't healthy.

"Ada turned you down. Twice, in fact. But Ada was fast. Ada would go with anyone. Except you. And that made you angry. Maybe not angry enough to kill. But angry enough to do harm. How dare she go with everyone but you?"

I was practically spitting now as I walked slowly closer. The miasma of flu that clung to me ever since that first day in the infirmary seemed to waft around me like a green cloud of chlorine gas. I willed him to inhale it. Willed him to take it in. To take in the poison we were suffering under because of him.

"But Ada didn't go with every boy who looked her way. She had more taste than that. She didn't trust you. Your letters scared her, so she destroyed them. I only saw the first few, when you thought you could charm her. But she never wrote back. She never returned your feelings, because while she may have been fast, and she may have liked boys more than she should, she also knew who to avoid. She knew you were trouble. She might have been fast, but she could tell you were evil."

Lucas's face twisted. At first, I couldn't tell if it was my vision going as off-kilter as my balance, or if it was really him. Finally, he pulled down the mask, showing that warped grin. The same look he'd given Ada as he leaned over her in the graveyard.

"You really are delusional. You're hallucinating, little mouse. Why don't you go back to your hole?"

I held up the button again. "You left this behind. I'm sure there's more evidence."

"The police sure didn't seem to think so. Especially not when Charlie told them it was an accident. They'd had their fun, sure. Then she went back. Must have slipped. Those stones get slippery when it frosts, you know."

"I don't like Charlie very much. But I think at heart he's probably a good person. He tried to fight you off. Tried to protect

Ada. And he thinks you're his friend, so he's trying to protect you, too. But unlike Ada, Charlie doesn't have very good taste in people."

He let out a bark of a laugh, closing the distance between us. "Right. The little whore, and the little mouse. Is it true what they say about your mother? That she lives in an asylum and doesn't talk?"

I didn't say anything, just stared him down. Or up. I only came up to the second button on his coat. Sure enough, from this close I could clearly see the eagle emblazoned on the black rubber.

He leaned in, licking his lips. "You know, I heard another rumor, from Mr. Katz. He's our history teacher, you know. He's lived here longer than anyone can remember. Knows all the local families. He says your feeble-minded mother gave herself to the gardener, and nine months later you came along."

The blow was sudden, fast. And it made every one of my fingers scream with pain.

Lucas howled, bending over to cup his bloody nose. "What the hell!"

This time I leaned in. "I'm not offended. It's the truth, and I can't be insulted by the truth. But the fact that you make my mother sound like a whore, when it wasn't her idea—when the gardener was a man just like you, a man the police thought had

328

done no wrong because the victim couldn't defend herself, couldn't speak up for the way she'd been wronged, that's the part I can't forgive."

I squeezed my fist so tightly around button, the rounded edges began to cut into my palm and the insides of my fingers.

Lucas glared up at me through his bruised eyes. "You little bitch. I'm going to kill you."

# Chapter Nineteen

*August 25, 1918*

*Dear Jules,*

*Be glad you don't like any of the boys at school. They are so
annoying, and far more trouble than they're worth.*

*That's why I never talk about my beaus. They cause nothing
but trouble. If you find a good one, then the other girls get jealous.
And if you find a bad one, well, that's bad enough, isn't it?*

*That's why I like you so much. You don't care. It doesn't make
any difference to you.*

*That was rude of me, wasn't it? I'm sorry. You know my
mouth—and now apparently, my pen—runs away with me
sometimes. I'm just so frustrated right now.*

*One of the boys sent me the most charming letters back at
school. A real flatterer, that one, telling me how pretty I am. But I
know he's a scoundrel. I've always known it. I thought we could
still have some fun, since it's summer and lord knows there's
nothing else to do around here, but no. He's even worse than I
thought. Boys like that aren't any fun, even when they're trying to
behave themselves. Especially then.*

*But then, nothing fun ever happens when we behave, does it?*

*I'm rambling now. I hope to see you soon. I might even see you before you get this letter. Wouldn't that be funny?*

*Love,*
*Ada*

He lunged for me, but I was already backing out of his reach. Leaving the food forgotten, I spun on my heel and ran down the hill. After only a few steps my boot slipped on something—a rock, some leaves, a root—it didn't matter. I went down, skidding and sliding and tumbling until I hit the bottom of the hill.

Disoriented, with the ground spinning under me, I struggled to my feet, pulling myself along with low hanging branches and tree trunks, anything I could reach.

Lucas bounded along behind, crashing through the underbrush and fallen leaves like a bull in a China shop. His shouted threats echoed off the bare trees.

Mud at the bottom of the hill sucked at my shoes, coating my knees and hands. I scrambled up the other side of the little valley, but Lucas was already gaining on me. He slid carefully down the hill, one leg stretched out to slow his descent. "I'll get you! Just wait, I'll get you!" he shouted.

I pulled myself over the crest of the next hill with the help of a little sapling, then raced off again. My head throbbed so badly, I thought I would be sick.

*Ada!* If ever there was a time I needed her help, it was now. The tumble down the hill had me disoriented. I thought if I kept moving forward, I would get back to the school. But I could hardly tell if I was traveling in a straight line. I couldn't find any sign of the path Bernice had pointed out to me.

The heavy clouds brought twilight on early. Or maybe I'd bumped my head. Or maybe it was the fever. I could hardly tell anymore. The fall seemed to have rattled something loose in my brain—I hadn't been scared earlier. For some reason, the danger of confronting Ada's killer hadn't occurred to me, but now it was very immediate. The vision of Ada's death came back suddenly and forcefully. I felt his hands around my throat, his fists on my face, like I was the one he'd killed.

My aching thighs clenched, as though he'd clamped one of those awful hands there, just below my hip.

I coughed. My chest burned. My toe caught on something and I fell again, landing hard on my hands and knees.

"Where are you? Come out, little mouse! I don't know who told you those things, but I'm going to teach you to keep your mouth shut," Lucas growled.

He'd come up on another part of the hill; hidden by the underbrush and boulders, he didn't see me. I crouched, keeping still, eyes closed, and waited for him to move with my heart in my throat.

"Come on! You know you can't run from me!"

I squeezed my eyes shut. My elbows shook under my weight, but I was too scared to move, too scared even to collapse. If I collapsed, he would hear me. He'd catch me. I wouldn't be able to outrun him, and he'd kill me, and I'd die and Ada's killer—and mine—would continue to walk free.

My head throbbed so badly, it was like someone repeatedly beating my brain with a baseball bat every time my pulse rang in my ears. I thought I was going to be sick. Bile rose in my throat, but Lucas stepped on a twig—too close. I swallowed it and tried to breathe as quietly as I could.

He paused, just on the other side of the bushes and tall grass I hid behind. He shouted again, swearing. I held my breath, shaking all over.

Lucas walked away.

I exhaled slowly, dropping back on my knees and ankles. Slowly, his voice began to fade as he continued to call for me, alternating been the type of noises one would make for luring a particularly annoying cat, and shouted threats.

Suddenly, his voice quieted. The sound of his tromping footsteps stopped. I thought he was a few yards to my left—maybe twenty-five or fifty, just beyond a stand of trees.

*He's waiting. He's waiting for you to make a move.* My breath rattled—fear or the flu, I couldn't tell which. If I could just slip off, get my bearings. I thought the school was just head, maybe a little to the left. If I could just keep my path from intersecting with Lucas's…

I coughed.

I couldn't help it. My lungs spasmed, and in a second he began bounding through the underbrush toward me.

I scrambled to my feet and tore off, climbing over boulders and leaping over a fallen log.

Was it the same log I'd passed with Bernice? I couldn't be sure. Why did trees all have to look the same?

Veering left just in case, I found what looked like a path and tore down it as fast as my straining lungs and aching legs could carry me.

By some miracle, the button was still in my fist. I held to it, my only proof. My good luck charm, if such a thing existed. It was the only proof I had, the only real evidence.

My feet slid over damp leaves. I crashed into a tree, bounced off and hit the ground. I rolled once or twice, but came up on my feet again, until something caught the back of my coat.

"Got you!" With a mighty yank that cinched the collar around my throat, he threw me to the ground. I landed face down, and the button flew out of my hand and into the layer of browning leaves.

"No!" I screamed, reaching for it, but Lucas was on me, his weight pinning my lower back as he grabbed for my neck. He couldn't get a good grip because of my layers, but he began pulling and twisting my scarf instead. I flailed, but couldn't reach him.

Black spots appeared in my vision. I tried to scream, but couldn't get enough breath. My back bent at an unnatural angle as I tried to lessen the strain on my throat, but he just pulled harder.

Suddenly, he let go. I flopped back onto my stomach, gasping. He backed away, rolling off me.

"Y—you—"

I crawled forward, retrieving the lost button.

Despite the sweat running down my face, I shivered.

"Get up."

The voice was female, familiar, but even as the words registered, I knew it couldn't be real.

But there—right there, inches from my face—were a pair of pointed black boots.

I followed them up a pair of black stockings to the hem of a light blue skirt and white blouse. To the ring of bruises around the neck, and Ada's damaged face.

"Get up," she said again, glancing down at me. "You need to run now."

"Who—how—what—" Lucas was nearly insensible with fear. "You're dead!

Ada glided toward him. "You're right. But I'm not the only one here, either."

Lucas took off running, kicking up dead leaves as he went. Ada followed, then vanished.

I stood, looking around, trying to decide which direction I needed to go. I thought true dusk might be beginning to fall.

Through the trees, a few lights glimmered—the school. They'd be lighting the lamps now. I hurried toward it, as fast as I could. The school had never seemed so welcoming before.

Lucas screamed, a short, sharp sound that stopped me in my tracks. Had he fallen? Or was it Ada again?

I looked around, trying to figure out where it had come from. If the school was straight ahead, then that meant…

The church. The graveyard.

My legs wobbled, but I turned left and started to run again.

By the time I reached the fence around the graveyard, I didn't think I could move another step. Everything hurt. The leaden sky was so thick and dark, I pulled out the flashlight to avoid falling on the uneven ground. There was no sign of Lucas anywhere.

I followed the fence around until I got to the back gate, then switched off the light and pushed it open, listening hard.

Somewhere, there was shuffling. Something moved in the dark, and I walked quickly toward it, the flashlight held tight in my right hand, ready to swing up and give him another good blow to the face if he appeared.

*I should just walk away.* The pastor's house was just on the other side of the gate, only a short walk. A light glowed in the kitchen; I could run for help. Surely if Pastor Brown thought I was in danger—real danger, he would help, despite his awful words about Ada on Sunday.

Yes. I would run for help. I would have him call the police, and then I could show them the button, and Lucas would be locked up, where he should be.

But the fastest way to get to the church and parsonage was to cut through the cemetery to the main gate.

The wind turned cold and a sudden strong gust nearly took me off my feet. I braced myself against a monument of an angel, listening again as Lucas's scream split the night.

Torn between helping him and saving myself, I hurried toward the sound.

The mausoleum door swung open, banging against the wall

with a sound like thunder. I switched on the light, tearing open the window.

Lucas cowered in one corner, half hidden behind the big stone coffin in the middle of the floor. Between us, a white figure hovered several inches above the concrete.

"Ada?"

She turned to me, eyes glowing with hatred the Gloria's did. She held one arm outstretched, tightly clenched, while Lucas clawed at his throat, like he was being choked.

"Ada, stop it!"

Instantly she was right in front of me. Her eyes, bright and dark and inhuman all at once, bored into me from mere inches away. I recoiled.

"P-please don't!" Lucas whimpered from his corner. "Please don't let her hurt me!"

Sidestepping Ada, I crouched down in front of him. "Ada asked you not to hurt her. Did Mildred Temple?"

Lucas's eyes widened. "Mildred? How—"

"You're the reason she left school, aren't you?"

He only stared at me.

"I saw what you did to Ada. She knew about Mildred, didn't she? She knew you hurt her. Was she willing to meet you, or did you have to ambush her the way you did Ada?"

338

"That—I don't know what she told you, but she's a liar. Whatever Ada told you, I didn't do it. I didn't hurt her."

I leaned in until we were almost nose to nose. "I saw your handprint on her thigh. You held her down and pulled up her skirt." Reaching up, I pulled down the collar of his coat and shirt, revealing three deep scratches on his neck. "And she dug her nails in. She fought you. She tried to stop you, but you liked hearing her scream. You enjoyed it."

For a moment, our eyes locked and in that instant the trouser-wetting fear in his eyes was overshadowed by anger. His fingers flexed.

I didn't have time to scream before he was on me again, pinning me against the casket plinth. I smashed the flashlight into his temple, but he didn't let go.

"You think anyone cares about those whores? You want to prove I killed her? The police have already been here, you idiot, and you know what they did? They spent a few minutes talking to Charlie, and he told them she fell. Slipped and fell, just like I told him to. And guess what? They walked away. Because Charlie and I, we've got futures ahead of us. My father went to Harvard, and that's where I'm going, too. And Charlie, his dad is on the city council and the school board. Do you really think they're going to do anything to him? Those poor, fallen girls. At least Ada won't have to live through her shame." A wicked grin twisted his lips. "Unlike your mom."

The black spots were back, overtaking my vision. I tried to raise the flashlight again, but it slipped from my limp fingers, too heavy to hold.

Then, all at once, Lucas gasped and went rigid. His face turned into a white mask of pain, eyes wide and unseeing, mouth searching for air. His hands dropped from my throat, and with one final gasp he toppled forward onto my shoulder, cracking his head on the plinth in the process.

I sucked in glorious cold air, shoving his heavy body to the floor. In the place where he'd been sitting, Ada hovered, watching me. I put a hand to my sore throat, knowing it was surely bruised.

I looked from her to him. "What did you do?" I asked. His dull eyes stared at the ceiling, unblinking. It was obvious he wasn't breathing.

Ada flexed her outstretched fingers. "He liked to think he held our hearts—our lives—in the palm of his hand. I just showed him what it's like when the tables are turned."

"Ada…"

"You know, he was right about one thing. No matter what we did, he never would have paid for his crimes. But this way, he'll have eternity for me to punish him."

She rose, floating above us, a brilliant vision, like a Valkyrie. An angel that avenged herself. She stared at Lucas, reaching for him once again. A weak pearly mist rose above his body. Ada gathered it up in her hands.

"Hurry back. The others need you. And you need them too."

I stood with some assistance from the coffin as Ada began to fade away.

"Jules? I'm sorry."

Sorry for killing him? Sorry for leaving me? I wasn't sure. All of it, I thought, as her face faded into nothing.

"I'm sorry, too."

***

It was a miracle even deaf old Pastor Brown didn't hear the noise or see the lights. But then, if he paid any attention to the mausoleum, maybe no one would have used it for their rendezvous. Maybe Ada would still be alive.

Either way, I couldn't be caught near Lucas's body. Checking to make sure I hadn't left any sign of my presence behind, I dragged myself out of the mausoleum and closed the door, following the well-worn path back to the school in the dark, not daring to turn the light back on until I was nearly at the school.

I could barely keep my eyes open. Every step took a monumental effort. At last, the lights came back into view. Shadows moved in the infirmary windows, a pantomime of images projected onto the flagstones as I passed the fountain where Ada died.

A figure waited outside the kitchen door. Headmistress Davenport watched silently as I shuffled toward her, unable to raise my feet any higher. My chest ached. My head hurt, and the ground was moving again. I couldn't tell if she was judging me, or just watching, as I slipped past her and reached for the door.

It swung open before I reached the knob. Ruthie stood on the other side. She blinked, eyes opening wide at the sight of me. "Julia! What happened?" She pulled me into the kitchen. I squinted against the bright light as she and Emily peeled off my layers and poured me a hot cup of broth—the last in the pot from the looks of it. I remembered the abandoned basket of food, and told them where to find it.

I wanted to tell them what had happened, but my teeth began to chatter so badly I couldn't get the words out. Ruthie put a hand to my forehead. "Goodness! You're burning up. Em, help me get her upstairs."

I stood up, and the floor rolled. I pitched forward. The last thing I saw were the ghosts of Mount Sinai—Mary, Sarah, Gloria,

the headmistress, and others I didn't have time to recognize—
drifting through the kitchen walls and out the back, marching
toward the academy like they were about to face the Kaiser's army.

***

I was so tired when I woke up, all I wanted to do was go back
to sleep. Bright sunshine streamed through unfamiliar windows.
Coughs echoed all around.

Blinking against the light, I tried to figure out where I was.
Someone had taken off my glasses, and everything was out of
focus. The sheets, bright white, were drenched in my sweat, and I
wore an unfamiliar nightgown.

On the nightstand was a pitcher, a glass of water, my
spectacles, and a stack of letters. I tried to reach for them, but
could hardly lift even a finger.

"Oh, good, you're awake. You gave us all quite a scare,
dearie," said an old woman. She was wearing an apron and carried
a basket of cookies, but didn't seem to be a nurse. A volunteer,
then.

"Are you thirsty?" She set down the basket and reached for the
pitcher and glass, filling it halfway. "Slowly, now." Sitting on the
edge of the bed, she helped me sit up and take a few sips. Just that

343

little bit left me utterly spent. She put a hand to my damp forehead. "There, that's much better."

I had so many questions, but I was so tired. I closed my eyes, just for a moment. When I opened them again, the woman was gone and the light coming through the windows had the orange tinge of twilight.

I tried to sit up, but my arms shook too much. I could barely lift my head. I reached for the water glass instead, and tried to drink a little. I spilled more than I drank, but put it back without dropping it. A large wet patch covered half my pillow, but it was nice and cool. I laid my cheek against it and closed my eyes again.

Time broke itself into segments. Darkness. Bright light. An empty ward; one that bustled with volunteers and nurses. I was in a hospital somewhere, a flu ward. At least it was better than the asylum the Headmistress had threatened me with.

Finally, I managed to pull myself up in bed and look around properly. The bed on my right was empty, but on the left a woman lay with her back to me, coughing hard. Across the aisle, more women of all ages lay on similar hard beds.

A light breeze blew against my neck. I reached up, panicking when I didn't feel my braids. My hair hung unevenly around my chin.

"It's all right. They cut it because of the fever," said the woman

344

next to me, rolling over. Her eyes were shadowed and bruised looking. Her hair had also been cut, it seemed.

"I—but—" I knew the logic. It was easier to care for. Helped keep the temperature down. But it was my *hair* and it was *gone*. What was left didn't even feel like mine. It was thin and dry, and every time I touched it, strands came out in my hand.

I took a deep breath, remembering what I'd read about the flu. The high fever caused many people to lose their hair. It would grow back.

Probably.

With my eyes still closed, I didn't see the people who came in then, just the squeak of a wheelchair as the nurse pushed it down the aisle. I opened them when the squeak turned, getting closer instead of further, coming down the aisle between my bed and the next.

"Grandfather!"

Several heads turned to look at us. Grandfather's eyes crinkled into a smile, then welled up with tears. "Oh, Julia. My girl," he said, holding out a hand to me. I took it. He pulled me toward him, giving me the tightest hug I could ever remember.

"Oh, Grandfather! I'm so glad you're all right. We didn't have any news for so long."

"I know. I was in a bad way there for a while. But I'm much

345

better now." He paused, panting a little, as though just those few words made him breathless. "Pneumonia. But it's clearing up now. They say I can go home next week. But then I heard they brought in an entire school, a whole school full of girls who were sick, and found out you were here. I convinced them to let me visit you. Though I don't think you knew I was here."

"No. I don't remember anything. What day is it?"

"Wednesday. The thirtieth, I think." He glanced up at the nurse pushing his wheelchair for confirmation, and she nodded.

"Yes. You got very lucky. We got a call for an ambulance on Friday night, and when it got there, there were only eight people left, trying to take care of thirty-five cases, with little food and no medicine. It had to be evacuated right away."

"Is everyone okay? What about Bernice? And Ruthie and Emily and Mary Anne? And the teachers? Mrs. Hodge?"

She held up her hands. "I don't have a list. Most of the girls are in the next room, but you were one of the most severe cases. There are a few more over there," she said, gesturing to the far end of the long room, but without my glasses I couldn't tell one white-clad lump in bed from another.

I reached for my glasses, but it didn't make much difference. They were too far away, too bundled up.

I turned back to grandfather. He was so thin and frail looking.

His gray hair had turned snow white with fever.

Someone called for the nurse. She glanced over her shoulder, then patted Grandfather's arm. "I'll leave you here for a few minutes more, but she needs her rest."

We both nodded. I was already feeling tired again, but wasn't ready for him to leave.

"What about grandmother? Have you heard anything from her?"

"She wrote me a letter. I guess they stopped the mail for a while, but it started running again yesterday." He pointed to the stack of letters on my nightstand. Some of them were in envelopes, while others were just folded slips of paper. "Looks like some of your friends are all right, at least. There hasn't been any word out of the asylum yet, but they announced in the paper this morning that the quarantine is lifted, so we should find out soon."

Eventually the nurse came back to wheel Grandfather back to his bed. I laid back down and was asleep in minutes.

Over the next few days, I slowly read the letters and messages on my nightstand. Bernice, Ruthie, and Emily were all well. They were at home for the time being, until the board could decide if they would reopen the school. The public schools, cinemas, and most churches remained closed, even though the quarantine was lifted. People were still avoiding public places.

Mary Anne, Miss Comstock, Mrs. Hodge, and Miss Newton all fell ill. By the time the ambulance arrived on Saturday morning to pick me up, there wasn't a single healthy adult in the entire school. Maureen was the only one in charge, trying to coordinate everything.

Oddly, when I woke up, the other girls from Mount Sinai lodged in the hospital made near-miraculous recoveries. The doctors and nurses said they'd never seen anything like it.

Unfortunately, the boys did not have the same luck. Two days after we were brought in, the Red Cross was called once more to Mount Sinai, this time taking away two students, the headmaster, and Pastor Brown. One of the boys survived, but the others all grew increasingly ill. By the first week of November, they were all dead. From what I heard later, Charlie Johnson was never really the same after.

Someone did report Lucas missing, and the police did come to ask me about it—apparently the cook told them he was supposed to walk me back to school.

I told the truth, as much as I could—that he'd attacked me, and I ran, and managed to lose him in the woods. I didn't say I went back to look for him, or what happened after. With the girl's school shut down and most of the boys sent home, it could be weeks or months or even years before anyone found him, and I was quite happy to keep it that way. I hoped Ada gave him hell.

The doctors sent me home on Armistice Day. For the first time in months the streets were crowded with happy people. Grandfather went home a few days earlier. Grandmother came to pick me up in a cab, and the first thing she did when we got home was even out the hair cut the nurses gave me at the hospital. Grandmother clucked her tongue as it curled under my ears, and her friends certainly didn't approve, but I'd gotten used to it short and was rather fond of my Castle bob. I didn't have to worry about braiding neatly or my inept pinning skills.

"It's a shame. All that pretty hair, gone," Grandmother sighed, putting her scissors away.

I checked my reflection in the window, reveling in how light and wonderful it felt. "I like it. Maybe after all these women with the flu recover, it will catch on."

"Heaven forbid. You look like a boy. But at least we've got you around to look at," Grandpa said with a wink, peering at me from over his newspaper. We were both weak, though I was making a quicker recovery. Grandfather still used the wheelchair, especially in the evenings when he got tired. We slept an awful lot.

The newspaper finally printed the list of the dead and ill at the asylum, but Mother's name wasn't on it. It would be some time before we got to visit, however. Grandmother and grandfather argued about bringing her home and hiring an in-home nurse. "Just think of how much money we're saving now that half the staff has gone to war." I thought it was supposed to be sarcasm, but had a feeling Grandmother wouldn't have to fight too hard to win that argument either way.

I twisted a strand of hair around my finger, my eyes refocusing on movement on the sidewalk. Bernice and Ruthie strolled up the walk to our front door. Bernice was holding a basket.

After they'd been let in, I took them up to my room. It still smelled a little dusty and neglected after so long away, but it was nice to be back in my own room. I wasn't sure where Grandmother would send me once the schools reopened, but I planned to ask to go someplace where I could live at home.

"I thought you would have gone home by now," I said to Bernice, poking around in the basket. We'd left the fruit and a pie from her mother in the kitchen, but there were also several books.

"I'm staying with my aunt for a little while. Mother and Father are in New York at the moment." She reached into the basket, plucking out a volume bound in green cloth. "My uncle runs a bookstore. I thought you might like this one, if you haven't read it yet."

"A Floating City," I read, examining the gold leaf on the cover.

"I also found a copy of Sherlock Holmes. This is only the first one, not the collected works, but I thought you would like it."

I held the books gingerly and smiled. "Thank you. I've been so bored the last few weeks. I've already finished my embroidery project, and I'm running out of books." The unicorn now hung above my desk. I hoped to one day rejoin it with the cardinal. They were all I had left from Ada, aside from her letters. I'd lost the flashlight and the button in the struggle with Lucas.

"Perish the thought!" Bernice put a hand to her forehead dramatically, pretending to swoon onto my bed. Ruthie giggled.

"Ha! There it is! I knew I'd get you to smile eventually," Bernice grinned, pointing at me. I tried to cover the evidence with my hand, but it was too late.

She nudged my leg with her foot. "Any more word from Ada?"

I shook my head. "No. I don't think she'll be showing up again. She got what she wanted, though I don't think in the way she expected." Her parents held a memorial service, and sent me an invitation, but by the time the post office delivered it and I got out of the hospital, it was already over. From what I understood, her body had been sent back to Lancaster but the other students and teachers who died at Mount Sinai would be buried alongside the rest of the parishioners who died in the epidemic.

"If you ever want to see her again, Miss Betsy has offered her services," Ruthie said, picking up one of the books and turning it over absently. "Mother and I went to see her yesterday. She said I 'needed solace after such a terrible ordeal.' I didn't tell her we snuck out to see Madame Marron, of course, but Miss Betsy did ask about you. She said she'd love to read your cards someday."

I thought of the Mount Sinai ghosts, of Ada and Lucas, and the ghost that still lingered in our attic and the guest room. Helping Ada was the first time I'd ever been able to set my strange ability to good use, but maybe it didn't have to be the last. After all, that seemed like a very good skill for a nurse to have, and with the school closed, I might ask Grandmother if I could start my training sooner, rather than later, now that I'd mostly conquered my fear of the flu.

"You've got that look again. It's too soon for that look," Bernice said, nudging me again.

"What look?"

"The one that says you're planning something. You just got out of the hospital, Jules. Can't it wait?"

I looked at her, and Ruthie. Mary Anne would be out of the hospital in a few days, and we already had plans, the four of us, to have tea.

"Sure. I think I can wait a few days."

# LIFTING THE BAN UP TO CITIES

## Local Authorities Can Lift Quarantine Says The State Board.

[By Associated Press to The Banner]

COLUMBUS, Oct. 31—Recognizing the improved condition throughout the state of the influenza epidemic, the state health department today decided to leave to local health authorities the matter of lifting quarantine regulations. In some communities it is expected a gradual lifting of the quarantine will begin at once.

This announcement was made by Acting Health Commissioner Bauman at the conclusion of a conference of the advisory council of the state health department with Bauman and Cox.

[The Democratic banner. (Mt. Vernon, Ohio) November 01, 1918]

353

# Author's Note

While the past hundred years have seen great strides in the way educators and society view people with developmental disabilities like Autism, young people and adults still struggle to be seen on equal footing with others.

As I write this, the medical community is re-evaluating how they define Autism, and realizing that the occurrence in girls and women is 100-150% higher than originally estimated. Females on the spectrum are more likely to be socialized in such a way that they "mask" or hide their autistic traits more effectively, and slip through screenings that usually catch boys with the condition.

Julia Grace could be one of those girls, even today. Students like her don't always get the help they need, and they grow into adults who lack effective coping mechanisms. A simple matter of slowing things down and respecting sensory overload, or explaining social expectations in advance is often all it takes to avoid a total meltdown.

While the UK has recently made great strides in working with autistics and their families, the US is lagging far behind. Regardless of where you are, I suggest you check the NHS's list of resources. In the US, our largest organization is Autism Speaks, which does not represent the autistic community and is frequently harmful to the people it claims to protect. At the time of this writing, AS does not have any autistic board members and has shown no interest in the first-person narrative and experience of living with autism. If you would like to know more about Autism Spectrum Disorders, or donate to help increase awareness and education, then I recommend visiting the Autistic Self Advocacy Network, which empowers people with autism to understand their needs, ask for help, and provide the support they need to function in a society that frequently doesn't understand or acknowledge their differences.

Every autistic experience is different. I've done my best to present Julia in as respectful a manner as possible. Many thanks to Kaelan Rhywiol for educating me on autism, answering my many questions, and checking this book for issues. All errors are my own.

Made in the USA
Middletown, DE
04 November 2020